Archie's Children

Beatrice Holloway

TSL Publications

Chapter 1

There was a knock at the door. Becky Wilson, soon to be Mrs Rebecca Ann Johnson, looked at Kevin. Kevin looked back at her and grinned as he said, 'Our first visitor. Will you go and answer that or shall I?'

Becky stood up. 'How about we go together and the first one there can open it?'

'You're on,' Kevin answered leaping to his feet.

Becky loved Kevin, or Kev as she called him, to bits even though he was sometimes a tad selfish – never thinking to put his laundry out or empty the waste bins or make her a cup of tea when she got home from the late shift. She loved his ready smile and how he made her laugh, especially when they both knew he was in the wrong. Like the time he was supposed to have met her at the station, but had allowed himself, 'Just one more beer with the boys,' as he put it, and was late, very late. So easily led, she thought, but that was how he was and she was happy to accept his faults.

Whooping with laughter, they got wedged in the doorway and jostled along the passageway bouncing off each other and the wall. There was another knock on the door, then another – louder and seemingly more demanding than the first. They looked at each other in surprise.

'Someone's in a hurry,' said Kevin as he unlatched the chain and opened the door. They stood in stunned silence – then simultaneously:

'Father!' Becky whispered.

'Dad?' questioned Kevin.

3

The man on the doorstep was tall and well built. His hair was wavy, greasy and long, hanging well past his slightly rounded shoulders. His face partially bearded, was weather-beaten, his eyebrows white and bushy. He was wearing a shabby coat that was too large and scuffed brown shoes. He could easily have been mistaken for a vagrant.

There was a smirk on his face and slyness in his voice. 'Well, well. What do we have here?' He put his foot over the threshold and Kev put up his hand to stop him. Archie Johnson barged past the pair of them, and they could smell alcohol on his breath as he grunted, 'I think not my son. There are things we got to discuss.' He made his way to the kitchen and the overpowering body odour, trailing after him, filled the air around them.

Becky gagged, turned white and groped for Kevin's hand. They looked at each other seeing shock on each other's face. Both were suddenly aware that the Archie, bursting into their lives was about to change their relationship. Becky was surprised and bewildered when Kev snatched his hand away from her. 'K ... Kev?' she stammered.

'That bugger's not staying here,' he shouted at her as he strode purposefully after the man.

Becky stumbled along behind him tripping in her useless, furry mules. 'Kev, wait. Hold on a mo.' Catching up with him she nudged him in the back. Breathlessly she said, 'You called him dad. How can that...?'

Fiercely he rounded on her, 'And you called him father. Now, you explain that if you can,' and he marched on into the kitchen.

Becky couldn't understand the change in Kevin, she had

never seen him so angry in all the time they had been together. Flare up of temper, yes, but he had never reacted so passionately before.

Kevin entered the kitchen closely followed by Becky. Archie had discarded his coat on the floor. He was drinking from a bottle of milk and was noisily opening and closing cupboards. 'Got anything to drink?' He looked at the bottle in his hand and shook his head. 'I could murder for a beer,' he growled as he prowled around the room. Becky pointed to the fridge. 'Get it,' he ordered, 'and a sandwich or something, there must be grub about somewhere in this dump.' He pushed her roughly across the kitchen. 'Go on girl, get on with it. On second thoughts an omelette would be tasty.' Becky looked about the room helplessly, and then at Kevin, who nodded to her to do as Archie had said.

Kevin was angry as he crossed the room and stood in front of his father. His hand was curled into a fist. Archie raised his eyebrows and his stance made it clear to Kevin that he was expecting, and ready, for a fight. It would be futile to strike the man Kevin realised. Instead, in a voice filled with disgust said, 'You stinking old man. You'll not eat anything in this house until you've cleaned up.'

Becky, already whipping up eggs, turned quickly, 'You're not letting him upstairs are you?'

Sarcastically, Kev answered, 'That's where the bath is Becky.'

'But...'

'Guard your tongue girl,' Archie said, 'or else I'll be handing out a slap or two.'

Slap! A word she knew well from the past. She longed to be defiant, but with tears in her eyes and paralysed with fear she watched as he strode towards her. He grabbed her wrist, and she could smell his bad breath as he bent his head close to hers and hissed, 'I need that food now. A bath can wait.' He let go of her and pushed her towards the cooker. His mean eyes glared at her. 'Now,' he bellowed.

Hoping that Kevin would intervene, say something to warn the old man off, she turned towards him. At once, she knew it was impossible. His head was bowed, his shoulders drooped. He lifted his head, but turned away from her quickly when he saw her pleading look. He was every bit afraid of his father as she was, and she understood.

Archie pulled out a chair and sat at the table. 'Now then, you...' he pointed at Kevin, 'you get the beer and you...' pointing at Becky, 'get that pan on the stove and hot food in front of me.' Kevin was sullen as he slammed the beer cans down on the table. 'Watch yourself, boy,' growled Archie as he pulled the ring off one and spilled some of the contents over the table.

He wolfed down the two-egg omelette Becky put in front of him making grunting noises of content as he did so. She went across the room and opened the window. She leaned on the sill, thrust her head out into the cool fresh air and breathed deeply. When she turned back into the room she saw that Kevin had sat down opposite Archie, warily looking at him. Archie had a broad grin on his face and she could see he had missing teeth and others black with decay. As she moved towards the kitchen door he grabbed her skirt.

'Get off,' she said firmly, and pulled the garment close.

'And where do you think you're going?' he demanded.

Although she was afraid of him she held her head high as she answered, 'I'm going upstairs to get some towels for your bath.'

Archie leaned back in his chair and patting his stomach said, 'Just like your mother.' He sniffed. 'Talking about your mother,' he began. Becky cringed, afraid of what he was going to say next. Archie leaned forward on his elbows. 'You know, in prison you get all sorts of deprivations, if you know what I mean. It's alright if you're, you know...' He winked and touched the side of his nose, 'The other way so to speak.'

In a firm but quiet voice, Kevin said, 'Your problem. I don't want to know.'

'Yes, my problem and I'm going to get my woman.' He sniffed again. 'She'll be so glad to see me, I'm sure. Won't she girl? So, she still in the same place?' Becky didn't answer and Archie asked again.

'No,' was the short reply.

'So where is she?' Becky ignored him and began to collect the mugs. Archie moved quickly, and grabbed her shoulder roughly. 'Where is she?'

Kevin rushed across to the pair. 'Get your hands off her, Dad. This is my house and I'll not have you chucking your weight around. Understand? Now sit down, and you...' he said pointing at Becky, 'Tell him.'

Surprisingly, Archie did as he was told with a curse under his breath.

'Tell him, Becky or I will.'

Becky took a deep breath. 'She's in Newcastle.' As she said this she saw the startled look on Kevin's face and mutely begged him not to contradict her.

'Newcastle!' Archie shouted. 'What's the silly cow doing there? It's over two hundred miles away.'

'Got herself a decent job, and away from you,' Becky

retorted.

'That's as may be, but I'll find her, don't you worry. And yes, I'll have me bath now. Run the water while you're up there, girl.' Looking at Kevin he went on, 'and when I come down again, we'll have a long talk you and me, lad.' Becky clamped her lips together as she realised that he had not included her. Kevin nodded, wondering what his father was going to say and what was he up to.

Chapter 2

They had met six years earlier at College. Kevin was supposed to have studied engineering, but his exam results were disappointing. Truth to tell he didn't bother much about getting a job where his meagre engineering skills could be used and advanced. No, he chose to work as a labourer as and when an opportunity arose. It was always by someone who knew someone needing a 'no questions asked' temporary worker. At eighteen his curly blond hair and sparkling blue eyes in a clean shaven face free of acne, had attracted many of the college girls. Whenever she saw him Becky's stomach had turned and fluttered. It had happened every day at college where she was training to be a nurse.

They began seeing each other at the end of the college year. Mary, Becky's best friend, was going to sing at the end of term concert this particular evening. As Becky had made her way towards the college gate intent on going home she knew she could never take part in the concert. She could sing well enough, but was too shy to sing in public and admired her friend's ease and confidence.

Earlier in the term a strong wind had been blowing. She had shaken back her long, dark hair which was being blown across her eyes and into her mouth. As she passed a group of boys lounging and smoking at the college gates, the wind had caught her pleated skirt. The skirt billowed and lifted – high enough to expose her panties. How the boys cheered and clapped. One boy had whistled, a whistle Becky was to hear again and again over the next few weeks, and she thought she would never forget that day. The lads couldn't have seen too much, but enough to see the top of her slender legs. Giving a small scream of dismay, she'd pulled her skirt down and ran to get away from their crude jokes.

Thinking about some of the jokes afterwards she knew they were childish and silly, but one lad, taller than the rest had called out to her, 'Hey, beautiful, you've got the longest legs I've ever seen. They must be worth a million.' Becky had briefly noticed his white, even teeth. 'Just like Madonna's,' he'd laughed.

'Give over Kev more like Batman's,' one lad shouted.

It was then that Becky, her face red with embarrassment and holding back tears, had run away. Much later she thought that the boy called Kev had meant his remarks to be a compliment, but couldn't be sure. That was the day Becky first saw him, a student in his last year and the cause of Becky's daily butterflies.

Every day since then, she had seen him. Often she saw him by himself leaning against the wall outside the college as if waiting, but he never spoke and turned away from her. If he was with the other lads he would stop fooling around and give out his distinctive whistle as she approached. Then she saw the others give him a sly poke or whisper something that made them fall about laughing. Often, she noticed, he would flush up, shuffle his feet, shove his hands in his pockets or attempt to thump someone. She assumed something crass had been said which Kev didn't approve of.

She'd heard he'd not done too well in his exams, but he would be starting work with an engineering company the following week. Today would be the last day she would be seeing him. As she approached the gates she hoped he would say something to her – anything would be fine, but a date would be more than perfect. Yes, there he was and the usual crowd of boys were with him joking and larking about.

Kev did speak to her and it was not what she was expecting. In a sing-song voice, he called out, 'It's W.I.N.D.Y...' and she watched as the boys grinned and nudged each other. 'Well, show us your undies girl,' Kev had shouted. Loud laughter greeted this remark. 'We won't get another chance will we lads?'

As Becky, wishing she was somewhere else and hating him, hurried away she saw Kev turn away and punch his fist into his other hand. His face was screwed up and she guessed he might be regretting his silly remarks. She realised it was too late to get to know him better. As she walked away she kept her head up, but was inwardly disappointed.

Later that evening she had decided to go to the concert, telling her mother that she was going to support Mary, 'I expect she's nervous, even though to look at her, you'd think she wasn't,' she said. 'I know I would be.' Backstage she searched everywhere for her friend and began to feel worried knowing Mary might be late. Suddenly the choir master had rushed up to her.

'Becky,' he said, 'Mary's lost her voice. Her mother phoned. Too much practising I think.' He grabbed her wrist. 'You could take her place.' As Becky shook her head, he said, 'Please, you sing well. And you were once in the choir. You don't like to sing in front of an audience, we understand that, everyone has nerves, believe me, but once you begin you'll be fine. I guarantee it. Honestly. Please.'

Again she shook her head, 'No. I can't. No, never,' she protested.

'Do it, please,' he begged. 'Sing for Mary, for the college. You'll be fine, I promise you.' Becky took a deep breath then slowly nodded. Nearly every evening she had sung with Mary as she practised so she knew the tune and words of 'Woman in Love' well enough. It would all be over in a few minutes she told herself.

When she stepped onto the stage she had trembled from head to foot and stood, feet apart, clutching her hands together, blinded by the spotlight. The piano softly played the introduction and Becky opened her mouth to sing. However, she only made a husky, raw sound in her throat. The audience stirred restlessly. To run away would be dreadful, but to stay was just as awful, she'd thought.

Becky bit her lip and looked over to the person playing the piano – Miss Smithers, one of her favourite tutors. Miss Smithers smiled encouragingly at her and whispered, 'Start again, dear. Take a deep breath.'

The audience waited. The opening music started again. Becky swallowed and began to sing. Her youthful voice was perfectly in tune. She sang with a depth of feeling from her heart. When she came to the end there was complete silence. Becky was bewildered, and for a moment she couldn't understand why. She turned to round to Miss Smithers who stood up and began to clap as she walked towards her.

'Congratulations my dear, well done,' she said as a roar of spontaneous and enthusiastic clapping and approving voices ripped through the air. Becky stood still pleased with the reaction. She felt herself going hot and then gave a broad smile as she acknowledged the audience's appreciation and gave the traditional bow. From the back of the hall came a distinct whistle. A whistle she would know anywhere. Kevin was in the hall and her heart lifted.

It was nearly dark when Becky set out for home. For the second time that day she made her way to the college gates. There were no lads there leaning against the wall, but as she passed by someone fell into step beside her and a warm hand gently took hers. 'I'll walk you home,' said Kev softly. They had been together ever since.

Kevin often teased her about her legs, no way were they long but they were in proportion to her height of five foot five and often her ankles were puffed after being on her feet all day in the hospital. Nothing like the film stars he pretended to compare them with. She had brown eyes, Kev called them, 'Malteser eyes, like chocolate – teaser's eyes, get it?' he said and he'd laughed at his little joke. She had a narrow waist and small firm breasts. 'Just perfect,' he'd murmur when he cradled them as he kissed her throat and whispered his love. For all his bravado with the college lads, she was surprised and pleased to learn that he couldn't abide any form of violence. He had told her he always walked away from confrontations.

They had planned their future carefully. They would save up and get a home together, get married, have a family, enjoy faraway holidays. Becky didn't want an engagement ring. Instead they exchanged tiny silver charms. Hers was a heart engraved with 'Forever' which she wore on a chain around her neck. Kevin's was a simple square with their entwined initials on. He had attached it to his watch. 'The best place,' he said, 'Every time I look at it I'll think of you.' When he saw her surprised face at this, he hastily added, 'Not that you're not in my thoughts twenty-four hours a day of course.'

It had taken six years to have got this far with their plans – a home of their own. Becky contributed the most as she had a steady job as a nurse in Trethorpe Hospital. She had odd moments of resentment when, on the rare occasions Kev did work, he hung on to most of his earnings. 'To have a night or two out with his mates,' he told her. As they lived so far from town, whenever work was offered he insisted he was picked up and brought home again in the evening. Not every would-be employer was willing to comply, so his opportunities of work were rare.

The house they finally chose, rather she fell in love with, was less than a mile from the village of Leddon, near Trethorpe, a small town three miles further on along the main road. It was a small, nineteenth century labourer's cottage and the outside walls were flint stones. In a lopsided frame with the old paintwork peeling in strips, hung the front door leaving a gap at the bottom. Kevin said it would have to be fixed before winter otherwise there would be a hell of a draught. Likewise the windows, sagging wooden frames, some covered in lichen and all needing a coat of paint. Kevin had sighed, envisaging more work when she'd pointed them out, and she had nudged him in the ribs and laughed. 'You're just being lazy. I'll help, you know I will.'

Kevin shrugged and gave a little grunt then put his arm around her and she knew she would probably get her way.

Inside were two bedrooms, one no more than a walk-in cupboard. The bathroom was even smaller. Downstairs there was a kitchen, and two reception rooms off a passageway. Floorboards creaked in nearly every room and the staircase.

Outside, there was a tiled path leading to the dilapidated front door and on each side of the path was an herbaceous border. Fading pinks, lupins of every colour, a few drooping hollyhocks, antirrhinums and pansies, their shy faces peeping out wherever there was a gap. When they inspected the back garden, there was a gnarled tree laden with ripening apples and a squared piece of garden, which Becky surmised had been a vegetable plot, now covered with rampant weeds. There was a stone birdbath and a feeding table on which an optimistic starling was perched and flew off when they appeared. It seemed to Becky that when she entered the cottage it enveloped her with a warm feeling of home and of safety. With Kevin and this lovely old cottage she was certain that their future together was going to be wonderful. Convinced they would be happy here, she had little trouble persuading Kevin that it was this cottage she wanted. 'Also,' she had added, 'it's well within our budget and I will be able to cycle to the hospital. That will save on fares.'

They moved in one late September day. It was sparsely furnished as their bank balance was empty at the moment, but they were content. The knock on the door was the first they'd had since moving in.

Chapter 3

Becky went into the bedroom she shared with Kevin and sat down on the edge of their bed. She heard Archie's heavy step as he came up the stairs, then the splashing of water. Quietly she got up and locked the bedroom door then sat down again.

That was one of the earliest of her memories. She must have been about six years old and playing with Molly, her doll, when her mother, Stella, had sat her down on the sofa beside her and said, 'Listen to me. Listen very carefully, darling.' Becky remembered staring at her mother as she heard the seriousness in her voice. 'I want you to promise me something.' Becky had nodded. 'When your father comes in...' her mother had hesitated. 'When he comes in, if I say to you, "Becky, go to bed at once" don't argue with me – just do as I say straight away and...' and wagging her finger she gave the next instruction. 'Remember this, this is very important, always lock your door and put the key in Molly's apron pocket. Promise me Becky, promise you will do it straight away.'

Becky gave a brief smile as she recalled her favourite doll, Molly. Her mother had given her an ice-lolly from the freezer when she had nodded and said, 'I promise, Mummy. I will, I will.'

It was a few years later when she realised the significance of her mother's insistence. Becky automatically got out of bed and locked her door when she heard her drunken father come in, always around midnight after the pubs and clubs had closed. He would be cursing and swearing and yelling for Stella. Her poor, dear mother was constantly tired, and always with bruises when he left them. There was one dreadful time when, after a beating from Archie, Stella had two broken ribs and a black eye. Becky was only twelve years old at the time and had taken her mother to the hospital. There was no disguising the fact she had been at the receiving end of someone's fists. Her mother had denied any such suggestions. Another time when Becky was fourteen she witnessed one of his attacks on Stella who hadn't been quick enough getting to him when he yelled for her.

'A bloody good slapping for you my girl when you get here,' Becky had heard him say.

She had followed her mother and saw her father lift his hand and slap Stella around the face. At first she had put her hands up to her head to protect herself but as his blows hammered down on her she fell to the floor. As Becky looked at Archie, she could see his eyes were red with anger and his body tense. It was as if he were deaf to Stella's cries and pleading. At first fear had stiffened Becky into a statue, and then she had raced to her mother's aid. She had begged him to stop and when he continued to thrash Stella, Becky had begun to beat him ineffectually with her fists. Archie had lashed out at her in his fury and her mother had whimpered, 'Go to bed Becky, at once.' In tears she had left her mother to her fate. As Becky remembered all this she felt ashamed of herself for abandoning her mother knowing she could not have done anything to help.

One day, a few years later, she asked her mother why she allowed Archie to beat her. Becky had been shocked by her answer. Stella had sighed heavily. 'He was grand to have as a boyfriend and I loved him a great deal. He showed signs of a temper because at first, I wouldn't give in to him. Then when I did, I saw little of him except when he wanted sex.' Becky had gasped when her mother said that.

'Oh, you know all about that at your age Becky. It happens. Anyway, you came along and I told him to clear off. But he wasn't having any of that. When he needed me, I mean sex, he'd come round and if I said no, he threatened to take you away.' Becky recalled Stella had patted her face at that point. 'I couldn't have that, could I? Not knowing where you were, who had you, were you loved? The very thought of life without you was unbearable, so I always gave in.' She had sighed, 'Then he took up serious drinking and let his temper govern his words and actions. There was nothing, nothing I could do.'

Becky had asked, 'Why didn't you go to the police? They would have stopped him.'

'Oh, I did, just the once. He was cautioned, promised them he would mend his ways and they believed him. He was always a bit of a charmer. As he told me later, after another slapping session, promises are made to be broken. He said if I did that again, he would see me dead and you in an orphanage. It was then that he stopped giving me money for your keep as a punishment, not that it was ever enough, but it meant I had to go out cleaning to make ends meet. I hated having to leave you, but as soon as you got a place in college I knew I had to soldier on. I am so proud of you.' Tears were coursing down Becky's face as she recalled her mother's words.

There were good times too, she told herself. Archie was a long distance lorry driver. Often he was away for weeks at a time and how the two of them enjoyed his absences. As the days lengthened into weeks though, they knew it wouldn't be long before he would be banging on the door.

Their luck changed dramatically. Archie was sent to prison, something to do with being arrested for grievous bodily harm. As the police investigated his background, they found he was also involved in counterfeit currency – his driving contracts took him all over the country, so he was able to 'spend' the notes and never be seen again in the area. Becky persuaded Stella to move home while he was serving his five year sentence. They had lived comfortably together in a small flat they had found across town, until she had moved out to be with Kevin.

Becky's eyes filled with tears again. She was fearful of what Archie might do now. She was certain the current situation was going to be manipulated to suit him regardless of Kevin's or her wishes. At the same time she realised that Stella might be in danger if he found out where she was living – especially as she had found Stuart, a decent, law abiding man.

'Friends only at the moment, we're letting things develop slowly,' Stella had told Becky and by the dreamy look on her face and the gentle way she spoke his name, Becky knew her mother was happy to be with him.

Slowly twisting the key so that it wouldn't grate she unlocked her door, stood still for a moment and listened. Archie was still in the bath. She crept past the bathroom, treading carefully trying to avoid the creaking floorboards. A brief vision of him leaping out of the bath not bothering to cover himself and dashing after her demanding to know what she was up to, came to her. Once down the stairs she saw that Kevin was still seated in the kitchen.

They had not yet had a land-line telephone installed and she knew she must get hold of the mobile phone they shared and turn it off without him knowing. Never before had she done anything so sneaky to Kevin, but a gut feeling told her to be wary. She crept into the sitting room where she knew she had left the phone and was relieved to see it was still on the arm of the sofa. Once it was safely tucked into her trouser pocket, she went into the kitchen. Kevin looked up at her and smiled briefly.

They had exchanged life stories long ago. Kevin had told her that his father was a company rep. Sometimes he was away from home on business. Jane, his mother had said he was abroad and when he came home there was a lot of fun. They went camping, they visited most of the London museums, had odd days at the seaside, visited the annual fun fairs and once they had a holiday in Spain.

When Kev was telling her this he said, 'It was a bit odd really. I mean when we got to the airport it was as if Dad didn't know what to do. You'd think he'd know the routine, booking in, passport checks, where to get a sandwich, and locating the departure lounge, things like that. Any experienced traveller would know, but I saw him looking positively bewildered searching for information.'

All of this had come to an end when his mother had found out that Archie had been unfaithful. All his days away were spent with a variety of women around the country. The discovery was made when Kevin was rushed into hospital with appendicitis. Sick with worry, Jane had telephoned Archie's main office wanting to know his exact whereabouts. They had given her a telephone number and when she phoned asking for Archie Johnson, the girl at the other end said he had left the office early as he had a date and could she take a message. Archie was in Dundee.

'There was a humdinger of a row,' Kevin had laughed when he told Becky this. 'He confessed and Mum wheedled out of him that there were two or three other women about the country. It was then Mum chucked him out of course, and we haven't seen him since. That was over four years ago.'

Becky sat down opposite Kevin, the only sound was the monotonous click of the battery run clock. She stretched out her hand to him. 'What are we going to do, Kev?' she whispered.

Before he could give an answer Archie's voice bellowed down the stairs.

'Where's the shaver our lad?'

Kevin snatched his hand away from hers and shrugged his shoulders. He scraped his chair back as he stood up. 'I don't know,' he snapped at her as he made his way to the door to answer his father.

It was ten minutes later when Archie came into the kitchen with his arm around Kevin's shoulders. He smelt of Kev's aftershave and was wearing his dressing gown which barely reached around his ample waist. Becky was dismayed, and was hoping that Kevin would insist that his father left. His father, not mine, not ever, I'll never call him father she told herself. Both men sat down at the table. There was a wheedling tone in Archie's voice as he said, 'A cup of tea would go down nicely, girl.'

Becky didn't move or answer as a flurry of rebellious thoughts flashed through her mind. Get it yourself, I'm not your servant, the kettle's over there, ask Kevin he seems to be your mate all of a sudden.

'Did you hear what I said girl? A cup of tea now, for your

dear old dad. How about it?'

'Kev will get it, won't you Kev?'

'It's your job to look after me, us men folk, me and Kev. Now, get on with it, girl or you'll be sorry.'

As she looked at Kev, she was surprised to see an impassive look on his face, that he was unable to look her in eye. Had his father said something to him when they were upstairs she wondered? She put the kettle on and set out a mug.

'Two mugs girl, Kev wants one, don't you Son?' After she had poured out three mugs of tea and found some biscuits the old man was demanding, he said, 'Right, now ain't this cosy? Me, with me son and daughter, all under one roof.' Becky cringed, Kevin gave a lopsided grin. 'Now as I see it, you two have set up house together, right?'

Kev nodded.

'And I suppose you've er... well, how do I put it...' he indicated Becky with a nod in her direction, 'had her so to speak.'

Becky went hot with embarrassment, her palms were sweaty and there was tightness in her throat. Kevin looked at her and she couldn't believe what she saw, his eyes were closed, face screwed up and she was sure she saw him shudder. After all these years did he now find her disgusting? Tears coursed down her face, as she heard Kev take a deep breath as he answered, 'Yes, but no more, not with my sister.'

'So, you know what that means don't you?' Archie looked expectantly in turn at their faces. 'Incest me dears, incest. You do you know that it's illegal don't you?'

They nodded together.

'But we didn't know it was like that, did we Beck?'

21

Becky managed to choke out, 'No, we didn't. We met each other at college as a matter of fact and fell for each other.'

'That's right,' Kevin agreed.

Archie sneered, 'That's as may be, but I tell you now, it is punishable with up to fourteen years imprisonment. In fact if the judge sees fit he can sentence a maximum penalty of life imprisonment in this country. It will be you my lad that'll end up inside, believe me.' He paused and pointed at Becky, 'Yes, and you won't escape either.' He waited for their reaction.

Kevin stood up abruptly. 'Not me, I'm not going inside for her.'

'You're right son. You ain't strong enough to stand up to the thugs in there, believe me. I could tell you a thing or two that, well...' he nodded knowingly.

Kevin's face turned white and Becky began to weep and covered her face. Between her wet fingers she looked at her father and saw he was grinning at their discomfort. When she looked at Kevin she was aware that he, who she acknowledged to herself, was weak but loved dearly, was already under the influence of their evil father and was rejecting her.

Archie took a noisy sip of his tea, banged the mug down on the table and rocking his chair on the two back legs said, 'Now, as I see it there is a way out of this mess.'

Kevin looked sharply at him and Becky's heart sank. The next few minutes proved her to be right – something unpleasant was about to be put forward by her father.

Stroking his now clean-shaven chin, he gazed up at the ceiling for a few moments as if thinking through an idea. 'Tell you what my dears,' he said, 'I'll keep your little secret. No need for anyone else to know is there?'

Neither answered.

'Of course, I can't promise to keep me mouth shut, but as I see it, I could be persuaded, if you get my meaning?'

It was Kevin who answered. 'We've no money Dad, none at all if that's what you're after.' He swept his arm around the room, 'We can only afford the mortgage and our food, that's all. There's no money to spare.'

Although her eyes were full of tears, Becky was more forthright. 'You do realise that you are blackmailing us.' She took a deep breath to hold back a sob before adding, 'for which you could go to prison as well.'

As quick as a flash Archie's chair clattered to the floor and he was on his feet. He was beside her in seconds. With his hands on her shoulders he began to shake her roughly. He let go suddenly when Kevin dragged him away and with anger in his voice said, 'No, I'm not having that Dad. Keep your hands off her. Understand?'

Archie sat down again and chuckled quietly. 'A chip off the old block, I knew it. Not afraid to say your piece when you're miffed are you?' There was pride in his voice as he added, 'My son.'

Becky's heart lifted for the few seconds, Kevin had come to her rescue, and he still cared she thought. What if Archie had started to hit her and Kevin hadn't intervened? She remembered that Kevin didn't like any sort of violence. Was that the reason he intervened she wondered? Thinking it might be so, her joy was short-lived.

'What I need...' Archie began, '...what I need is a roof over me head, a permanent one. So, in exchange for me keeping me mouth shut, bed and board would suit very well.' He raised his eyebrows and looked at Kevin first, then Becky. 'Well,' he demanded. 'What do you say to that? Neat arrangement I'm thinking.'

Kevin spoke first. 'We've no extra beds.'

Becky added, 'And no bedding, only what is on ours.'

Archie laughed, shook his head in disbelief and laughed again.

'Shut up,' muttered Kevin.

Becky went and stood beside him to search out his hand for comfort. She was hurt when he glared at her and snatched it away again and put it in his pocket.

'I've had a little wander around upstairs,' said Archie. 'Now as I see it, me and the lad can have the bed and you miss, can sleep in the little room.'

She gasped. 'Don't worry, I'll let you have the duvet, me and him can snuggle up a bit. We'll be fine, won't we boy?'

Before Kevin could answer, Becky had rushed across to where Archie was sitting and with her arms akimbo and feet apart confronted him. She spoke slowly and emphatically, 'No. No, no.' she said firmly. Choosing her words carefully she went on, 'You do know that you are suggesting incest with your own son don't you? And by heaven if you ever get into bed with him I'll make sure the authorities know. I'll don't care what will happen to any of us after that.' It was a guess. There, that's got him she said to herself as she noted the shock and surprise on Archie's face.

The look changed quickly to one of anger but before he could say or do anything, Kevin spoke up. 'She's right Dad, we could be in bother. Let her have the bedroom. We'll manage. I'll sleep in the little room and you can sleep on the settee.'

Archie was astounded at her outburst and spluttered,

24

'You know I wouldn't touch you. You know that don't you son?'

Kevin shrugged his shoulders before saying, 'I'll sleep on the sofa.' He saw his father's eyes narrow and added, 'Just for now until we think of something else.'

'What? How can I be sure that you don't go sneaking into her bed again?'

Kevin looked at Becky who watched him close his eyes and shake his head. 'No, never again. I'll never touch her again. She's my sister, half sister at that. My God what have we done? It disgusts me to even think about it now. Never again.' He turned to Becky with a fierce look on his face. 'Never, understand? You make me ashamed of myself.'

No one spoke. At the harshness of his words Becky felt faint, her legs buckled under her and she groped for a chair. As soon as she had recovered, she made her way across the kitchen.

'And now where are you going?' demanded Archie.

Skirting around him she mumbled, 'Too bed.'

'I've things to say to you, girl. You wait 'til I say you can go.'

Becky ignored him and when she reached the foot of the stairs heard him push his chair back.

'Come back here, I...' he yelled after her.

She heard Kevin's voice interrupted him, 'Leave her be. She's on early shift tomorrow, starts at six.'

As she made her way upstairs she heard Archie mutter something, then some murmuring between them.

Intent on cleaning her teeth and rinsing her face she entered the bathroom. The first thing to meet her eye was the heap of dirty clothes Archie had left on the floor. She opened the window and threw the lot into the garden and left the window open. Immediately she washed her hands saying 'Ugh' over and over again as she did so. The next thing she noticed was the dirty scum lining the bathtub. Disgusted, she ignored it and, after cleaning her teeth, took her toothbrush, flannel and her personal toiletries into the bedroom with her. Before undressing she locked her door and put the mobile phone on the pillow.

As soon as she got into bed she punched in her mother's number and pulled the covers over her head. Stella answered immediately.

'Darling, I was going to ring you in the morning. I have some marvellous news for you. I...'

Quickly Becky interrupted her. Whispering urgently, she said, 'Wait, please wait. Don't ring me on this number again mother. Archie...' she choked on saying his name. '...Archie has turned up. He is so hateful, I hate him.' There was urgency in her voice when she went on, 'We mustn't ever let him know where you are. You understand don't you?'

'Oh my God,' whispered Stella. 'You mean he's actually in the house with you now?'

Becky, her voice hollow with misery answered, 'Yes, Mum. Here, in my house.' There was a momentary silence between them, each filled with their own thoughts, Becky of her father and Stella's of a violent ex-lover.

Hoping that she could not be heard, Becky spoke quietly, 'Don't ever phone me on this one again, will you? Phone me at the hospital, you've got the number and they'll put you through.'

'Yes, of course, a good idea, love. No way do I want anything to do with that evil man ever again.'

'He's already mentioned your name.' Becky could almost see her mother shudder and there was a moment's silence before Stella said,

'Listen, Becky. The good news is, well, I... we, Stuart and I.' Now Becky could hear the excitement in Stella's breathless voice. 'We're getting married. Brought the date forward,' she said, 'because he's been offered that contract in Australia. If all goes well, the firm is prepared to keep him on. So Becky,' she squealed with joy, 'we are leaving in two weeks.'

Becky was shocked and quiet as she took in the news. Her mother was going far away, but she would be safe from Archie. It was obvious that she was very happy.

'So soon? But what shall I do now without you?' she whispered back.

'Come with us,' her mother answered promptly.

'I can't leave Kevin with him.' She took a deep breath. 'I haven't told you the worst piece of news, Mum,' and began to softly cry.

'Oh God. Don't cry darling. But it is a wonderful new start for me isn't it?'

'Of course you must go. I'm... I'm really happy for you. You deserve a break and you will have no fears and you'll have Stuart to look after you.'

'I'm so glad to hear you say that. But what were you going to say. Something more is upsetting you isn't there?'

'Oh Mum,' she paused, 'He, Archie...' She stopped and in a hushed voice said, 'I can't bear it, Mum. He, Archie...' Becky burst into fresh sobs. 'Mum, Archie is Kevin's father too.'

There was a gasp at the other end of the telephone. Shocked and in disbelief Stella said, 'Oh my God. My God.

The wicked bastard.'

'That's not all Mum. He's blackmailing us into giving him a home.'

'Get rid of him. You've got to get away from of him.'

'How?'

'Leave. Leave the house.'

'I can't. I'm not sure how Kevin feels about me now. He's so easily led. That man, I can't ever call him father, already he has Kevin on his side I think.'

Becky heard the stairs creak and heard one of them enter the bathroom. She knew at once who it was when Archie's voice bellowed around the house. 'Where's me bleeding clothes gone?'

'Got to go Mum,' she whispered down the phone. 'I'll speak again tomorrow. 'Bye.'

Kevin raced up the stairs at the sound of his father's angry voice. 'What's up?' he panted.

'Me clothes. That silly little bitch has chucked them out of the window. Look.'

'Well, they really are past it aren't they? Look at them. You can't really blame her can you?'

Archie's voice roared across the landing, 'There's a twenty pound note in one of them pockets. Any tramp could have spotted that coat. It's a good coat is that? Any-one could have taken it and me money. Silly cow. What was she thinking? A bloody good hiding so she knows who's boss is what she needs. Mark my words, I'll see to her one of these days for this.'

'She meant no harm.' Kevin muttered and as Archie leaned out of the window grumbling, Kevin said, 'I'll nip down and get them. Once you've rescued your money I'll put them through the machine. They'll be dry by morning.'

Again, Becky thought that Kevin had, in a small way, protected her. At the same time she smiled to herself knowing that she had caused Archie a small measure of anxiety.

Next morning, Becky left for the hospital earlier than usual on her second-hand bicycle. She packed her clean underwear and uniform carefully into a backpack and made sure she had the mobile phone with her. She decided she would breakfast and have a shower at the hospital. It was customary for Becky to leave a note for Kevin on the window sill when she left early. Usually they started with, 'Love you', followed by a message like, 'Peel potatoes and put bins out' or something similar. This morning the letter merely said, 'Clean the bathroom. Buy some mince for dinner. Get rid of him'. She hesitated before setting down a five pound note.

Later in the day during her break, Becky telephoned her mother. 'So, Mum, when's the wedding to be?'

'We've arranged it for next Wednesday.' Anxiously Stella continued, 'You will be there won't you? Eleven at The Registrar's Office, just behind the Town Hall. You know it don't you?'

'Don't worry. I'll be there somehow. When are you leaving for Australia, Mum?'

'On the following Saturday.'

Becky gave a gasp. 'As soon as that? Oh, God. You mean I've got to manage on my own. Who else is there for me talk to? You're the only one who knows the truth.' There was a catch in her voice as she said, 'I can't... I just can't tell anybody else about... Kevin and Archie.'

It was hard for Stella to hear her daughter's distress. 'Try not to get upset, my love. When everything is settled, perhaps you could come over. Emigrate yourself. You've good qualifications and you're young, just what the Australian immigration people are looking for.'

Becky sniffed back her tears. 'But...'

'Don't say but. Think about it. Tell you what. Tomorrow I'll come to the hospital to see you. I'll wait until your lunch break and we'll have a talk then.' There was a moment's silence only broken when she said softly, 'Is he still so awful?'

She couldn't see Becky's nod but heard her say, 'He's more than that Mother. He's a monster. I hate him.' She looked at her watch and said hurriedly, 'I've got to go, promise you'll come tomorrow.'

'I will, I promise. Bye for now darling.'

Chapter 4

'What's for breakfast then?' asked Archie yawning, and pulling the inadequate dressing gown around himself, as he entered the kitchen. 'Cold in here boy. No heating on?'

'Can't afford it, not in the summer months any road.' Kevin began emptying the washing machine and shaking out his father's clean, but crumpled, clothes.

'Breakfast? What you got?'

'You had the eggs last night. I doubt there's anything else in the fridge.' He pointed to the fridge. 'Look for yourself.'

Archie peered in. 'There's a bit of cheese, cut the rind off that and we can have it toasted on bread. You got bread I hope?' Kevin nodded. 'Well get on with it. Can't hang about all day. We got things to do.' He paused for a moment and then asked, 'You got a job to go to?' Before Kevin could answer he went on, 'Well it don't matter none 'cos I got plans for us boy, big plans.'

Shrugging his shoulders, Kevin replied, 'I work sometimes. A mate sorts something out for me now and again.'

'You play your cards right lad, and you'll never work again, mark my words.' Whilst waiting for his food Archie wandered over to the window and spotted Becky's note. He read it and went over to Kevin. 'You read this?' he asked as he thrust the note into Kevin's hand. 'Cheeky little madam. Cleaning's her job, you tell her.' He peered into Kev's face. 'Oh, don't tell me you do all that stuff?' Anticipating Kev's confirmation, added, 'you daft sod.' He looked at the note again. 'And look what else she says, "Get rid of him". She means me. Well, she has another think coming.'

When they had finished eating, Archie put on his clean clothes and looked down at himself and sniffed, 'Can't go out in this little lot. Look at them. I'm sure they've shrunk. So here's what you do.' He picked up the discarded dressing gown and fished in the pockets for his twenty pound note. 'Now, you take this and get down to the charity shop. Find me some decent trousers, a jacket, not a suit, can't abide them, and a couple of shirts. I'll use your socks so don't bother with them, but look out for a decent pair of shoes size nine, black with laces.' He hesitated, 'Yes, That'll do for now and when you get back well have a nice long talk.' He winked and touched the side of his nose, 'We'll start with how to make easy money. You'll soon get the hang of it.'

Kevin was indignant. 'What! Me? You must be joking. It's three miles into town and I've got a puncture.'

'Don't tell me you can't mend a puncture, lad. I remember showing you when you was knee high.' He gave out a sigh, 'Of course, if you had a car it would be different.' He paused, 'No reason why you shouldn't have one in a week or so, I'm thinking.'

Kevin's face lit up. 'What do you mean? You got cash somewhere?' He grinned, 'You crafty old bugger.'

Archie grinned back. 'A little, but I know how we can get more.' He sniffed, 'With your help of course,' he added, as he ducked his head and winked again, making Kevin feel a little uneasy.

Between them they mended the puncture, squabbling and grumbling a little as they tried to prise the obstinate tyre back onto the rim. Wiping his hands on the clean tea towel, Archie said, 'You got that note safe?'

Kevin nodded.

'With the change bring in a couple of take-aways. I like a bit of Chinese myself, big helpings at that.'

'Do you really expect to have some change when I've bought all that gear? You must be having a laugh.'

There was a serious tone with a hint of menace when Archie said, 'You see to it boy, that there is some change.' He hesitated, 'You was caught, if I remember, when you was a kid for shop lifting. Can't be that hard in a busy charity shop can it?' After a moment or two he added, ''sides you can spend that fiver she left.'

'I don't do that sort of thing now. I've grown up a bit you know. Anyway, Becky wouldn't like it.'

'Becky wouldn't like it,' mimicked Archie. 'What the hell does it matter what that little madam says? You're going to have to think again about your situation with that girl. For a start, you can forget any more larking around in the bedroom.' Again he sniffed. 'For meself, I can't think what you sees in her.'

'She pays most of the bills, the place is in her name and I've nowhere else to go.' He was quiet for a second before saying, 'and nor do you, do you?'

'Well, seeing as you put it like that...' Kevin was already sitting on the saddle and wobbled as Archie gave him and the bike a shove. 'Now, get on with it.'

Propping his bicycle outside, Kevin reluctantly entered the charity shop, desperately trying to pluck up courage to steal some gear for Archie. It was all right for Archie to give orders, saying, 'It's only borrowing, you can give it back when I've got proper stuff,' or when Kevin argued called it, 'A bit of pilfering no one would miss.' Kevin was sure he would be seen and besides he'd nothing to put any clobber in, and he certainly wasn't going to try something on and walk out with whatever on his back. He began rummaging through the men's clothing, picking out a jacket a shirt, and a tie then put them all back. The rack across the shop had more men's stuff, and he wandered over to have a look. Again he pulled out what he thought might be suitable, looked around, saw the assistant who smiled at him and unnerved him. With two strides he was out of the door. Nervously, he drummed his fingers on the bike's saddle. It had to be done, there was no way he could go home empty handed to Archie. He would buy what he could and they would have to make do for their dinner. Mince was what Becky had in mind and that would be fine.

As he stepped back into the shop the friendly assistant came over. 'Is there anything I can help you with? I could see you were undecided. Perhaps I can assist.'

'Er, no. No thanks,' he replied.

'Is it men's clothing you had in mind? For yourself?'

Kevin never knew where the idea came from as the words fell into place. 'It's my father, he's lost everything in a fire.' He gave a brief smile. 'Now he needs everything, even a roof over his head.' He paused. 'He's coming out of hospital tomorrow. Nothing I've got will fit him, he's twice my size.'

The assistant gasped. 'Why, that's dreadful, poor man.' She looked furtively around the shop, before saying, 'Good. No one here at present. It wouldn't do to let other customers know of our unspoken policy.' When she saw Kevin's questioning look she said. 'Look here. We have a selection of stuff out the back that... well, it just isn't selling. I could find you some clothing from the pile if you like. We're always happy to help anyone who is need. What do you say? '

Kevin nodded and with relief thought this is an answer to my prayers.

'Follow me,' she said leading him into the back room.

It wasn't long before Kevin's arms were full of very suitable clothes for his father. The assistant thrust them into three carrier bags. 'Sorry there's no underwear, only really tatty stuff which we put out straightaway for shredding.'

Kevin stammered his thanks and put his hand in his pocket. 'No, no charge. I'm sure there is a lot more your poor father needs.'

'But...' Kevin began.

Patting his arm, she said, 'Next time you're passing, perhaps you could drop a small donation in. We are always glad to have a contribution.'

Kevin was ashamed and delighted – ashamed at his deceit, but delighted with the results. 'I'll do that, I promise.' It was said with sincerity, but he wasn't sure it would ever happen. One thing he was certain of, he was never going to tell Archie about this bit of luck.

When Becky arrived home she wrinkled her nose at the smell of stale food lingering in the hallway. In the kitchen she was disgusted to see brown paper carriers stuffed with cold leftover food and sauce encrusted foil dishes. Compressing her lips she made her way to the sitting-room where she found Archie asleep and was surprised to see how better dressed he was, even sporting a colourful waistcoat. Kevin was lounging in an armchair drinking from a can of lager and watching football on the television. Angrily, she snatched the can from him.

He spluttered and sat upright, 'What the hell...'

'Where's the mince?' she hissed through clenched teeth. Turning and pointing at Archie she added, 'and what's he still doing here?'

Shrugging his shoulders and in a guarded whisper Kevin replied, 'I said he could stay for a day or two until he got himself sorted out, so stop getting in a strop.'

She leaned over him quietly emphasising every word. 'I want him out Kevin. He'll bring big trouble down on us.' She watched as Kevin wriggled uncomfortably, and his eyes moved away from hers. 'What's he said already?'

'He's our dad, Becky,' he mumbled.

'Never! Never will I ever say he is my father. Never, understand?'

'Blood's thicker than water, Becky, we owe.'

'You what? We owe? His blood is contaminated, filled with hate and violence and spite.' They glared at each other then Kevin looked away.

'So, where's the mince?'

Kevin frowned and shook his head. 'What you on about?'

'The mince, Kevin for dinner.'

'We fancied some Chinese earlier so he said not to worry about food.' He turned back to the television, 'Look at that,' he exclaimed as someone sprinted across the pitch. 'Man, can that guy run. I...' She strode across the room and pulled the TV plug out.

'Hey, I was watching that,' he protested loudly.

'Where's my money?'

Kevin sat up abruptly. 'Money? What money?'

Becky couldn't believe his feigned innocence and gave him a sharp poke in his shoulder shouting, 'The five pounds I left you.'

Both of them turned round as Archie mumbled and stretched his arms. 'What's all the racket? A bloke needs his rest.' He opened his eyes wide and looking at Becky said, 'I might have guessed. You're back and starting trouble already.'

With eyes flashing with anger she pointed a wagging finger at him, 'And you, you should be gone from here. I prayed all day long that you would have left, but no, thoughtless bastard that you are, you're intent on tormenting us, aren't you?'

Archie frowned, 'Don't know about that, but let's get this straight, I'm here for the duration my girl, so get used to it.'

'So, what do you suggest I eat for my supper? Scraps from this mess you've left?'

'You're the one with money, feed yourself I say,' he hesitated for a moment then added, 'Of course, we expect you to contribute to the weekend grub.' He turned to

Kevin, 'but me and the lad will manage in the week, won't we lad?' And laughed as he saw Kevin squirm as he understood what the old man was hinting at.

Becky looked at Kevin and knew that Archie had somehow got a hold on him already. 'In that case,' she retorted, 'when you eat here I suggest you clear up afterwards, because there's no way I'm going to.' Tired and hungry, she made herself two slices of toast and a cup of cocoa and went up to her room.

As she left the kitchen, she saw Kevin on his feet collecting up the foil dishes and heard Archie say, 'Gawd, boy. You don't have to do everything she says. You got to break some of them bad habits of yours.'

She was a little surprised to see that an attempt had been made to clean the bathroom. Before falling asleep she thought that she would probably fare better with her daily meals at the hospital than with the two men downstairs.

Chapter 5

Passing through the kitchen on her way to work the next morning Becky saw the receipt amounting to eight pounds twenty-five pence for the Chinese meal. This puzzled her as she had left only five pounds and Archie had twenty – there was no way Archie could have been kitted out, without cash from somewhere. In the charity shop she had seen men's suits at the very least four pounds and Archie's smart almost new jacket and trousers were probably more. Men's shoes were anything from three pounds, and he also had two shirts. It didn't add up.

As planned her mother arrived in good time and waited

in the staff restaurant until her daughter was free to join her. Breathlessly, Becky said, 'I've only got forty minutes. Let's get in the queue.'

They waited to be served, Stella told Becky of their disappointments, then their excitement when at last they had received their residents' papers for Australia. Stella was laughing as she told of the packing of his and her treasured pieces and wondering what to take was causing them to bicker. 'For instance, why on earth does he want to take his badminton cups with him? I mean, it's not as if he is going to play anymore.'

Becky smiled. 'And what are you taking that he thinks isn't necessary?' widening her eyes her mother protested,

'My collection of dressed dolls.'

Becky laughed outright. 'Mum! You can't take all of them. You must have at least twenty, more I bet. I'm with Stuart on this one.'

Embarrassed, Stella mumbled, 'Well, I like them.'

After a minute or two, Becky said, 'Why don't you take a couple, your favourites and put the rest in the charity shop? That way you know whoever buys them really wants them and will look after them, same as you've done.'

Stella brightened. 'Good idea. I'll do that, but it will take ages to decide which of the little darlings will get left behind,' and they laughed together.

They paid for their sandwiches, yoghurt and coffee. The noise of cluttering dishes and loud, animated voices filled the restaurant and they searched desperately for a quiet place to eat and talk. They decided to eat outside and found a picnic table, climbed into the attached benches and sat down facing each other.

At first they ate in silence until Stella said, 'Becky, I've been thinking.' She looked at her daughter. 'You must get away from that house. Those two men together are going to make your life a misery.'

There was an almost guilty look on Becky's face as she quietly answered, 'I know what you are saying, Mum but...' She hesitated then whispered, 'I can't. I can't leave Kevin, he needs me.'

'Rubbish. He's twenty-three years old for God's sake! Old enough to look out for himself,' adding softly, 'and about time too.'

'Oh, I know he's weak and now that his father is around I'm sure he'll be led into trouble.'

'There's nothing you can do about it my girl. Kevin won't take any notice of what you say. In fact, I can almost hear that wretched man wheedling, cajoling and even threatening him.' She paused, 'Listen to me, get away from both of them.'

'Where shall I go? You're off to Australia. I don't know anyone else who can put me up.' Biting her lip she said, 'If I did, how can I explain the whys and wherefores of leaving Kevin. Some of my friends know we're a couple. Some have even met him.'

Stella shrugged. 'You find somewhere as soon as possible. I'd like to see you settled before I leave.' Tears filled Becky's eyes and Stella's heart constricted. 'Don't cry my love, they're not worth it.' She handed Becky a tissue, 'Dry your eyes now. What you could do is find somewhere for, let's say, a year and then apply to come out to Australia and live with us. You have lots in your favour, you're a trained nurse and they, the authorities, are looking for skilled people. Also as I shall be there you will have a family sponsor. I'm sure it will work out. What do you think?'

'It's no good, Mum. I...' She dropped her head, unable to look at Stella, and lowered her voice. 'I love him.'

Stella threw herself back and lifted her arms above her head in exasperation. 'Really, Becky, do be sensible. Nothing more can come of your relationship with Kevin. He doesn't love you, you know that. In fact, he can't love you. Even if he did it would be so wrong.'

Aghast at the mention of the word 'relationship' Becky said, 'You're not going to tell anyone are you? I don't want anyone to know he is my brother.'

'No, of course not. But I'm warning you, you must never, ever let him near you again. Do you hear?' Softly, she added, 'It's against the law, love.'

Becky nodded and whispered, 'I know, but I still love him.'

'Listen to me. I thought that about Archie for years,' she said. 'When you love someone, you'd do anything and everything for them just to keep them close.' She closed her eyes for a moment, and bit her lip. 'Well, I did Becky, and I paid dearly for doing so. Believe me, there's no future for you with Kevin, darling. There, I've said my piece.' She compressed her lips to prevent herself saying anything more.

They sipped their coffee in silence for a few moments before Stella leaned forward, put her hand over Becky's and said, 'You will be at my wedding won't you, Becky? Next Wednesday. It's in the morning, at eleven.'

Becky nodded. 'I'll swop shifts with someone, probably someone on nights. It won't be difficult. There's one or two owe me.'

Stella looked quizzically at her daughter. 'What will you wear? Something in apple green or perhaps blue. I saw a lovely linen suit in blue.' She looked into Becky's face and smiled. 'I think the green will go better with your brown eyes.' She clapped her hands before saying, 'I've got a good idea. Let's meet up on Saturday and I'll treat you to an outfit. What do you say?'

Becky's face lit up. She wiped away the tears as she said, 'That would be great. A bit of shopping with you is always fun. Yes, okay. Something good for me to look forward to. I was dreading having to be around Archie on my day off.' She could see her mother was pleased with her answer. Becky's heart was aching. She had lost Kevin and now her mother would soon be lost to her as well.

Fiddling with her engagement ring Stella was a little embarrassed and unsure, but knew what she had to say, 'By the way, I don't want Kevin at the Registrar Office. Do you mind?'

Becky shook her head, 'And I was thinking. If we buy something on Saturday...'

Stella laughed, 'Oh, we will, believe me. You shall be a princess on my special day.'

'Well then, would you mind awfully taking whatever it is home with you?'

'Of course, I know what's in your mind. If they see something special they'll get suspicious and start asking awkward questions. Right?'

Becky lifted her shoulders and gave out a long sigh, 'I'm afraid so. I'll come round to your place early and dress there.' She stood up, bent over her mother and kissed her on the forehead. 'Got to go now, Mum. See you on Saturday.'

'I'll be there, by the memorial about ten,' then added to Becky's departing back, 'and don't be late.'

After Becky had left the next morning and the men had finished their breakfast, Archie leaned forward on his elbow and stroking his chin, thoughtfully asked, 'You got any change over from yesterday's little trip?'

Kevin nodded.

'How much? Enough for some ciggies?'

'I shouldn't think so.'

'How much have you got then?'

'A quid and a bit of silver,' Kevin answered as he started to wash the dishes.

There was silence for a few moments and Kevin, glancing over his shoulder, could see Archie was deep in thought. After a while he stirred himself and rocking on the back legs of his chair pointed at Kevin and said, 'As I see it mate, you'll have to go shopping again, same as yesterday so to speak,' he hesitated, 'and for God's sake stop fussing with them dishes.'

Kevin wiped his hands and leaning back against the sink said, 'What do you mean? I aren't going thieving.'

Archie laughed until the tears rolled down his face, 'Thieving,' he spluttered, 'You're not thieving, you don't know the meaning of the word.' Then touching the side of his nose added, 'Remember, you're just borrowing without asking.'

Kevin's face grew red. 'You can call it what you like but in my book it's thieving,' he muttered.

'The biggest joke inside...' Archie cocked his head to one side, 'you know where I mean?' Kevin nodded. 'Well, the biggest joke the old lags used to tell was when a bloke was convicted of shoplifting he told the judge, "God helps those who help themselves".' Ruefully he added, 'Didn't make any difference though, poor devil still got two years.' He stood up, went across to Kevin and put his arm around his son's shoulders.

Kevin shrugged him off. 'No, Dad, I'm not going.' Archie muttered something under his breath and moved away from him.

Kevin watched him as he began searching the room opening drawers and cupboards, running his hand along the window-sill and lifting old magazines before asking, 'Where's the phone? I thought you had a mobile some-where?'

'We have. Becky phones me sometimes from the hospital if she's going to be late, and he too began searching. 'It's usually on the telly in the other room. I'll take a look. He was surprised that it was not in its customary place. He lifted the cushions, checked behind the furniture and curtains. 'She must have taken it with her,' he mumbled.

'Well, that's your first job then. Get us a mobile.'

'What!' exclaimed Kevin.

'Yes, a mobile. Now listen to me lad. I know a bloke who'll pay us for anything we want to flog. Get it? Knock something off and we'll have cash.' He stabbed Kevin a couple of times in the chest with his index finger. 'Cash boy for that car you wanted. Think about it.' He stopped then added, 'Yes, a car would be useful,' he said quietly to himself, 'we could get a lot more stuff if we had a car.'

Kevin stomped out of the room yelling, 'No, no, no.' He was shocked at the speed with which Archie grabbed him.

'None of your lip boy, understand. You just do as you're told.' Tightening his grip on Kevin's arm until he winced he said, 'Sit down, and listen.'

Uncertain and feeling somehow defeated, Kevin slumped into a chair, scowled at his father and rubbed his arm. Archie went back into the kitchen and returned with a glass of water. 'Here, you're all right. Nothing to worry about. Mind you, if I wanted to hurt you, and hurt you bad, make no mistake, I can and I will. Got it?'

Kevin went white knowing now that his father was capable of carrying out his threat. Pushing himself further down in the chair, he took the glass and nodded.

Archie sensed his son's fear and saw the tears glistening in his eyes. He gave a sigh, 'I thought you were tougher than that boy. He gave Kevin a friendly pat on the arm. 'Now, listen. We need two phones really. One for you and one for me so's we can keep in touch.'

Kevin swallowed nervously.

'Today we need some grub. Supermarket's your best bet. Yes, that mini mart, they haven't cameras about yet. Not like those big supermarkets. You'd best check first. Couple of tins in yer trouser pockets will do.' He sat down, saying, 'Let me think for a minute how best to get a mobile.' A few minutes later he said, 'Got it.' and rubbed his palms together. 'What you have to do...'

Kevin stood up intent on walking away, but Archie pushed him back into his chair.

'As I was saying, what you have to do is wait outside a school. High school would be best. Some of those rich, little devils got phones these days. Texting each other day and night is what I hear, even in the classroom. Pick out a rich looking kid, he'll have the most up to date one. Wait till he...' he hesitated, ''course it could be a girl,' he mused. 'Anyway, cycle up as close as possible and snatch it out of their hand and get yourself away as fast as possible.'

It all sounded plausible, even easy to Kevin, but he didn't say a word.

'I think if you go about two o'clock, supermarket first and buy something, some eggs for tomorrow's breakfast would be nice, nick a tin of ham and...' he chewed his lip, '...and, oh anything.' As an afterthought he added, 'and get me some fags.' Kevin waited for him to go on. 'That should take you no more than ten, twenty minutes. Make your way to the school. You know one don't you?'

Kevin replied, 'The college might be better.'

'Oh, beginning to think for yourself now are you?' Archie half sneered and half laughed. 'Stay away from groups, they'll see you're a loner and have you quicker than you can blink. Pick on someone smaller than yourself if you can, just in case they try to give you a thump. Understand?'

'Yes, Dad. It makes sense, I can see that,' but he was uneasy at the plans Archie was making.

'Good, now put the kettle on I'm parched and then we'll discuss our future. It's all beginning to look up for us boy.'

After a meagre lunch, cheese again, Archie grumbled 'We got to do better than this.'

Kevin reluctantly pulled on his sweatshirt with a hood and jeans. Dragging his bicycle to the road, he fiddled with the brakes, tested the tyres and tugged at the chain.

Archie watched him. 'You're wasting time, my son. It won't do. The sooner you get started the sooner you'll be back here, safe with your father.' Kevin glared at him, mounted his bike and reluctantly made his way towards Trethorpe.

The mini supermarket was full of shoppers, mostly young women making their purchases before picking up their children from the afternoon nursery session. This made it easier for Kevin to conceal the ham and a couple of pre-packed processed meat cartons. In his loose top he secreted some sausages, thinking to himself that he might as well get something he liked. The cigarettes were more difficult to obtain as they were served at a separate counter, but luck was on his side. He watched an elderly gentleman buy a packet of twenty, put them in the trolley and wheel it around the store filling it with goods as he meandered up and down the aisles. Just once he carelessly left the trolley to reach up for a cereal packet and, without hesitation, Kevin strolled by, took the cigarettes and strolled on. Picking up half a dozen eggs, he made his way to the tills, paid for them and left. He was relieved that no one challenged him.

The box containing the eggs was in a carrier bag which he hung on the handlebars. This kept banging against the front wheel and he realised this would be a hindrance if he needed a fast get-away. He stopped and put the box, along with the rest of the illicit haul, in the carrier attached behind the saddle.

The college had not yet churned its students out of the main entrance and there was another ten minutes to go. Kevin sat astride the saddle, with his feet firmly on the ground, and waited, tapping his foot impatiently and wiping his sweaty brow with his arm. As he did so he noticed his hands were shaking. Quickly he pushed them into his trouser pockets. There was a sick feeling in his stomach wishing he was somewhere else. That's it, he told himself, I hate him and I'm never going to carry out any more of his plans again. There were a number of people waiting at the entrance and Kevin avoided looking directly at them, afraid someone might recognise him. I shouldn't be here he told himself, to hell with Archie, but he knew he couldn't go home and face his father, who would either be angry or spitefully jeering at his inadequacy.

The bell was distinctly heard marking the end of the afternoon lectures. In no time at all students were pouring out of the main doors. Kevin waited and watched. There, that's the one he told himself. The person he had chosen was obviously very popular as the boys were slapping him on the shoulders – so he must be good at sports, Kevin surmised. There was no mistaking the adoring looks of the girls each vying for a smile or word from Kevin's chosen victim. Kevin hated him on sight. As the group got closer Kevin heard a mobile ring. Sure enough it belonged to the boy he'd picked out who fumbled in his jeans to locate and answer it. As he did so, the crowd gradually left him until he was finally alone, talking into his phone and walking towards the nearby park. Kevin let him go by, waited until he was a fair distance ahead, then mounted his bike and began to follow him. I'll get him in the park. I'll race past him and snatch the mobile without stopping, he thought. He'll have a hell of a job trying to catch me.

It didn't happen as he had planned. Carefully he followed his quarry into the park, but as he passed some bushes he heard a scuffle and someone whimpering. He stopped to check, and found a group of lads surrounding a young boy clinging desperately to his mobile – a thin, sniffling lad looking far too young to be a college student. The others were mocking him, pulling at his clothes and one tipped his books out of a plastic bag as another began to tear up his paperwork. Kevin's first instinct was to fly into the group and land a few punches, something he had never done before, but the unfairness he was witnessing made him angry. He hesitated, briefly questioning himself as to whether he was afraid of having pain inflicted on himself or if he was just cowardly. Instead he yelled out, 'You lot, clear off.' The gang scattered and in their haste to get away bumping into each other as they looked back to see who had shouted.

'You all right?' asked Kevin putting his cycle down on the ground. The boy hung his head and Kevin briefly felt sorry for him. 'Tell you what you should do, you should call the cops. They'd soon sort that lot out for you. Do they often come after you?' The boy nodded.

It was at that moment that Kevin had an idea, a brilliant idea, he told himself. 'If you like I'll call them for you. Look at all those your torn papers – they your course work?' The boy gave another nod. 'Well then that's a good enough reason to report them. Give me your phone and I'll call them right away. Okay?' He picked up his bicycle, swung his leg over the crossbar and sat on the saddle balancing with one foot on the ground and put his out hand.

With relief the boy handed over the phone and for a moment Kevin felt a twinge of remorse seeing the boy's look of gratitude. At last, a phone was in his hand and he cycled away as fast as he could. Kevin couldn't believe he could pedal so fast or be so devious.

Once he was in the quiet lane leading to his home, he jumped off his bike, threw it on the ground and sat on the grassy kerbside. Sitting quietly, at first with his mouth wide open with shock, he couldn't believe what he had done. He threw himself back onto the ground and began laughing. He'd done it and he was elated, he no longer felt as if he were a failure and the feelings of inadequacy and frustration lifted from him. In his mind he could see that gullible, little youth, so easy to take advantage of. I suppose, he thought, that's how I must have been when I was that age, but not anymore.

As soon as he arrived home Archie took everything from him. 'See, told you it's be easy,' was all he said.

Something held Kevin back from telling Archie the details of his success, but he knew that next time he would not suffer quite so much from nerves.

'Tomorrow,' said Archie. Kevin's heart sank. 'Tomorrow, I'll take the bike and see what's what about that town. See if there are any worthwhile pickings.' Picking up the phone he said, 'In the meantime, I'll phone my mate. See what he's after at the moment. He's pretty fair when paying out, that's why I deal with him.' He winked at Kevin. 'Get them sausages into a frying pan Kev, let's celebrate.'

Chapter 6

Archie was restless, prowling about the downstairs rooms itching to be doing something, anything to ease his boredom. He glanced at his watch and saw it was nearly six o'clock, nearly time for their evening meal before Becky got home.

Kevin was in the garden, tidying up, orders from Becky, Archie suspected. We need a bloody car, he muttered to himself, so's I can go out with the lad and show him how to make real money, useful money. The problem, he thought, was Kevin, sniffling little coward, afraid of his own shadow I reckon. If only he would...

There was a tap on the window and Archie turned towards it. He saw a young man around Kevin's age and went across the room to open it. 'Who are you and what do you want?' he demanded, 'We don't buy at the door.'

There was a look of surprise on the man's face as he raised his eyebrows. 'I might ask the same of you. What are you doing in Kev's house? He's my mate. Does he know you're in there?'

Archie stroked his chin. 'Kev's mate you say? Didn't know he had any. I'm his dad.'

The man put his head on one side and frowned.

Archie could see he was puzzled. 'Didn't tell you he had a father, did he?' There was a shake of the head. Archie sniffed. 'No, suppose not.' He nodded his head in the direction of the garden, 'He's down there, digging or something.' The man started to walk towards the back of the house, ''Ere, wait on. I'll come with you.'

Grinning, when he saw his friend, Kevin said, 'Hi Ryan. See you've met my dad.' He straightened his back and rubbed his hands covered in dry earth down his trouser legs. 'What brings you here? I do hope it's a night out with the lads. I reckon I deserve a treat.'

Ryan gave a rueful laugh. 'Nothing like that I'm afraid. In fact, quite the opposite.'

'I'm parched. Let's go up to the house and have some tea. You can talk to me while the kettle's boiling,' said Kevin. Together they walked back, with Archie trailing closely behind them. Kevin pointed to a chair. 'Take a seat. Won't be long. So what's it all about?'

Ryan moved some newspapers off the seat and said, 'I'm working on the new supermarket site just out of town. Know where I mean?'

Kevin nodded and noted Archie's head was swinging between the two of them.

'Well,' Ryan continued, 'They're looking for some labourers and... So mate, I thought you might be interested.'

'He isn't a labourer.' Both lads turned in surprise at Archie's sharp words.

For some reason Ryan was annoyed at Archie's remarks and retorted, 'And he's no Einstein either Mr Johnson.'

Kevin laughed outright. 'Got you there, Dad.' He turned to Ryan, 'When?' he asked.

'Monday. Early start. You on?'

Before he could reply, Archie growled, 'How much?'

Ryan, affronted again by Archie's interference, said, 'None of your business, mate.'

Kevin sensed the tension growing between them, and shaking his head as if in warning to Ryan said, 'Just his way. Take no notice.'

I said, 'How much?' Archie repeated.

Kevin gave a sigh. 'What's the hourly rate and for how long?' The kettle bubbled on the hob demanding attention. He went across to pour its contents over the tea bags.

'I'll pick you up as usual if you're coming,' Ryan said, deliberately not answering the money question.

Archie was surprised by his offer, and there was a gleam in his eye as he asked, 'You got wheels?'

With a bit of a swagger and pride Ryan answered, 'Yes, got myself a runabout a few months ago.'

'I suppose you wouldn't let me have a...'

'Not likely,' was the swift reply. 'One driver only and that's me.'

Archie shrugged. 'Only asking. So, what's the rate of pay then for a...a labourer? A first class one, I might add.'

When Ryan hesitated, Kevin intervened and said, 'Fifty quid a day as usual?' Ryan nodded.

Archie's face lit up. 'Fifty quid! Blimey boy, you'll soon

have a car of yer own at that rate.' He turned to Ryan, 'How long for?'

'I would say definitely a week, maybe two.'

'He'll be there. What time you picking him up?'

Kevin, had a resigned look on his face as Ryan turned to him, 'Half seven as usual?' He said as he swallowed his tea rapidly, and began to make for the door.

Kevin followed him, 'I'll come to the door with you.'

'Just a minute,' Archie called after them, ''Ere you, Ryan, ask your governor if he needs another labourer. I'm pretty handy to have around. You ask him, son.'

The two men looked at each other and Kevin mouthed, 'Don't you dare. A few days rest from him will be heaven.'

'Glad you said that,' Ryan whispered back. 'I...well to be honest Kev, I haven't taken to your old man at all. Something about him...sets me on edge somehow.'

Kevin leaned into Ryan and mouthed, 'Becky hates him.'

Ryan laughed. 'Not surprised at that. Oh, and by the way it's sixty quid a day.'

Kevin's face lit up, there was no way he was going to tell Archie that bit of news. 'See you Monday then, without fail,' and slapped his friend's back.

'Hurry up boy,' Archie called from the kitchen. When Kevin entered the room Archie said, 'That's all settled then. Now, how about another cuppa?'

Becky was tired and beyond caring about anything by the time she reached home. Home? Hardly, she thought, not anymore. All that happiness and those dreams she and Kevin had not so long ago. It was impossible to go back or to go forward now they knew of their illicit circumstances. Commonsense told her it was a good thing they found out before they'd got any further, like marriage or a family.

Closing the front door softly she made her way along the passage to the kitchen in order to make herself a hot chocolate and a sandwich. She was startled when Kevin suddenly poked his head out of the living room door. Furtively, he looked to see if Archie was about. There was a note of urgency in his voice as he said, 'Becky. In here, quick.'

Becky's heart soared. He'd spoken to her for the first time without ill humour since Archie had arrived. He cares she told herself, Kevin still cares about me. After she had entered the room, Kevin quietly closed the door behind her.

Trying hard to hide the love she still felt and, at the same time, feeling that she would never forget his recent churlishness, she asked, 'What do you want Kevin? I'm tired and ready for my bed.'

Kevin cleared his throat, glanced nervously at the closed door. 'I want to know if you'll still be on the early shift next week.'

'You know the shifts run in four week cycles. Yes, of course I'm on early's next week.'

Kevin sighed and smiled with relief. 'Good,' he said, 'That's what I was hoping.'

Becky was quiet for a moment puzzled by his pleased reaction, wondering why it was so important for him to know. 'Why? What are you up to?' she demanded.

Perching himself on the edge of an armchair he said, 'Keep your voice down.'

'Tell me what you're up to then,' she asked in a low voice.

'Ryan came by.'

'Oh, I see and you don't want that...beast to know.' She watched Kevin's face redden as he went on the defensive.

'You mean Archie, our father.'

'Yours, Kevin. I won't ever call him my father.'

Kevin raised his arm and began to bite the side of his thumb. She noticed, as his sleeve slide down his arm, that the charm was no longer on his watch. Of course, she told herself, he had to get rid of it now that we are no longer together, and she was saddened as she remembered their happiness on the engagement day.

He looked intently at her. 'It's like this Becky. I'll be at work and I just don't like the idea of you being here alone with Archie.'

Becky looked at him in amazement. 'What's that suppose to mean?'

'I'm afraid for you.'

'What?' she exclaimed and again her heart soared. He cares, he cares she told herself.

'Listen Becky, just stop winding him up.' He hesitated, hung his head and muttered, 'I'm afraid he'll lash out at you one of these days.' He looked up into her face, 'and next week and probably the week after, I'll not be here to stop him.'

'I can look after myself you know,' she retorted.

There was a note of sarcasm in Kev's voice as he drawled, 'Like your mother thought and look what happened to her.' He saw the brief flash of consternation on her face and softening his voice said, 'Please Becky, keep your thoughts to yourself around him. Understand?'

Becky nodded, 'I'll stay out of his way, Kev. Don't you worry.' She longed to be in his arms, she couldn't make herself believe that it would never happen again.

'God only knows what he'll get up to here on his own. Keeps talking about going into town, but as there's no buses. I can't see him walking the three miles so it's very unlikely. I expect he'll be stir crazy by the time one of us gets home.'

Becky gave a snort of derision, 'Something, surely he's used to.'

Kevin stood up and ignoring her jibe said, 'And by the way, he's been asking about your mother. Wants to see her, he says. He's already asked me for her address.'

Becky drew her breath in sharply and snapped back, 'You didn't...?'

'No, I didn't. I said I didn't know. I never go to see her because you always go on your own.'

'Thanks,' she said as she made her way to the kitchen. She edged passed Archie who had quietly appeared at the doorway and eyed them suspiciously.

As Becky hurried away she heard him say, 'What you Two been up to? No hanky-panky I trust.'

Becky seethed with hatred at his implied hint.

Later, locked in her room, she heard voices and a scuffle in the garden below. Carefully pulling back the curtains and looking out she was amazed to see Kevin holding onto the saddle of his bike as Archie, wobbling, was trying to keep his balance on it. 'I'll ride this bloody thing you see if I don't,' she heard him say.

Standing by the window she watched their efforts, Archie getting redder and redder with frustration and Kev tight lipped with exasperation. When Archie fell off the bike Becky laughed out loud, and hastily stood back from the window. Throwing herself on to her bed she hugged herself with glee, knowing she'd remember forever, Archie falling into a bed of nettles they hadn't got round to clearing yet. The look of amazement on his face as the handlebars turned into him, his legs beating the air for grip and his hands flailing the nettles from his face.

Shortly afterwards she realised it was first time she had laughed, really laughed out loud since Archie arrived. If only she could have shared the moment with Kev, how they would have laughed together she thought. Kev would have happily performed the scene again and again chortling all the while. She smiled to herself as the pictures flashed before her again, and she giggled happily.

Chapter 7

In order to meet her mother as promised, after cleaning the bath which wasn't as grimy as she had expected, Becky bathed and dressed herself in a sleeveless dress patterned in varying shades of beige, brown and tan with narrow shoulder straps. It was her only good piece in the wardrobe, the rest were at least four years old. Saving so hard for the future she had made do with what she had. The dress bought to go to a friend's wedding just over a year ago still looked pristine. Becky sighed as she put it on, things were so different then. She and Kevin were so happy, holding hands during the ceremony. He had turned to her and whispered, 'We'll be next.' Now, everything had changed.

Throwing a lightweight jacket over her shoulders she came down the stairs and saw Archie, lounging against the frame of the open front door flicking ash from his cigarette into the garden. He stood up sharply as she approached.

'And where might you be off to, may I ask?' he demanded. Becky ignored him and tried to pass. He moved and blocked the doorway putting his hand up with fingers outspread to stop her. 'I asked you a question. Quite nicely I thought, and now I want an answer, if you please.' There was no mistaking his tone.

Becky shrugged, 'You want me to cook dinner tonight, with what? Someone's got to do some proper shopping.' She stopped for a moment and looking straight into his unsmiling face, added, 'Of course, if you'd rather do the cooking yourself, I can always get myself something at the hospital.'

Archie took a step towards her. His eyes narrowed as he said, 'You're a lippy little bitch aren't you?'

Becky tossed her head and with her nose in the air tried to push past him. He grabbed her arm, 'Don't you dare touch me,' she hissed.

The hold on her arm tightened, Archie thrust his face into hers as she tried to pull herself free.

It was then Kevin put in an appearance, 'What's going on? You two not at it again are you?'

As Archie dropped his hand he whispered to her, 'You wait, my girl. I'll sort you out one of these days.' Then turning to Kevin and smiling brightly added, 'Off you go then, steak will do nicely for dinner won't it lad?' Becky didn't hesitate, she grabbed her bicycle and rode away as dignified as she could. The encounter with Archie had unnerved her and she realised that Kevin was right – she could easily be targeted and God knows what Archie might do if Kevin wasn't around.

As soon as Becky reached town she saw Stella waiting patiently at the memorial. She jumped off her bike, padlocked it to the iron bicycle stand and gave her mother a hug.

Linking her arm through her daughter's and almost pulling her along, Stella said, 'Coffee first, I'm gasping for my coffee. Let's go to "Beth's Buns" they do the most marvellous pastries there.'

They set out along the high street. As they were passing The Bridal Boutique, Becky stopped and gave out a low moan. The problems of cancelling the wedding and explaining the reasons were brought home to her again.

'What? Whatever is the matter?' asked Stella, full of concern as she looked at her daughter's stricken face.

Becky stood still gazing into the shop window. Then turning to her mother, her face white, her eyes full of tears said in a faint voice, 'My wedding dress. My beautiful dress...' Almost sobbing she added, 'I'll never be able to wear it now, will I?'

Stella didn't know how to comfort Becky and gently agreed with her saying. 'No, darling, you won't.' She watched Becky swallow a sob, 'But listen to me.'

With her shoulders drooped, Becky placed her hands on the window and peered inside.

Stella shook her arm, 'Listen, you will be a bride one day.' Becky glared at her. 'Believe me, there is someone out there for you. You'll see. All this trouble and upset will eventually pass.'

'I can't even begin to think when,' Becky snapped. 'He keeps saying he's there forever.'

'Nonsense. Not forever.' She paused for a moment and gave a little chuckle. 'Why, you never know he might keel over and die, fall under a bus or something.'

There was a hint of a smile on Becky's face as she turned to Stella and retorted, 'Well he'd better not end up in my ward.'

'Come on, let's go inside and see if we can get your money back.'

When they entered the shop, the first thing they saw were four wedding dresses, encased in plastic protectors, waiting for collection. Tears welled up in Becky's eyes again. 'That one,' she whispered, 'That's the one I chose. The ivory satin with cap sleeves and tiny rosebuds embroidered down the bodice.' She pointed, 'That one, see?'

Stella held her hand and nodded. 'It's beautiful darling, but...'

'I know.'

A young assistant came over to them, 'Can I help?' she enquired with a smile.

Stella answered, 'I should like to see whoever is in charge, please.'

The girl looked crestfallen.

'Oh dear,' Stella exclaimed, 'I'm sure that another time you could help, but I think on this occasion we ought to speak with someone, shall we say, with a little more experience?'

The girl nodded, 'I'll get her for you, the manageress. Would you like to sit down while you're waiting?' They took their seats as the girl went away.

A woman in her mid-thirties, neatly dressed with a tape measure draped around her neck, came towards them with a smile. 'How may I help you?' she asked. Then recognising Becky, said, 'Oh, The ivory dress. You came in a few weeks ago, if I remember rightly.' She smiled brightly as she went on, 'I remember what dress goes with whose face, but I'm sorry your name escapes me.'

Becky swallowed the hard lump in her throat, 'Becky,' she whispered, 'Becky Wilson.'

'Yes, I remember now. Have you come to try on the dress? Don't worry, a lot of my customers lose weight before their special day? It's no problem to take the dress in.' She looked keenly at Becky and gave a little laugh, 'or let it out that happens sometimes. The girl finds herself expecting and well...'

Firmly, Stella interrupted, 'Nothing like that, I can assure you,'

The manageress turned to Becky, 'So, what is it my dear? Just passing and wanted to see the lovely creation?' She went across to the dress, took it down and brought it over to them. She pulled the plastic cover up from the hem and stroked the material. 'It really is beautiful,' she murmured. 'You will look stunning in it.' Becky burst into tears and the dress was hastily pulled away, and replaced on the rail.

Stella handed Becky a tissue, then taking a deep breath turned to the assistant and said, 'Unfortunately, my daughter has to cancel the wedding.' She was stunned when the manageress laughed.

'My dear,' she said turning to Becky, 'I hear that so often and usually it turns out that the couple have a quarrel, begin to cancel their wedding plans and before you know it, everything is back on again.' Becky, her face red and eyes swollen shook her head.

Stella stood up and picking up her handbag, said with dignity, 'That definitely will not be so in this situation I can assure you.' Pulling Becky to her feet added, 'I should like a refund. – I believe there is a refund?' The manageress opened her mouth to speak, but Stella went on, 'The cheque should be made out to Miss R. Wilson.' Again the woman began to protest, and again Stella forestalled her,

'We'll wait shall we, while you make it out.' She smiled at Becky, 'Then darling, we really must go and get that coffee we promised ourselves.'

In the coffee shop, Becky stirred her coffee round and round watching the frothy milk disappearing, her face etched with misery. Stella felt helpless as she watched her unhappy daughter. She stretched her hand across the table and closed it over Becky's. 'Listen love, today we are meant to be enjoying ourselves. So...' she took a breath and smiled brightly at Becky, 'Let's get the worst over with first, shall we?' She leaned back in her chair, lifted her mug and took a sip before going on. 'Now, what else have we to cancel so that you can put everything behind you?' She gazed into Becky's face. 'Cake? Flowers? Cars?' Becky lifted her head and Stella saw her cheeks wet with fresh tears. 'Come on, darling,' she coaxed. 'Let's get it all over with.'

Becky nodded and mumbled, 'Everything, even the honeymoon.'

'All booked locally?'

'Except the cake. My friend at the hospital and I were going to make it together. I'll have to tell her something I suppose. Tell her it's all off.'

'Right. Finish your coffee and we'll start at one end of the town and work our way along shall we?' She saw Becky give an unwilling nod. 'As we go along we'll look out for something dressy for you and something for me to go away in.'

Becky burst out, 'I can't. I can't. How can I go to your wedding and be happy when my own is, is...?'

Stella stood up. 'Come on. You've got to face up to things and...' she paused, 'and on my wedding day, I hope you will be glad for me, my pet.'

The girls in the flower boutique were obviously curious their faces alight with a possible scandal to pass on. Stella hedged round their enquiries. As the owner of the shop returned the deposit she said to Becky, 'If you change your mind,' she hesitated, 'or have found someone else, shall we say...' she smiled brightly, 'well you know you can rely on us for an excellent service.'

When Stella and Becky were once again outside the shop, Stella could hardly contain her indignation. 'If... No, when you do find someone else, you'd damn well better find another florist. What cheek! I'm glad she's not doing mine, I'd cancel straight away. Insensitive madam.'

Becky shrugged her shoulders. Although she knew her mother was right cancelling her well laid plans, it still hurt. Nevertheless, she thought, I'm spared the ordeal of doing it all by myself.

The visit to the car hire firm was short. 'No problem,' the man said as he opened his appointments diary and put a pen through entry. 'Only a provisional booking as far as I can see. Your bloke didn't leave a deposit.' He lifted his head and saw the look of misery on Becky's face, 'All the best,' he added. And it was all over, so little fuss Becky thought, and typical of Kevin not to have left a deposit.

They had a light lunch and by mid-afternoon they were exhausted, content with their purchases. Becky had chosen a cream linen suit, a blouse patterned with small, blue flowers, a blue clutch purse and strappy open-toed shoes. Stella's going away outfit was in dusky pink, a straight dress with cap sleeves and two rows of drawn thread across the bodice. The matching three-quarter length coat had three rows of drawn thread from the shoulders down over the bodice stopping at the bust line. It was perfect and each agreed that the other looked sensational. Stella also bought herself a couple of jumpers, a pair of lined trousers and a furry hat and Becky raised her eyebrows in surprise. 'Well,' Stella laughed, 'It's winter in Australia; I'd look pretty daft if I arrived in a sleeveless dress.' They made their plans for the wedding day, and Stella collected up all their shopping and hailed a taxi.

It was nearly four o'clock and Becky still had to get something for the evening meal. The butcher's shop was empty except for the assistant in his trade uniform of a blue and white striped apron and white trilby hat. He was busily wiping down the tiled counter but when he saw Becky he laughed, and said, 'Well, here she is at last, the queen of my heart.'

Becky felt herself going red and took time searching in her bag for her purse to hide her embarrassment. When she raised her head she saw he was leaning over the counter and grinning at her. 'Sorry,' he said, 'I didn't mean to offend you. What can I get you?'

She hadn't really thought about what they were going to eat. Well, she thought, I've had a busy day, don't feel like cooking anything really and they don't deserve anything, so it'll be spag bol. Hastily she said, 'A pound of mince – good mince mind. None of that fatty stuff.'

'Tell you what, if I get the best steak out and mince it up for you will you tell me your name?'

'Do you own this shop or are you just the manager?'

'I'm the manager,' he replied turning to the back of the shop and choosing a piece of prime steak. 'Mind you, I may not be the best looking guy in here, but I'm the only one talking to you, so, are you going to tell me your name or not?'

'Do you usually want to know all your customers' names?'

He turned back to her and she noted his blond curly hair escaping from under his hat. His blue eyes looked directly into hers. She wasn't sure what she read in them – definitely a challenge and she was very much aware of his interest in her. 'Only the ones I fancy.'

A little unnerved, she quickly got out her purse and asked, 'How much do I owe you?'

'Will you be in next week sometime?' he said as he wrapped the meat. 'Two pound, twenty-one.'

She handed over the cash and didn't answer.

He smiled as he murmured, 'Great. I'll look forward to seeing you again, queen of my heart.'

Becky cycled home her thoughts in turmoil. Someone, someone of the opposite sex had taken an interest in her. She'd only ever known Kevin, never dreamed anyone else would be interested in her. The butcher had definitely made a pass, well something like she imagined was a pass. And didn't he say he was looking forward to seeing her next week. The short repartee between them had made her uneasy. she told herself that she would not be going in that shop again. Nevertheless, there was no denying that he had somehow made her lonely feelings diminish a little and she gave a small satisfactory smile.

The three of them, Becky, Kevin and Archie sat down together at the evening meal. Few words were spoken between them. Becky found herself daydreaming and gave a ghost of a smile. The two men looked at her then at each other. Archie raised his eyebrows as if questioning and Kevin shook his head from side to side as if to say, 'I know as much as you.'

Noting the pantomime between them, Becky pulled herself together, washed her own dishes and made her way to bed.

Chapter 8

Kevin and Becky arrived at the front gate together on the Monday after their respective day's work. As Kevin jumped out of Ryan's car, he was surprised to see Becky arriving at the same time.

'You're late,' he accused. 'Where've you been?'

Becky propped her bike against the hedge inside the garden. 'You told me to keep out of his way so I've volunteered for overtime this week,' she sniffed, 'Not that it's any of your business.'

Opening the door ahead of her Kevin stood back to let her enter, and nearly bumped into her when she stood stock still inside the entrance hall.

'What's up now?' Kevin in grumbled. 'Move will you?'

Becky pointed and said nothing. Kevin looked beyond her and turned back to her in surprise. Archie had taken over the spare downstairs room. By putting a single bed and a chest of drawers into the room he had turned it into a bedroom for himself. Archie stood by the door, grinning and obviously proud of what he had done. Nobody spoke. Kevin shrugged his shoulders which seemed to indicate to Becky that he didn't care.

Archie tapped his nose as he looked at Kevin and said, 'Tell you about it later.'

Becky felt both sick and outraged at Archie's audacity, but knew it was useless to make a fuss. Instead she narrowed her lips and flounced her way upstairs to her own room. A bedsit, that's what I'm reduced to now she thought bitterly, in my own home. Admitting to herself that she was curious as to how Archie had so quickly arranged the downstairs room she decided to find out.

'Later,' he'd said.

She had been in the house long enough to know by heart where give-away creaking floor boards were and every stair that softly groaned under weight, the third, sixth and seventh. Each time she heard a floorboard give she knew almost instantly who and where one of the two men were.

It was over half an hour later that she heard the two of them talking in the kitchen. Carefully treading her way down the stairs and along the passage, she made her way to the kitchen door which someone hadn't fully closed.

They were both eating jacket potatoes with a cheese wedge. 'This isn't grub for a fella to go to work on,' moaned Kevin.

'Don't tell me, tell her.'

With his mouth full, Kevin started to complain about his boring sandwiches he had made in haste that morning, to which Archie replied, 'As I said before, don't tell me, tell her. It's about time that little madam was made to know her place.'

Kevin stopped chewing, 'Which is...?' He asked looking squarely up into Archie's face.

Archie shrugged, 'What women should do – look after their men folk, cleaning, mending, seeing to their grub.'

Becky was outraged, desperately wanting to vent her anger, but was mollified a little when Kevin answered, 'But she's working full time. This week she told me she was doing overtime. We can't expect her to wait on us hand and foot.'

Archie pushed his plate away, picked up his mug and took a mouthful of tea. 'Overtime,' he said thoughtfully. Briskly he added, 'On the other hand lad, you're in work now, so she could easily stay home and do as I...we say. What do you think?'

'I've two maybe three week's work, that's all. What'll we do then if there isn't anything else...?' He took another mouthful of food before adding, 'and what about you? Are you going to find something? Put your share into the kitty? You can't expect us to go on giving you free food and lodgings,' he paused, 'who said you could take over that front room, and where did the money come from to buy that bed? You've got a nerve, you know. God only knows what Becky thinks about it.'

Archie gave a sly snigger. 'Thought your old dad useless didn't you. Well, I'd been wondering how I could be more comfortable and you kept moaning you wanted a proper bed instead of that sofa affair.'

'So would you if you had to sleep on it.'

'No doubt. So anyway,' he stopped to take another swallow of tea. 'As I was saying,' he began, 'now that I've mastered that bicycle contraption – I could ride a bike when I was a lad, you know.'

Kevin nodded.

'Made my way into town, found a furniture shop and saw just what I wanted – a decent bed. Went in and chatted up the manager. Got him to take forty quid off and put down a deposit.'

'Oh? And where did that come from?'

'I'm not daft you know. Kept back a few quid.' He was quiet for a moment. 'Not got much left. Going to have to do something about that.' He did not smile as he looked at Kevin and said, 'Got some plans about that. We'll talk about them later.'

Kevin felt himself going cold, guessing he would be coerced into a criminal act. He kept silent hoping Archie's plans would be kept on hold indefinitely.

'Well, I said to myself, my boy is working so is she, one of them can pay the rest on the never-never. What do you think?'

'You old fool,' exclaimed Kevin. 'Do you really think Becky will be willing to pay for something for you? She truly hates you, you know.'

'Well, you'll have to persuade her then.'

'She has her own bank account; I can't make her pay up.'

'It's either that son, or you'll have to find the rest, won't you?

Kevin sighed, 'Don't you understand Dad, this job is not permanent so I can't make any promises.'

'As I said before, I got a plan, and mates who can help out, but of course, if madam could be persuaded, then there'll be all the more for us.'

'But...' Kevin in began to protest.

Archie held up his hand to stop Kevin saying anything further. 'Listen will you. When I was in the town, I managed to get a little something myself.' Out of his pocket he produced a woman's purse and opened it. 'See?' he questioned. 'Fifty-four pounds and some coins and see this?' He tipped the purse over the table and a gold ring with three diamonds fell out. 'Why that's in there I can't think, but I know someone who'll give me a fair price for it.'

Becky had heard enough and crept away. Back in her room she was both tearful and a little afraid. She was fearful of Archie's threats to keep her at home to be at his beck and call, but was determined this would not happen. At the same time she wondered if she could stand up to the two of them. She promised herself she would. Her tears were not only for herself, she hated Kevin being dragged into Archie's cunning plans, and his boasting about stealing a purse. His disclosure of the theft didn't surprise her in the least, nor did his lack of sympathy for the victim or his lack of guilt. Briefly she wondered if she should contact the police, but something, she didn't know what, held her back, probably the knowledge of Archie's uncontrollable temper and what he could do if he found out.

The two men in the kitchen continued to talk then argue. The argument came about when Archie mentioned purchasing a car. 'I've been looking in the paper for a sound second-hand car. You could pick one up for a couple of hundred at the end of the week,' he told Kevin. 'Boy, once we have wheels we can plan all sorts of little dodges.' He was thoughtful for a minute. 'No, not little dodges – something much more rewarding perhaps?'

Kevin stood up, wiped his mouth and took his plate across to the sink. Turning to his father he shook his head from side to side a number of times before saying, 'Dad, there is no way we can buy car at the weekend. I've other things to do with my money and...'

'What sort of things? Now look here my son...'

Kevin noted the raised tone of Archie 's voice and answered carefully, 'I need some new clothes for a start. Do you know how long I've had these work boots? I'll tell you, since I left college. My bike needs new tyres and no doubt Becky will be looking for something towards the food – our food yours and mine.'

'Okay, forget her for a start.' Archie was quiet for a moment. 'Well the weekend after then. We could look at a few then, right?'

Kevin was beginning to get exasperated. 'I may well be out of work by then. Besides,' he added, 'have you thought about road tax and insurance? They will dig a hole into any money I might have.'

Archie laughed, 'A lot of blokes don't bother about that sort of thing. They just get in and drive,' but before Kevin could interrupt added, 'and they get away with it.'

'And eventually get caught.' Kevin pent up with resentment took a step forward, but remembering his father was quick tempered and stronger than himself, stopped. A confrontation with the old man was not advisable. Containing his own temper, he took a deep breath and said, 'If, and I say if we...I get a car, it will be mine. Understand? I will drive it, no one else and that means it will be properly licensed so that should we get stopped by the law at any time, we shall have the proper documents. Now, do you understand my meaning?'

Archie looked at his son almost in awe. 'Blimey boy, you're ahead of me. That's good thinking that is.'

'Good, at last you understand. Leave the car business to me. If I've got the cash I'll see what's about in a few weeks time. So until then, for heaven's sake shut up about it will you?'

Archie was satisfied and his answer was a cheerful. 'Right. Right you are boy.'

Chapter 9

Becky was pleasantly surprised when she and her mother arrived at the local registrar's office. There was a luxurious, red pile carpet on which stood more than a dozen gilt painted chairs with matching velvet cushions. At each end of the long table covered with a pristine damask cloth, was a vase of white and red long stemmed gladioli. A smaller vase holding roses was set in front of a large open book in the centre of the table.

During the ceremony Becky did her best not to think of her own wedding plans. Deep within herself she was miserable and a little jealous of her mother's day, and swallowed the little sobs that welled up in her throat. At the same time she told herself that her mother deserved every moment of happiness. She watched as Stella and Stuart signed the registrar's book, then turn to each other, their faces alight with happiness, and kissed. There were no more than fourteen guests, a couple of Stella's friends along with Becky, the remainder were Stuart's relatives. All clapped and surrounded the couple showering them with good wishes.

There was a short journey to the reception. The cars carrying the guests drove through a pair of large, wrought-iron gates then along a wide sweeping driveway. The wedding breakfast, a luncheon, was held in the eighteenth century Gibson country house standing in an acre of well maintained gardens. Everyone climbed the wide curved staircase to the reception room where Stella and Stuart were waiting to greet them. Becky hugged her mother and quickly embraced Stuart, who, with a wide grin on his face, said, 'At last, I have a daughter. Makes a change from the three boys I have to suffer. Though I don't see much of them, what with them all working abroad somewhere.' He turned to the young men behind him. 'But as you can see, they made the effort today to support their old man.' There was soft laughter from behind him and Becky saw three grinning faces, all showing affection for their father.

Looking around the room Becky was attracted to the magnificent marble fireplace its hearth covered with dozens of vases of flowers. There was an elaborate candelabra, ornate cornicing and oak beams along with other original features. Around the room were some antique artefacts and furniture. The high, open, beautifully stained glass fanlights made the room light and airy. Soft pastel colours on the walls added to the restful and graceful atmosphere of the room. The bridal couple were teased about their love story that they had printed on the back of the souvenir menus – how they had met, conventionally at the office, their first date – the local drama group's production of *Kiss me Kate*. There was a great deal of laughter at the recording of the proposal, not on Stuart's bended knee, but last winter when he was red and streaming with a cold, 'Man flu, he said,' Stella added.

After a glass of champagne followed by a glass of wine, Becky realised she was beginning to enjoy herself. As she sipped her wine she was joined by one of the grinning faces she'd seen earlier. 'Hi,' he said, as he smiled and sat beside her. 'My father forgot his manners and didn't introduce you to me, so here I am – Ian.'

Becky smiled back at him and put out her hand to shake his as she said, 'Becky, daughter of the bride.' She took a sip from her glass before asking, 'And what are your brothers' names?'

Ian sat up abruptly then leaned towards her and still smiling said, 'Brothers? I don't have any brothers – least not any that count when it comes to getting to know pretty girls.'

In quick succession, Becky registered surprise at his attempted lie and then embarrassment. The wine though, had relaxed her and she quickly answered, 'What are you doing talking to me then?'

Ian glanced slowly around the room, 'Yes,' he said, 'I was right. Pretty girls, and as far as I can see there is only one in this room.'

Becky hiccupped then giggled.

'Now, tell me something about yourself. You're a nurse I believe. Got the bedside manner, I hope. Perhaps you'd like to practise on...'

He stopped abruptly when two young men hauled him to his feet. Both perched on the now empty chair beside her. 'Has he been trying his luck? Chatting you up or something?' one of them asked.

Becky looked at the two newcomers – Ian's brothers. There was no mistaking the resemblance between them. 'Well,' she began, 'he was quite charming really.'

Ian smirked and shrugged his shoulders as his two brothers roared with laughter. 'See, I've got charm. The lady said so.'

One of the boys pushed him away and the other said, 'Clear off.'

As Ian sauntered away he called over his shoulder to her, 'I'll not be far away Becky, so find me and give me your telephone number later. Right?'

'I shouldn't if I were you. He's always breaking girls' hearts. You're too good for the likes of him. I'm Paul and this is John. May we call you Rebecca?'

As she shook hands first with Paul then John she said, 'Becky is fine.' Looking at the pair of them and raising her eyebrows she said, 'I wonder what sort of character reference Ian would give either of you.'

They both laughed, 'The same I dare say as we've given him,' said John, 'Although I expect he would add to Paul's that he is already engaged to be married next year.'

'Yes, but...'

Giving his brother a friendly punch on the arm, John said, 'No buts. You're out of the market.' He smiled at Becky who thought it remarkable that the three brothers had the same open smile – a smile with clear sincerity. By their banter she knew that they were close. 'Now me,' John continued, 'I'm free...'

'Only at the moment.'

'Shut up.' John turned back to Becky. 'As I was saying, I'm free this evening if you'd like to have a late dinner with me.'

Becky was in turmoil. It had been a very long time since anyone other than Kevin had shown any interest in her and she had forgotten how to react, flirt even, with the opposite sex. Briefly she thought of the butcher, did he count, she wondered? Her mind told her to go, her heart told her she couldn't – she still somehow felt she should be faithful to Kevin. Come to think of it, he wouldn't like what was happening – nor would her father. And yet, it would be wonderful to go on a date. She shook her head regretfully. 'Sorry,' she said, 'I have to work.'

'Ah, yes.' John sighed and leaned back in the chair, then

added brightly, 'But hey, let me have your telephone number and we can arrange another time. Yes?'

Becky drained the last of her wine before answering. 'I don't think...'

'There, told you so,' interrupted Paul, 'she's already spoken for.' As Becky was about to explain, he went on, 'Stands to reason, an attractive girl like you must have someone special.' He looked at her and added, 'I'm right aren't I? There's a bloke somewhere in your life isn't there?'

Becky stood up and looked at one then the other, and gave a brief nod of her head. She was pleased, when looking past their shoulders, to see her mother beckoning. 'Please excuse me will you? My mother wants me. I do believe they are leaving.' They stood up as she edged past them and hurried towards the newly-weds.

Both Stella and Becky were in tears as they said their good-byes. Stella begged her to leave, 'Those dreadful men. They will make you unhappy and I feel you will not be safe especially with Archie around. Promise me you will? Leave them darling, and make your way to Australia. We'll take care of you, and help you find work. You'll love it. Promise?' Becky nodded as she wiped her tears away with a soggy tissue. After further farewells to friends both left. Stella to a new life with her husband, and Becky to the hospital to start the late shift.

Chapter 10

'Becks not home yet?' were the first words Kevin uttered when he arrived home the same evening.

'Becks not home yet?' mimicked Archie. 'Never mind

about your poor old dad here on his own all day.' Putting down a bowl of soup and a wedge of bread in front of Kevin, he said, 'Here's your grub. Eat it while it's hot and no she ain't in yet. Probably working on, doing the late shift.' Kevin heard him muttering almost to himself, 'She'd better be, or I'll be asking some awkward questions and...' He sniffed, scratched his nose and added, 'That's all there is. You'll have to make do with sandwiches if you want anything else.'

'For the love of God,' Kevin burst out. 'What have you been doing all day?'

'Archie raised his eyebrows and compressed his lips before saying, 'Making plans boy.'

'Surely you could've got some sort of meal together. Just because I'm not here all day waiting on you hand and foot doesn't mean...'

'What do you mean waiting on me hand and foot? That day isn't likely to arrive. You'd be lost if I wasn't around to tell you what to do.' He hesitated, 'Like that missy used to.'

'Her name is Rebecca in case you've forgotten. He wiped out his bowl with the remaining piece of bread, sighed and leaned back in his chair. 'You can ride the bike now, you could've gone to the shops and got something to cook.'

'Oh, and who's going to pay for it? I notice she don't leave out any cash now,' There was an emphasis on the word 'she'.

'No, because she knows and I know that you've got some of your own.'

'If you mean that twenty quid note I had, it's gone.'

'Come off it! Who do you think you're kidding? You've got more stashed away somewhere, I know it.'

'None of your business, 'sides you got plenty now between you. Her doing overtime and you...how much a day did you say?'

'None of your business,' Kevin retorted as he left the room and made his way to the sitting room.

He switched on the television, sat in the armchair, hung his legs over the armrest, leaned back and closed his eyes. He heard the clatter of dishes as Archie rinsed them. That's a first, he told himself, but it wasn't long before Archie joined him. At first all Kevin could hear was the tell-tale sound of newspaper pages being turned over, far too fast for Archie to be doing any serious reading. Archie coughed and Kevin half-opened his eyes to watch and inwardly smiled as he saw his father lean towards him to check if he was asleep, then sigh in frustration thinking he was.

Kevin opened his eyes, 'What?' he mumbled, 'what's up with you?'

Archie 's face brightened, 'Good, you're awake.'

'Yes, I'm awake. You made sure of that with your fiddling about with the paper and coughing and sighing. What do you want now?'

There was a cunning look on Archie's face along with hardness about his eyes, as he asked, 'Did you ever get girlie an engagement ring?'

Kevin swung his legs back and sat up straight, alert. 'What sort of fool question is that?'

'Simple enough, lad. Has she got an engagement ring or not?'

'Never had any spare dosh for that sort of thing. Bought the telly instead.'

Rubbing his chin thoughtfully, Archie said, 'Thought not.' He stood up and turned the television off before adding, 'Good.' He sat down again and clasped his hands together and leaned forward, his head, twisted so he could see Kevin's face. 'I got an idea about that,' he said.

'Ain't interested, you know that.' He turned his head away from Archie's hypnotic eyes and added, 'Don't want to know.'

'But this is different.' Archie got up and went to the door, checked that Becky was not in the passageway, even taking a step or two to listen at the bottom of the stairs to ensure she had not come home and crept up to her room, as she usually did. Wants to avoid me, he told himself, but I'm up to all her tricks. Confident that they had the house to themselves, he closed the door firmly as an added pre-caution, and walked across to Kevin. Standing behind him Archie put his hand on Kevin's shoulder bent over and quietly whispered his latest plan in Kevin's ear. When he had finished, Kevin shrugged his hand off, leaned back in the chair and put his hands behind his head.

'You're a clever old bugger, I'll give you that,' he said, 'but I don't know. Not sure I want to get into that sort of carry-on.'

Archie stomped about the room and slapped his head. 'What do I have to say or do to convince you. It won't be difficult I promise. You...' He stabbed his finger at Kevin, 'The way you carry on I can't believe you're my son. No, not at all, too soft an upbringing that's your trouble. First your mother spoiling you, and making sure you stayed on the straight and narrow. Yes, she turned you into a prissy little fool. Then that little hussy got her claws into you, telling you what to do. You need to toughen up lad. This is noth-ing to what we can do together if you play your cards right. Get a bit of spine in yer back for God's sake.'

'That's enough,' Kevin shouted as he jumped to his feet.

'You were never around for my upbringing.' He paused, took a deep breath to hold back his mounting anger, 'No, and if you had been where would I find myself now, eh, tell me that?' In three strides he was at the door then added, 'in bloody prison no doubt.' He made his way to the kitchen, found a mug, filled it with cold water and took two good gulps causing him to splutter. Archie followed him.

'See what I mean? Any other bloke would have had a can of something handy, but not you, you softy.' He sat down and watched Kevin wipe his mouth then his shirt, rinse the mug, dry it and put it back on the shelf. 'Just give it some thought, lad. Work it out in your own mind and you'll see it'll work.'

Kevin shook his head twice. 'I'll think about it.'

There was a touch of glee in Archie's voice as he said, 'Good lad.' Again he rubbed his chin thoughtfully, 'Of course, it'll be even better when you get us a car.'

'My car, you mean.'

'Aye, aye, something like that.'

Kevin, shoulders and head down brushed past him. 'Just shut up will you.'

Chapter 11

After finishing her shift on Saturday, Becky called in at the supermarket. She was surprised by the amount of goods she had bought and had a struggle placing the carrier bags around her bicycle. What she hadn't bought was meat for dinner that evening, and pondered if this had been a deliberate omission as there had been a good selection in the supermarket. Deliberate, so that she had to call into the only fresh butcher's in town, the butcher who last week had, through his silly banter, lifted her spirits.

It was around two thirty when she reached the shop. The doorbell pinged as she entered and he came out wiping his hands on a bloodied piece of muslin. He grinned, 'I knew you'd be back.' Becky didn't speak. 'So, what can I get my princess today?' he asked.

'I forgot to pick up some mince in the supermarket,' she said as a small thrill reached her heart.

'Forgot! No, no. I reckon you was desperate to see me again.'

Shaking her head she answered, 'I don't think so. I've got a hungry...' she hesitated, '...family,' not wanting to admit to a father and stepbrother at home.

'So, its mince again is it? If there are grown men in your family surely they'd like a steak or chops, definitely something to get their teeth into.'

Becky muttered something to herself.

'What's that you say?'

Still muttering she said, 'They'll eat steak when they pay for it.'

'Ah! I see. Just you working is it?' He turned and washed his hands properly, reached for the tray of mince and scooped some up. 'How much do you want then?'

'A pound should be enough I think.'

'And what are you going to do with a pound of mince?'

'Not sure yet,' but after a few moments said, 'shepherd's pie, I think.'

'Yes lovely. Put plenty of mash on top that should fill them up.' As he wrapped the mince he added, 'My...' he stopped suddenly before going on to say, 'My mother always made that for me and my brothers when I was a kid.

Always filled us up that did.'

Becky handed over the money and he passed her the meat. As she made for the door, she felt disappointed. He had not attempted to tease her today, and she resigned herself to the fact that last week was just a ploy for her custom.

As the bell pinged when she opened the door to leave she heard him call out, 'You still haven't told me your name.' He came out from behind the counter, leaned across her and closed the door. Becky noted the seriousness of his tone when he said, 'I'm Michael Govan. Mike to most of my friends.'

Becky couldn't help it. She gave him a full smile as she answered, 'Rebecca Wilson, Becky to my friends.'

'And are we friends?'

There was a hint of shyness in her voice, hardly audible, 'Yes, Mike I think we could be.'

'Well then Becky, we close at three on Saturdays. You can see the place is empty. I've scrubbed up all the counters so I reckon I could treat you to a cup of tea in the High Street. What do you say?'

'I don't know. I...'

'What's to stop you?' He eyed her loaded bike. 'Tell you what. Leave your bike here inside the shop. I'll lock up and it'll be quite safe.'

She shook her head.

'Aw! Come on. Half an hour that's all I want. Just to get to know you a bit better.' He put his head on one side, 'Please. Come on, please.'

Why not, she asked herself and gave in to his cajoling. 'Half an hour only mind, then I must get home. They'll be wondering where I am.'

They had tea and scones at the nearby 'Tea Rooms'. Becky was impressed with Mike's good manners, taking her coat, settling her in a chair and offering her the menu.

'A cup of tea please,' she said. 'That's all I really want and a sit down.'

The waitress came over and looking keenly at Becky asked, 'So something special today, Mike?'

'Hi, Jan, a pot of tea for four.' Jan laughed. 'The cups are so small, I need two or three refills,' he explained to Becky. 'And we'll have some of those fat scones, please.' He smiled at Becky. 'You can manage one of those, can't you?' Turning to the waitress and grinning he said, 'What happens to a scone when I've eaten it?'

She shook her head, 'Oh really Michael, not another one of your terrible jokes.'

'Now, don't be like that. Want the answer?'

With a resigned sigh, 'Go on then. Hurry up. I'm busy.'

'Okay. Got this off the Internet. What happens to a scone when I've eaten it? Answer: It's gone.' Both Becky and the waitress gave a loud groan.

'You sure you want to stay with this horror?' the girl asked Becky.

Becky pursed her lips before answering, 'I suppose so if I want tea.'

When the loaded tray arrived, Mike decided he would pour and she was to help herself to a scone. She spread thick cream thinly on hers and topped it with a meagre amount of strawberry jam.

'Oh, come on. You can do better than that. Here let me.' He promptly dolloped a large helping of cream on top.

Becky eyed it then raised it to her mouth and took a bite. Hearing a snort, she looked up and saw Mike grinning,

'What?' she demanded.

'Well you do look a picture. I wish I had a camera. You've squashed the cream out and it's all over your chin.' He stopped laughing and gazed at her, 'Quite fetching actually.'

Beck grabbed the paper serviette, wiped her mouth quickly and gave a brief smile. Mike was laughing again as he said, 'I was right. I guessed you needed cheering up.'

'What do you mean?' she snapped.

'You've a lovely smile, a bit like the Mona Lisa's.'

'Don't be soft.'

'Seriously, I mean it. But yours is a bit sadder somehow, as if...well, I don't know. It's as if something pretty rough has happened to you.'

Becky turned away from him briefly then turned back to him, 'Something like that,' she said quietly.

'Want to talk about it?' She shook her head. He lifted the teapot. 'Another?' and poured when she nodded.

'You know Becky; you do have a lovely smile. I noticed it straight away last week. I'm so glad you came back to the shop today. Better still, when you said we could be friends I was really chuffed.'

Becky smiled at him. 'Yes, we can be friends.'

There was a contented sigh from Mike as he leaned back in his chair. 'Mind you, I wouldn't say no to a little more than friends.'

'If you don't shut up you'll not even have a customer, let alone a friend,' she retorted.

Suddenly he sat up. 'So you need cheering up. Here are a couple of jokes. Bet you laugh.'

'Go on then. I expect they're corny especially when you beef them up.'

Mike couldn't believe his ears. 'Do you realise what you just said?' he asked.

She grinned at him. 'I'm not as daft as you think.'

'That's very good. I'll try it out on my mates. Corned beef. Ha. Ha.'

'Let's hear yours then,' she said as she reached for her cup.

'Right, here goes. Our local butcher is selling meat on hire purchase – but you have to have a joint account!'

Sipping her tea and looking at him over the rim of her cup Becky murmured, 'Not bad.'

'How about this then? A man walks into a butcher's and says, "Have you got a sheep's head?" and the butcher replies, "No, it's just the way I brush my hair."' He looked at Becky who was straight faced. 'No? Oh well, just trying to keep you amused.'

Relenting she gave a little giggle, 'Where on earth do you get such lame jokes?'

'I belong to a local Butchers' Club of sorts. We all try to outdo each other with daft jokes. I thought they were quite good. Not mine, one of the others read them somewhere.' He stood up and stretched out his hand for her. 'Shall we go?'

The bike was rescued from the shop and they turned to each other to say goodbye. It was obvious from Mike's leaning towards her that he was expecting a kiss. Becky backed away from him and mounted her bicycle. Holding on to the frame, he ventured, 'I'll see next week perhaps?'

Pursing her lips she looked at him sideways and answered. 'Maybe.'

'Better still,' he went on, 'how about meeting me in the week. Just for a walk or something. More tea if you like.

Wednesday is my day off. Are you free say after, two?'

Becky was thoughtful for a moment before saying, 'Alright. I'd like that. I'll come straight from work.'

Sighing with relief he said, 'Great. I'll meet you here then. I'll wait until you arrive then we'll plan something. Right?'

She gave a wave as she left him and thought to herself, I've got a date. I must be mad. I don't want another man in my life, ever. There was however, a ghost of a smile as she pedalled home, a smile that came unbidden as she cooked supper.

It was late afternoon on Saturday and Archie and Kevin had cycled to the town. 'Right, now. You know what you've do, don't you?' Archie said.

Archie had taken Becky's bike as soon as she arrived home, saying only, 'You're late,' as he let her struggle with the over-full carrier bags and made his way to Kevin waiting at the gate.

Just before they set out Archie said, 'I phoned for an appointment on Wednesday, so they're expecting me.' As he looked keenly into Kevin's unhappy face, he said, 'For the love of God, cheer up will you.' He leaned over and slapped Kev's face playfully. 'It'll be a doddle. I sussed the place out proper. Went back twice to make sure. Trust your old dad, son, will you?'

Kevin shrugged his shoulders. He fingered the little silver talisman in his pocket. He didn't know why he kept it, but to feel it in his hand comforted him. 'I don't know. It all seems a bit risky to me.'

'Well, I'll tell you something for nothing boy. It won't work unless you cheer up. You got to go in there all cheerful, cocky, look as if you know what you're doing. Understand?'

Archie leaned the bicycle against the window. They were outside the premises of 'Hear That?' a consulting suite in town where people were assessed for and were sold hearing aids. He turned the bike round into the direction of home. 'There, ready for a quick getaway. You make sure you do the same, right?'

There was a fleeting look of panic which was replaced with doubt on Kevin's face. Shrugging his shoulders Kevin looked carefully around. The town was emptying of shoppers and a few people jostled, laughed, scolded and scurried past them. It took him only a moment to realise that there would be few witnesses about and that the road was practically clear for a swift getaway. He straightened his shoulders and said, 'Give you a couple of minutes, you said and I come in, right?'

'Yes, yes. That's right son.' He lightly punched Kevin's shoulder. 'Good boy. I knew you'd got it in you. Right, tonight we'll have a few more bob in our pockets.' He straightened his jacket, smoothed his hair and as he began to walk towards the door said, 'We'll soon have that car.' Calling over his shoulder he added, 'Then we'll really get going, making some real money.'

In a sullen tone, Kevin said, 'We don't need to do this. I got work for another two maybe three weeks. I'll have enough then.' He caught up with Archie and tugged at his sleeve. 'Come on Dad. Let's leave it,' but Archie was already stepping through the doorway. Kevin sighed and cycled slowly up the high street then back as Archie booked in for a hearing test.

The receptionist looked up and smiled at him. 'Mr...?' she asked. Archie was amused to see her enunciating very carefully in a slow measured voice, louder than necessary for his perfectly good hearing.

'Blimey miss. I ain't that bad. I can hear you proper if you talk normal like, it's just sometimes I miss bits on the telly.'

'Sorry, sorry,' she said. 'Sometimes we get someone in who has great difficulty understanding me.' She reached for a pen, 'Now, before you see the consultant, I need a few details.'

'Right you are. Go ahead. I'm listening.' He chortled, 'Get it'?' he asked.

'Shall we get on with it Mr...?' After answering all the usual questions of full name, address, date of birth and a list of symptoms, he lied to all, she said, 'If you take a seat just at the end of that corridor, Mr Saunders will be with you in a minute. He is just finishing up with another client.'

Archie checked the table. Yes, what he was after was beside the telephone, and smiled to himself as he headed to the seat that had been pointed out.

As he sat down he heard the door open and the receptionist asking, 'Can I help you?'

He sighed with relief when he heard Kevin's cheerful voice say, 'That's my dad down there, come for a hearing test. Will it be all right if I wait for him in here?'

'Of course, take a seat. He should be seen shortly, won't be long.'

Kevin too, surveyed the desk and saw what Archie meant. There was a selection of magazines on the low table and picking up the top one he glanced quickly at the pictures, desperately trying to hide his agitation. Two or three minutes passed. Each felt like an hour to him, before he heard Archie calling the receptionist 'Here miss, can you help?' As she scurried along the short passage to answer him, Kevin was elated. It was going to work. Quickly he snatched up the unguarded tin cash box, left the premises, mounted his bike and made his way home as fast as possible.

Arriving home about half an hour later, Kevin asked Archie what happened. 'I asked her for the lav and she pointed it out. Then she went back to her desk and blow me, she noticed the box had gone almost at once.' Archie chortled, 'Screaming fit to bust, silly cow. First rule in business – never leave the cash box unattended.' He glanced around the kitchen, 'Where's her ladyship then?'

'I think she's in her room, got the radio on by the sounds of it. Go on, what happened next?'

'Had her fooled alright. Course, her yelling brought the bloke out of his little room and the woman client. Both rushed after him – and me as well, so I told them to call the police quick, they might just catch him.'

Kevin stared at his father in disbelief. 'You what?'

'Well I had to say something didn't I? The girl asked if you were my son. I got all indignant like, and told her my son wouldn't dream of stealing.'

'Do you think the police will be able to trace anything back to us?'

'What this local lot? Not likely. Right, that's enough. Put the kettle on there's a good lad. Got parched cycling up that bloody hill.' Rubbing his hands together he asked for the box.

Kev went into the sitting room. Archie followed him and watched him reached under the sofa. 'Thought it best to hide it from Becky.'

'Quite right too. She'd be asking some very awkward

questions,' Archie answered as he snatched the box from Kevin. 'Let's see what we got here then shall we?' He sat down and placed the box on his thighs and slowly opened it. 'Blimey, looks like a good haul here, boy.' He began counting the notes and tipped the coins onto the floor. 'You count that little lot,' he instructed.

Under his breath Kevin heard him counting, 'Seventy-two, seventy-three...' When he had finished he leaned back with a grin on his face, 'Bet you'll never guess how much we got in here,' he said.

Kevin raised his eyebrows. 'So...?'

'Near on a hundred.'

The amount surprised Kevin, 'How come that much? I mean...'

'She should have put some of those notes in the safe especially towards the end of the day. Careless, that's what I think. Fancy leaving all that cash on show.'

'It wasn't on...'

'You know what I mean.' There was a clattering from the kitchen. 'Now, say no more. Madam's around. Hope she's cooking something decent for supper,' he said as he stuffed the notes into the inner pocket of his jacket. 'Keep that little lot out of sight. How much you got in silver then?'

'Not as much as you, about nine quid I reckon.'

'Not bad, not bad at all for a day's work.'

Archie was surprised at how fast Kevin moved. Jumping in front of him, he pulled on Archie's lapels and said, 'Hang on a minute.'

'What's up with you now?' Archie grunted.

'How come you get to keep all the money? I think, seeing as I did the actual stealing I should have at least half.'

'You do, do you? Well, I was the brains behind this little

scam.' He sighed as he reached into his jacket, 'You're right of course,' he said as he thumbed through a good number of notes and handed them over, 'but you make sure you put it towards that car.'

'If you're so keen for me to have a car I reckon you should give me all of it,' Kevin countered.

'In your dreams. I want to find myself a lady friend, and have some fun.' They laughed as they both made their way to the kitchen each with different thoughts.

The air seemed charged throughout their meal. Both men noticed Becky's enigmatic smile. 'She's up to something,' muttered Archie to Kevin. 'We're going to have to keep an eye on that one.'

Chapter 12

Michael was standing outside the closed butcher's shop when Becky arrived on Wednesday afternoon. It was great to see the obvious anxiety on his face that changed quickly to delight when he saw her coming towards him. She gave a wave and smiled as she saw him take his hands out of his pocket, lift and pull back his shoulders and smile back.

At first it seemed as if both were shy and embarrassed until he said, 'Hey what am I thinking of, letting you stand there propping up your bike? Let's get rid of it and decide where to go shall we?' He unlocked the shop door and pushed the bike inside. 'There,' he said, 'safe as houses till we get back.'

Becky muttered her thanks.

'Now,' he said as he tucked her arm through his, 'what would you like to do?'

Becky tried to withdraw her arm, but he firmly gripped it against his side. 'I thought maybe an afternoon's bowling?' She said nothing. He glanced at her sensible working flat shoes. 'Or maybe you'd prefer a walk along the river bank then a cup of tea. What do think?'

'The walk, please, would be lovely. It's so warm and not so noisy. Because of all the bustling, busy time in the hospital, I'd prefer something quieter. Yes, a walk would be fine.'

Avoiding the centre of town they strolled along back alleys until they reached the river towpath saying little on the way. Slowly they walked along the almost empty river side. Michael gave a nervous cough. 'So, Becky, you're a nurse?'

'Yes, I love it. The only drawback is the shift work. Next week I start a late shift, then after that it'll be nights.'

'Which shift is your favourite? I bet it's not nights.'

Laughing, she answered, 'How did you guess? It's not the working nights, it's trying to sleep during the day.' She frowned a little as she thought about her next night duty rota – if Kevin was still working, she would be alone in the house with Archie and anything could happen.

Michael stopped walking and looked into her face, 'What are you thinking about? You're lost in a daydream there.'

Shrugging, she answered, 'Nothing special. Just on nights it's a bit difficult to get enough sleep. My...' she gave an inward shudder, 'Archie, and sometimes my brother Kevin, if they don't have work to go to they're a bit noisy about the house.'

'Yes, I remember now, you said something about them paying their way if they wanted steak for dinner. Was the shepherd's pie up to standard? Bet that mince softened up nicely.'

'I don't believe they noticed. They seemed very excited about whatever they'd been doing, though they didn't tell me what. They're interested in buying a car, so I guess that's what it was all about.'

They walked on and Becky glancing at him now and again decided that, yes, she liked him. He was polite and friendly and, she recalled, he could be quite funny.

'Do you like your job, Michael? Butchering I mean. Don't you sometimes feel, oh I don't know, feel a little remorseful at the slaughter of the animals?'

'No, not really. I don't actually kill them myself you know and, well I suppose someone's got to do it. I just cut up the carcasses and sell them. I mean, what would people do with all those dead animals anyway if they weren't culled? They don't get contraceptives you know. They'd just keep breeding.' He smiled. 'In any case I like a good meaty dinner myself along with thousands of other folk.' He kicked a stone along the path in front of him, before adding, 'Like it? It's a job, but I got some plans.'

'Like what?'

'I've always fancied owning a wine bar. Not a pub, a proper wine bar somewhere in the sun.'

'Like Cornwall or Devon, plenty of sunshine there in the summer.'

'No. There'd be no real trade in the winter months only the locals, so there'd not be much profit in that. No, I was thinking somewhere abroad. Spain or Portugal, even a Greek island.'

'All sounds very ambitious to me, but a lovely idea.' She turned to him, and he heard the dreamlike tone in her voice as she went on, 'Sun and wine, heaven. Think you'll get there?'

He lifted his shoulders, 'Might do. You never know what's around the corner.' In the distance they could see a small café. 'Come on now my lady; let's have a cup of tea before we go back.'

When they returned to the shop and retrieved her bike, he said, 'Next Wednesday, how about going to the pictures? We could meet up at say, two thirtyish, see a film and afterwards we could have a little supper.' He looked at her, waiting for her answer, and was pleased when she nodded.

'I'll let you know if there'd be any change in the plan.'

'What sort of change do you mean?'

Giving out a sigh she answered, 'Well, they like to know exactly what I'm doing. I don't think they'd be too pleased to think I was out with a fellow.'

'Don't tell him, them. Surely they're not that bad.'

Becky raised her eyebrows and nodded. 'Archie's moods change by the minute. I can only guess how he is and I stay well out of his way when it's obvious he's in a temper.'

Taking her hand, Mike exclaimed, 'Please tell me he doesn't hit you.' There was no answer, 'Please, say no.'

Becky saw his agitation, 'No, he hasn't struck me, but I have to say I am sometimes afraid of him and his moods.'

'What about your brother? Surely he wouldn't let anything happen to you.'

Becky turned away from him.

'Just what is going on in that house of yours?' Mike demanded. 'I mean, in this day and age and you gone eighteen. It sounds to me as if there is some sort of hold over you.' He tugged on her hand, 'Is there?' he could see tears filling her eyes. 'Tell me, please. Maybe I can help.'

Pulling her hand away from his and mounting her bicycle, she answered, 'You wouldn't understand. It's not easy.'

'Try me. I tell you now, if anyone threatened my sister they would see the end of my fist pretty smartly, I promise.' Becky didn't give an answer and as she began to pedal away, he called out to her, 'I'll be there on Wednesday and I'll wait all day if I have to.' He was pleased to see her wave as she turned the corner.

After preparing herself a meal, a jacket potato in the microwave, then topped with cheese she sat at the kitchen table thinking about the afternoon. Archie prowled around the kitchen then finally stood beside her chair. 'Why you home earlier tonight?' he asked. 'I mean, I'm not daft, you always arrive with Kevin, like as if you're avoiding me.' He pulled on her arm, 'So what you been up to?'

Becky tugged her arm away, 'Let go,' she hissed, 'and mind your own business.'

'Ha,' he said as he screwed up his eyes, stared at her and shook his head, 'You are my business. Make no mistake there, my girl. I'm keeping an eye on you.'

He can't possibly know about Michael can he, she asked herself? She knew he would not tolerate her having a boyfriend, any friend in fact. What was wrong with him? Jealous, possessive, afraid? Afraid of what? Surely not losing her love or respect. He must know I loathe him. Carefully she wiped her mouth before answering, 'Someone came in early and relieved me, so I could get away a bit sooner.' She turned her head away from his gaze. 'Satisfied?' she heard him grunt as he let go of her arm.

Kevin arrived home and sensed at once the taut atmosphere. 'What's up with you two now?'

Becky shrugged and Archie said, 'About time you came in. Put the kettle on. I've got some ham and we can have some chips with it.' He began getting the plates out as Becky quietly left them to it.

Chapter 13

The alarm, a gentle pinging then getting louder, woke Becky at one o'clock. When they had first made arrangements to meet up on Wednesday, she hadn't been sure that she really wanted to see Michael again. The reason for this wavering was that she felt he was hoping for more. What they had at the moment was a warm friendship, and she was not ready for any sort of relationship – never again, she had warned herself. After washing and dressing she packed her uniform carefully into the cardboard box, provided to keep it pristine, ready to strap it on to her bicycle. Yes, she thought, I shall go. How could I assume more after only two outings with him? A quick cup of coffee and a couple of slices of well-buttered toast and she was ready.

As she made her way to the front door, Archie stepped out of his room his bulk filling the narrow passageway. Her heart sunk. She knew what was coming, the usual inquisition of where, what and when of her life. Holding her head high and clutching her shoulder bag and uniform box she edged past him, but was suddenly shocked when he tightly gripped her upper arm and dragged her back to his side. With his face close to hers, he sneered,

'Nearly got away with it, didn't you? Thought you'd sneak out, but I got keen hearing my girl. I heard the alarm go off and I thought, hello, she's up to something again.

We saw the signs, me and the lad. All prim and proper like, up to something I told him, you can bet on it.'

Becky experienced a brief feeling of panic. He heard the alarm? He could only have heard it if he were outside her room – it wasn't that loud a noise. Her mind took on all sorts of reasons, none of them offering a legitimate excuse. Thank goodness she still locked her door. Turning her head away from his cigarette laden breathe and she was sure there was a hint of whisky as well; she struggled to free herself from his painful hold. 'Let go,' she hissed. 'I'm going to be late.'

'Just who do you think you're kidding? You never go to work dressed like that or put on that amount of muck on your face.' He shook her arm, 'So, where you off to? Let me see,' he looked at his watch, 'Nearly eight hours before your shift.' He shook her again, more roughly. 'Come on girl, tell me now. You know I'll get it out of you one way or another.'

His words made Becky go cold. She knew only too well from her childhood what he was capable of. Still trying to pull away from him, she thought quickly, if he thinks a boy is involved I don't know what he would do, and made up her mind to tell half truths. 'I'm going to the pictures.'

'To the pictures!' he snorted. 'I don't believe that my lady.' Increasing the pressure on her arm with his strong grip making her wince and shaking her, he demanded. 'Now, the truth girl, or you're not leaving this house again. I mean it. No going to the hospital and no shopping. Understand?'

She gave a miserable nod.

'So...?'

'I'm going to the pictures with a friend. Afterwards we

are going out for a meal before work. Okay?'

Suspiciously, Archie asked, 'Name? What's their name?'

In a quiet voice, she answered, 'Michelle.' There she thought, not quite the truth, but enough. 'And if you don't mind, I'm going to be late.'

Archie let go of her arm and she hurried to the door hearing him call out loudly after her, 'If I find out you been lying my girl, you can expect big trouble.'

Don't I know it, she said to herself as she pedalled as fast as she could towards the butcher's shop and Michael. She was surprised and pleased to see him waiting beside a car.

'Thought I'd bring the car,' he said, 'So that after the show we could go out of town for dinner. That all right with you? There'll be plenty of time to get you back for the hospital.'

'Lovely idea,' and they both clambered into the car.

After the picture show they made their way through the countryside to a small restaurant serving home-cooked meals. Becky slipped off her coat as he ordered a beer for himself and a fruit drink for her. She told him she couldn't go on duty after any intake of alcohol. 'Makes sense,' he agreed. 'Be bloody awful if you made a mistake with some-one's medicine, wouldn't it?' It was then he spotted the bruises. 'My God, what's happened there?' he asked point-ing at her arms. 'Who the hell did that?' He looked at her keenly. 'Please don't tell me it was your brother.' She shook her head, 'An anxious patient then?' Again she shook her head. 'No, not your father? Surely not?' Becky heard the disbelief in his voice and turned away as she nodded so that he wouldn't see the tears starting.

They were quiet for a few moments, the drinks arrived and menu cards thrust into their hands. 'Later,' said

Michael to the waiter. 'Give us a few minutes will you? Thanks.'

Michael reached across the table for her hand, 'Why?' he asked softly. 'What on earth had you done?'

It took a few minutes for Becky to tell him what had happened, 'So you see,' she said, 'we shall have to be careful. I don't know what he'd do to you and I have a good idea what he would do to me. There's no way I want to give up my job. I would be a prisoner, that's what he's like. He did it to my mother. Left her for weeks on end then turned up suddenly and treated her like a slave. All the time he was away she daren't go out in case he turned up. He'd threatened to take me away if she showed any signs of defying him and, as she told me later, she couldn't take that chance, knowing he'd probably treat me the same in time.'

Lifting her head she looked at Michael. His face was white and she could see he was angry by his compressed lips and jutting jaw. 'Forget it Mike, it doesn't mean that I won't be seeing you. Of course I will. Like I said, we shall have to be more careful.'

She heard him mutter something and asked him to repeat it.

'I'd like to thrash him, mangle him so that he couldn't hurt you again.'

'He'd love that,' she said too quickly. 'Oh, yes. In no time at all he'd have his prison cronies onto you. Smash the shop up as well as you, and think nothing of robbing the till. No, Mike, please don't go along with that idea.'

She saw him relax a little; he smiled at her, an artful smile. 'There must be a way of getting back at him. Give me time. I'll think of something.' He handed her the menu, 'Now, what shall we have to eat? You choose something hearty and meaty for me, a master butcher, and I'm starving.'

Later, when they returned to the shop, Michael asked, 'What about Saturday? Will I see you then?'

'Of course. I've got to shop haven't I? Mind you, it will be late afternoon as I shall sleep for as long as possible. Saturday nights are always busy at the hospital.'

'Why don't I phone you to see if you're a right?'

Becky was thoughtful for a few moments, 'Tell you what, give me your telephone number and I can phone you. I have a mobile I keep at work.'

She was surprised when he said, 'I'll give you the shop number. I'm often here late into the night.' He tore off a piece of the corner of the menu and wrote it down. 'Here you are, keep it safe.'

Mike kissed her gently on the lips when they parted, but Becky found it difficult to respond.

Chapter 14

There was a sound of a spluttering motor outside and Becky rushed to the window as Archie raced to the door. What they saw brought dismay to Becky and delight to Archie. Smiling broadly, Kevin stood beside a car belching out black smoke from the exhaust.

'Blimey! At last,' was Archie's first gleeful response, followed by, 'it's a bit ancient ain't it?'

Kevin, refusing to be discouraged said, 'It needs a bit of work I know, but the bloke I got it from says it goes like the wind when it's tip-top.' He turned and ran his hand over the black car's body. 'Let me have it cheap as he hasn't time to do it up himself. Got himself a lovely little green sports car instead.'

'I will say it was sensible of you to get a black one. I mean a green or red one would be a bit of a giveaway when we...well, when we want to get away a bit smartish.'

Kevin gave a deep sigh. He knew only too well what was being hinted at. He didn't like the criminal activities his father instigated. Nor did he consider himself a criminal. At the same time, he always got a thrill at 'getting away with it'.

Archie seated himself in the driver's seat and twisted the steering wheel like a child. Climbing out, he went to the back of the car and opened the boot. 'Pity he didn't leave some tools. We could have had a go now at improving it.'

'Ryan is coming round later to have a look and see what he can do. He reckons there's not much wrong with it. He's pretty good with maintenance and stuff, does all his own.'

Archie nodded. 'We'll watch him then, see what he does. You might learn something from him.'

'I think it best if you leave it all to me and him, Dad. You two don't see eye to eye and I don't want you upsetting him.'

'You got a point there, son. He's a cocky little bugger at the best of times. One of these days...'

Kevin turned off the engine and as he walked into the house with Archie at his side said, 'Oh, shut up.'

It was midweek and Becky had spent the afternoon with Michael. As usual they had gone for a walk, found somewhere secluded and talked a great deal. He had asked her about her brother and father. Becky had shrugged and told him that nothing much had changed. 'Except for one thing,' she suddenly remembered. 'Kevin has bought a car, an old banger affair. I don't believe it is even roadworthy.

It splutters and backfires all the time. I even saw a flame shoot out of the exhaust pipe one day.'

Michael laughed at her description and confessed his first car was the same. 'But when I'd finished getting it up to a proper standard, it went like the something on Brands Hatch racing circuit. My mates were quite envious. They didn't think I'd ever get it on the road.'

'Just like Kev's been doing with his friend and now he is getting out and about. Already Archie is beginning to tell him to drive me to work, but I insist on cycling. I told them it was good exercise.' She was thoughtful for a moment before saying, 'Michael, if I ever come into the shop with one of them, please treat me as a customer, no one special. They'll soon realise if we're interested in each other, and I wouldn't be surprised if Archie banned me from going out altogether. He's threatened to keep me home and just keep house for them before. Promise?' Michael nodded his head and promised, before making a clumsy attempt to kiss her.

Time was what Becky needed, time to be sure that she was ready for a serious relationship. Even if such a relationship developed, there couldn't possibly be any love on her side. No, she was determined never to fall in love. She had never told Michael the true situation at home, that her stepbrother had once been her lover or that her father was blackmailing them over the secret.

Michael sighed and murmured, 'I'll be very careful, I'll never force you to do anything, ever.' He tucked her arm close to his side as he added, 'that's because I love you.' He felt her stiffen and try to draw her arm away. 'It's alright,' he said softly, 'I will wait forever if need be.'

To be fair he was, she admitted to herself, very patient. She knew the day would come when she would give in to his gentle persuasion.

The unease that Becky had been experiencing was confirmed the following Saturday, her day off. She intended to cycle into town, have a little wander around and end up with a visit to the butcher's and a chat with Michael. It was not to be.

Archie was at the table when she came into the kitchen. 'Saturday jaunt is it?' he asked.

Ignoring him, Becky boiled the kettle and made herself some coffee.

'I'll have one of those,' he said pointing to her steaming mug.

Again she ignored him.

'Did you hear what I said?' There was a belligerent tone in his voice.

Becky did no more than point to the kettle.

'You cheeky cow,' he growled but didn't move to make himself a drink. 'And another thing I asked you a question. Going to town this afternoon are you?' Becky nodded.

'Me and Kevin have been thinking what with you working an all...'

Becky waited not knowing what to expect but knew he had something in mind, something to do with her.

'So we've arranged it so that he can take you shopping on Saturdays from now on in the car,' he went on. He narrowed his eyes as he looked searching for her reaction. 'Save you carrying all that stuff and you so tired after your night shift. Good idea, we thought, shows we care a bit about you.'

Becky, hoping panic didn't show in her face, turned her back to him before replying, 'I'm going on my own. Gives me a bit longer away from you two. I can manage thank you.'

Archie picked at the skin around his fingernails. 'That's what's bothering me,' he said, 'You on your own. Why anything could happen to you. No, my girl you need protecting.' He stood and crept up behind her back, and in a low, menacing voice said, 'You do as you're told. No arguing. Remember what happened to your mother when she answered back?'

Becky moved away from him, 'If you want to spy on me, I've nothing to hide. Kev is welcome...' and as an afterthought, 'but not you.'

'We'll see how it goes today, shall we?' and he yelled out, 'Kevin.'

Becky swore to herself, but decided to go along with them. She had made her plans with Mike and was determined to make Kevin's trip a misery. Putting on a cheerful smile she waited by the car door for him to open it. At first he ignored her and tapping her foot she said, 'If you insist on being my chauffeur, I expect you to behave like one.'

Archie grinned. 'Hoity toity madam.' Turning to Kevin, he said, 'Open the door you idiot.'

The car spluttered and backfired all the way to town leaving a trail of smoke. 'I thought you'd fixed the car,' said Becky. Kevin glanced at her and she shouted, 'Watch the road you fool.'

'Your fault. Are you complaining? You can walk if you like, I don't care.' he shrugged before saying, 'Anyway it'll do for now. Getting something better soon.'

Once the car had been parked, he asked, 'Where to now? And hurry up, I got things to do myself today.'

Becky smiled to herself as she was intent on going to make his life a misery today. 'First, I'm getting myself a decent coffee,' and marched off catching him off guard, so he had to scurry after her. The best coffee shop was crowded and she had to wait to be served. Kevin sat down. 'A white coffee and one of those Danish pastries please,' she ordered.

As she sat down with her drink and cake, Kevin couldn't believe his eyes. 'But, but...' he stammered. 'Where's...?' he stood up, 'You mean bitch,' he muttered as he left to join the long queue. When he returned, Becky had finished her drink and was putting on her coat and heading for the door. 'Hang on a bit,' Kevin called after her, 'I haven't even started my coffee.'

Becky waved to him, 'Too bad,' she laughed.

Archie would be mad as hell if he let Becky out of his sight. He took a quick swallow of his drink and spluttered as the hot liquid burned the back of his throat. Swearing under his breath, he chased after Becky.

Becky had no intention of buying anything, but entered a large department store. Starting in the basement, she viewed the garden section. She tested a garden swing with a canopy over the top and large comfortable cushions designed for two. After asking for its price and laughing at the salesman's patter, she shook her head as Kevin looked on. Next she sauntered around the kitchen department, picking up saucepans, fingering cutlery and compared the prices of weighing scales. 'We could do with one of those,' she said, 'and then you and...and him can see who's got the biggest portion instead of arguing every mealtime.'

Embarrassed, Kevin snapped, 'We don't. Hurry up will you.'

Becky spent almost an hour in the shop and bought nothing at all. Before leaving the store, Becky took herself off to the ladies. It was named 'Ladies Rest Room' and furnished with a couple of easy chairs and a coffee table. Becky took her time refreshing her make-up and tidying her hair. She also made a hasty phone call to Mike. 'Hi,' she began. She stopped him as he began to speak. 'Listen, I can't stop to chat. I just want to warn you that my brother is with me today. Be careful won't you? You promised.'

When he answered, she could sense he was smiling, 'Don't worry. I'll be as good as gold.'

There were a few magazines on the table and she sat down for a few moments and read the letters page in one of them. When she finally left the room, she could sense Kevin getting madder and madder, and she enjoyed seeing him trying to keep patient.

Luck was on her side. Miriam Hunt, a nurse on a different shift and always the first to know hospital gossip, rushed up and began a long saga on the latest, scandalous romance at the hospital. Usually, Becky cut her short, but today it suited her to stop and listen. She laughed or gave nods of disapproval as the story unfolded, very aware of Kevin striding and back and forth, mouthing to her to 'Hurry up.' At last Miriam waved goodbye and Kevin muttered, 'Silly bitch,' as Becky promised she would relay any further news on the liaison they'd been discussing.

As there were a few groceries to get and she made her way to the supermarket, knowing that at this time of the day it would be crowded, and a long queue at the till. Kevin trailed miserably behind her, made a few suggestions which she ignored, or asked him if he was prepared to pay for anything extra. He always shook his head. Becky had not had lunch so she told him, 'I'm getting myself a sandwich and a drink, then I'm going to the park to eat and read the paper. Do you want anything?' he nodded, and she put out her hand. 'Well, I'm not paying for yours. What do you want?'

'Whatever,' he mumbled. 'You know what I like. Anything will do.'

It was gone two o'clock when they finally reached the butcher's. All the while they were walking towards it Kevin was moaning. 'Do you realise it's going to cost a packet in parking? We've been out nearly four hours.'

'Too bad,' she replied. 'It wasn't my idea.'

'Nor mine,' he retorted hotly.

'Then why bother to spy on me. You can see how I spend my time. My time, to be away from you two morons.'

'The old man would whack you for that.'

Becky looked at him closely as she said softly, 'And you'd let him?'

Stopping suddenly, Kevin shuffled his feet and shoved his hands in his pockets before saying, 'Not if you asked for it.' He tugged her arm, 'Listen, he is determined to keep you at home. He doesn't want you to meet anyone, have a boyfriend, not even a girl friend. He thinks you owe him.'

Becky pulled away from him saying, 'Well, you can tell him otherwise now can't you,' and marched away.

As they entered the shop, Becky's stomach tightened. Michael was just finishing serving a customer with his usual bantering. 'You'll be your old man's best friend for life when you dish this little lot in front of him,' he told the elderly lady. 'He might even take you to the pictures if you're lucky.' Wrapping the meat up swiftly, and taking her money he bid her a good day, and rushed round to open the door for her.

Back behind the counter he glanced at Becky, nodded to

Kevin, and said, 'Now what can I get you? A nice joint for the weekend? Got a lovely selection of pork.'

Becky relaxed. Thankfully Mike had heeded her frantic warning. At his words, Kevin said, 'Now you're talking. How about a roast for a change, Becky?'

'I thought something like spaghetti bolognaise.'

'Not bloody mince again. The old man will go bananas.'

Mike looked from one to the other. He picked up a piece of frying steak. 'How about a nice juicy steak then? Just right for a loving couple on a Saturday night.'

Kevin shrugged. 'With her? Not likely, she's my sister.'

'Right. Bet anything you like you've got a girl. Need to build your strength.' He winked at Kevin, 'know what I mean?'

Kevin laughed. 'Steak will do nicely for what I've got in mind. Not got a date yet, but you never know what'll turn up.' Together they laughed.

Becky was overcome with fury. Cross about what Mike was implying and at Kevin for encouraging him. 'A pound of mince, please,' she said tartly.

'A pound of mince, it is then,' said Mike and pulled a long face at Kevin.

'For God's sake, Becky let's have some decent food for once.'

Rounding on him she snapped, 'Steak if you're paying, mince if I am. You choose.' Her eyes widened when Kevin pulled out his bulging wallet. For a brief moment she wondered how he had so much, then thought of Archie and made a few wild guesses.

'Shove a couple on the scales, mate. One for me old man and one for me.'

'What about her?'

Kevin was shocked and pushed her away. 'She's only my sister and a pain in the neck.'

'Ain't that true of all women?' Mike joked.

Becky elbowed Kevin sharply in the ribs. 'One you couldn't manage without. And yes, I'd like a steak too.'

'Three prime steaks it is then,' and before Kevin could protest, he deliberately picked the biggest and thickest off the tray.

As Kevin paid and replaced his wallet, Becky said, 'Seeing as you're so flush, you can pay the electric bill on the way home.' She watched as Kevin scowled, knowing he didn't want to, but couldn't think of a way out. Mike rushed round the counter to open the door for them to leave, tipped his hat and as Becky passed him, winked.

They made one more stop on the way to the car park. Kevin, intent on picking up a girl that night, decided he wanted something new to wear. It amused Becky to see he had bought a new blue T-shirt, cheap and nasty, and she knew she would never look at anyone who would wear such a garment. He won't get much luck with that, she told herself, and realised she was glad at the thought.

Archie met them at the door. 'You took your time. What you been up too?'

Kevin stomped into the house and Archie raised his eyebrows. 'Ask her,' he snarled. 'Led me a proper dance around town. I'm not doing it again. If you want to know what' she's up to, you go.'

As he made his way up the stairs, Archie called after him, 'Now what you doing? I got to talk to you. Had an idea. I think...' he stopped when he saw Becky, 'Been playing the lad up have you? I've a good mind to...'

Kevin yelled down the stairs, 'I'm going to have a bath.

Leave her be, she's got steaks to fry up before I go out.'

Archie stood back to let her pass and said in a low, threatening tone, 'He won't always be around, my girl.'

Chapter 15

When Becky arrived home the next day, Sunday, she was surprised to see Kevin nursing a black eye. At one time she would have rushed to his aid, bathed and smeared ointment on his injury. Instead, she hardened her heart. 'Well, that's a beauty. I suppose you're not going to tell me how you got it?'

Kevin winced as he lifted his head, 'Mind your own business,' he lisped through swollen lips. Becky shrugged, one day she would know she was sure. Leaving him to suffer she smiled briefly as she knew Archie would do nothing. He'll probably be proud of him she thought.

The headlines in the daily paper next day said it all. *"A violent mugging left a man with a broken jaw"* she read. The paper had been left on the table in the staff restaurant and she had at first glanced it and then, shocked, read on. *"Walking past the Swan Hotel in the early hours of Sunday morning, after seeing his girlfriend safely home, Mr Peter Welsh was violently mugged. A man approached him, greeted him and suddenly began repeatedly punching him in the face. The victim said the attacker, armed with a length of wood, demanded his wallet. Mr Welsh was knocked to the ground as he resisted the younger man. He was pushed into the gutter and kicked several times about his body. The police are seeking a man in his early twenties, clean shaven and wearing a blue T-shirt, a hooded jacket and light coloured trousers, with possible bruises about his face and body."*

Becky threw the paper onto the kitchen table. There was an intense discussion in progress between Kevin and Archie in hushed tones. Becky looked at the pair and leaning on the table asked, 'Another one of your schemes for easy money?'

Kevin snatched the newspaper from the table. Archie tried to stop him.

'What you got there?' he demanded.

Becky noticed the flicker of unease on Kevin's red face as he muttered, 'Nothing much.'

'Well, let's 'ave a look then,' and Archie snatched the paper. Becky and Kevin watched as, at first, Archie gave a grim smile, then scowled. He glanced up at Kevin who had prudently moved out of his reach. 'You silly, bugger. You deserve to get caught, blue T-shirt it says, and you still wearing it.' He read on, 'It says here that you got a hiding.' He stood up and moved towards Kevin. At first Becky was amused when Kevin sheltered behind her, but she moved away quickly. Archie stood in front of Kevin and bunched up the shirt. 'A real cheap give away this is, you stupid, stupid...' he sighed. 'And I suppose that's where you got your fat lip. Not some tart's slap as you made out.' Letting go of Kevin, he sat down at the table, 'Now, as I was saying earlier, all you got to do for easy money is...' he stopped suddenly. 'You, girl, clear off. We got things to discuss.'

'Such as?'

It was then, caught off her guard, that Kevin shoved her and she fell to the ground. She felt her face, and found her cheekbone was grazed and on her lower lip, tasted blood. Kevin helped her up, saying over and over again that he was sorry.

'Go to hell,' she snarled, 'both of you.' As she left the room she heard Archie snigger, 'At last, mate. You're showing her who's the boss.'

'Shut up,' was Kevin's reply.

When, on Wednesday, she met up with Mike as usual in the shop, her cheekbone was speckled with minute scabs, and her lip still a little swollen. Mike was both sympathetic and angry.

'Which of those bastards did this?' he asked, as he tenderly stroked the other side of her face. 'I'll kill the pair of them for this. Honest I will.'

She laughed. 'You won't believe me, but neither of them touched me. I fell.'

Bluntly he answered, 'No, I don't believe you. I'm quite sure one of them hit you and I've a good mind to sort it out.'

She drew back when he tried to kiss her. 'Steady on,' she said. 'The inside of my lip is still a bit tender.'

'Sorry, so sorry. Let's get out of here. I'm so angry though, at the way they treat you. One of these days I'll... I'll do something I swear.'

After a long walk along the river bank they made their way to their favourite tea room. Mike ordered and then leaned back in his chair. Becky didn't say anything as, deep in thought, he drummed his fingers on the chair arm. Once the waitress had delivered their tea and pastries and Becky had filled their cups, Mike smiled at her as he said, 'I've had a bit of an idea.'

Raising her eyebrows she said, 'I hope it's nothing to do with revenge on those two. Honestly, it wasn't them.'

'But I bet they caused it somehow, didn't they?' He

peered at her intently. 'Didn't they?' She didn't answer. 'Becky?' She kept still and held his gaze. 'I thought so.'

He took a sip of his tea then a bite out of his teacake. Becky was startled to see a change come over him. It was, she thought, as if he's had a eureka moment. He was chuckling to himself as he took her hand and said, very carefully, 'Do you like plenty of sun, sand and sangria?'

'Who doesn't?' she pointed the teapot at him and he nodded. Pouring for both of them she went on, 'So, what are you up to, Mike? A holiday?' she stretched. 'Oh boy, I'd love a holiday.'

'Something like that.' He took his lower lip between his fingers and looked keenly at her. Becky sensed he was making up his mind to say something of importance. Something, she felt, that might alter their future together.

Taking her hand, he said, 'I've been thinking about this a lot just lately.'

Becky tilted her head. 'And...?'

Mike put down his cup and reached for her hand as he took a deep breath. 'And...' He hesitated. 'How do feel about starting up a wine bar in Spain? I told you once that was a dream of mine.'

With wide eyes, Becky asked, 'You're joking?'

'No, no I'm not. Listen Becky we could make a go of it if we work really hard together.'

'I take it you have some money for this...this dream of yours because I haven't a bean.'

There was a glint in Mike's eye as he stroked her thumb and said, 'Oh, but you have my darling. Lots of it.'

At first, he saw puzzlement on her face and then a frown. 'Not that I know of,' she said.

Pursing his lips he looked away from her then turned

back. 'If we have the cash will you come with me or not?'

'Of course,' at the same time thinking it would never be possible.

'Right, here's what we'll do. We'll open a bank account in your name, because most of the money will probably be yours.'

He ignored the sarcasm in her voice when she answered, 'Really!'

Every week, I'll give you some cash to bank. Anything from, say, twenty pounds or more.'

Becky couldn't believe what he'd said, and asked, 'Where will you get that amount from?'

'That's my business.'

'And where is my money coming from?'

'I've thought about that,' he grinned. 'Just stop paying the mortgage.'

'But that's my home.'

'And home to those other two sponging off you.'

'But, but...'

'You can go at least three, maybe six months before the bank starts chasing you for the money, and, hopefully, we shall be gone by then. They will either have to pay up or find somewhere else. Why should you care?'

For a few moments Becky was thoughtful. She remembered how she and Kev managed with just the basics to get a home of their own. Becky had contributed the most as she had a steady nursing job. She had odd moments of resentment, when, on the rare occasions Kev did work, he hung on to most of his earnings to have a night or two out with his mates. But his opportunities of casual work were rare.

'I'm in digs, so I've nothing like that to fall back on, but

I do have some savings.'

For a few moments Becky was thoughtful and suddenly beamed at him. It could work, she told herself, and I'll be free of them. She nodded to Mike. 'Okay. I like the idea. A career-move, landlady of a bar.'

He went round to her and gave her a bear hug. 'Good girl. I thought it might appeal.' He paid for their tea and they made their way slowly back to the shop discussing their future. 'I've just thought of another idea for the kitty,' he said, stopping and holding her back in excitement. 'Don't pay any more gas or electric bills, or water for that matter.'

'But we'll be cut off,' she protested.

'Not for a good while, at least three months. These companies make allowances for all sorts.'

'Like what?'

'Like illnesses or holidays or...or bankruptcy. I don't know, but they do.'

'You seem to have it all worked out.'

'At first it was only a dream, but I think we can do it. I promise I'll pay my share, Becky, honestly.'

A new beginning, someone who cared, away from the two miserable men in her life –a chance not to be missed she told herself later as she gave in to Mike's desires. Her body was indifferent to his love making, but, she told herself, I'll grow to love him, I'm sure.

It was the roar of Kev's car and the screeching of tyres as he braked, that woke Becky. Half asleep she looked at her bedside clock that showed it was just past two o'clock. Turning and pulling the covers over herself, she was more than a little miffed at the disturbance. It was her first full night in her own bed for over two weeks. On Monday the three turn-around shift pattern meant she would be starting work at six in the morning.

Trying to settle, she heard Kevin enter the house, but he was not alone. There was giggly laughter and whispering on the stairs. Worse was to come. It was obvious Kevin had a female companion and it wasn't long before Becky realised that there was frantic lovemaking in the room next to her own. Tears welled up as she remembered Kevin's arms around her, how he could arouse her and how they would gently laugh and tease each other after their breathtaking sessions.

The following morning there was no sign of the girl. Kevin was humming and Becky thought him a little smug. Archie grinned, he too must have heard they'd had a visitor and his prying question of, 'Good night, was it son?' grated on Becky.

Kevin looked down at his hands, turned them over then lifted his head. 'You could say that,' he smirked as he turned his head and looked at Becky.

Archie winked at Kevin. 'Thought so. Good was she?' and a knowing, lewd look passed between them.

Becky glared at the two of them, tossed back her hair and marched out of the room. Their coarse laughter followed her. Yes, she told herself, I probably am a bit jealous, but comforted herself as she remembered own plans. Plans that she had every intention of carrying out, and what's more, she thought with satisfaction, those two will soon be homeless.

Chapter 16

Becky was surprised how the bank balance in her name grew. Every week Mike handed over cash, sometimes as much as twenty, but usually around seven or ten pounds a week. There were brief moments of guilt when she passed the bank, and didn't enter to pay the mortgage. Gas, electric and water bills arrived at the house which Becky schooled herself to ignore.

Arriving home one evening, Archie confronted her with a buff envelope the words in red 'Final Demand' clearly visible just above her name in the cellophane window. 'What's this?' he demanded. 'You not paid the mortgage?'

Coolly she answered, 'I forgot. In any case, you seem to have plenty of cash these days, you pay it.'

Archie flared. 'Watch your tongue girl and get that paid up tomorrow, you hear? You want to end up on the streets?'

She shrugged.

'Don't care do you? Well, you know what street girls are for don't you?'

Becky gritted her teeth, wishing she had the courage to slam her fist into his face. Instead, in a low voice she said, 'Well, you'd know all about that wouldn't you? It wasn't just my mother you were unfaithful with was it – street girls as well it seems.'

Archie made a quick move towards her, fists at the ready, but she raced up the stairs and locked her bedroom door as usual. It was over five minutes before he stopped yelling up the stairs and cursing her.

Although she was a little afraid and trembling, she consoled herself with looking at her bank balance and dreaming of the future with Mike. Mike had suggested she put the house up for sale, but after discussing this idea, it was agreed that she shouldn't start approaching agents until the day before leaving, and after this evening's outburst knew it was better to wait.

Mike told her over and over again that he loved her. 'You are beautiful,' he whispered. 'The only one I ever want for the rest of my life.' pulling her closer he added, 'I love you, darling.'

Wriggling out of his arms, she laughed. 'Bet you say that to all the girls.'

He gave a mock horrified grin, 'Only to the customers over eighty.'

There was no sexual satisfaction for Becky. Left unmoved she told herself that in time, she would grow to love him. I suppose, in a way I do love him, he is kind and gentle. When I'm feeling down he makes me laugh. Remembering the two men at home, there was no comparison. Mike was always clean, fussy about his clothes and there was always a smell of gorgeous aftershave on smooth cheeks. He trusts me too, all that money he insists on putting in my name, he never shows greed or meanness, ever. Any girl would be proud to be with him. She knew she was very lucky, but love? She sighed inwardly.

Everything was changing. Kevin seemed to bring home a different girl every weekend. Becky could only guess this was so. It was the giggles, hushed tones and sometimes noisy shrieking during the carrying-ons in the room next to hers confirmed her suspicions. There was continued bickering between Kevin and Archie. Odd comings and goings at all times of the day, sometimes at night after a series of telephone calls. Often there were visitors. Well-dressed men, obviously uncomfortable in their striped suits, and displaying flashy rings and smoking cigars. Individuals who seemed unfamiliar with the wealth they were displaying. It was as if they were acting the part of sharp businessmen that somehow didn't quite ring true. Gathered in the sitting room, there was often laughter, arguments and heads together in hushed conversations, one or two glancing around as if suspecting a listener. Becky left them to it and she no longer bothered to eavesdrop.

Archie sat at the breakfast table enjoying a fry-up. He wiped up the spilt egg yolk with the last piece of bread and gave a satisfactory yawn. He went to the window to check if he could see Becky's bicycle. It was missing, so he knew she had already left for the hospital. Picking at his teeth he turned to Kevin. 'Some time ago I asked you to think about going into a jeweller's shop and...'

Kevin coloured up, he didn't want to answer, didn't want to get involved in Archie's mad ideas. It was bad enough having to fetch and carry, heaven only knew what, in his car. Archie never told him what, but he often suspected by the size of the packets it could only be drugs or jewellery even paper cash. To be honest, he didn't want to know, didn't want to get involved more than necessary. Archie always flashed his wallet around after these 'little contracts,' as he called them and, Kevin reminded himself, was often generous with his thanks. Indeed, Archie gave him enough so that he didn't have to put himself out for legitimate work. Kevin shrugged as he answered, 'Not really. I reckon we're doing alright as we are.'

'Yes, I know boy, but this would be for us. Just us two.

All we get will be ours. We won't have to share with the others.'

Kevin turned away and was startled when Archie banged on the table.

'Look at me will you? Stop dithering around,' he bellowed. 'Lowering his voice he said, 'you're still a bit soft aren't you? What you afraid of? Getting caught and your precious sister disowning you? Prison?' He looked into Kevin's face, paused for a moment when he saw the look of scorn. He jumped to his feet and made a grab for Kevin as he said, 'I'll wipe that look of your face you...'

But with his hands curled into fists Kevin was ready for him. 'Lay one finger on me and so help me you'll see how soft I am, believe me,' he threatened.

Archie sat down and grinned. 'Blimey. Had you going for a moment there, didn't I?' He lit a cigarette and blew smoke towards the ceiling. 'What do you say then? Shall we sort the local jeweller out?'

There was a reluctant nod from Kevin.

'You remember what you got to do?'

'Most, but we'll go over it again before Saturday.'

'Nothing to worry about. Only a burglar alarm as far as I could see.'

It was almost closing time when Kevin parked the car outside the jeweller's shop on Saturday afternoon. Archie stayed in the car. 'Give me three or four minutes at the most. Don't hang about,' he ordered his father, as he stepped out onto the pavement.

He pushed the shop door open and a bell pinged. A young woman behind the counter smiled at him. 'We're just about to close sir,' she said.

Pretending to be rushed and flustered, in a breathless

voice Kevin said, 'Oh don't say that. I need to buy an engagement ring. I want to propose to my girl tonight.' He smiled as he added, 'It's her birthday today. I thought it would be such a surprise.' He fished in his pocket, 'Look,' he said holding out an envelope, 'I've already got her tickets for *Jesus Christ Superstar*. She's going to love it.' He put his hands on the counter and leaned towards the girl. 'Come on, show me a few rings. I won't take long, I promise,' he coaxed. She glanced up at the wall clock, turned and unlocked a cabinet behind her.

She placed a tray of rings on the counter, saying, 'See if there's anything there you...' she gave a little chuckle, 'I mean your girl might like.'

Kevin fingered a few and picked out one, put it back and chose another. Not satisfied he said, 'These are fine, but I was thinking of paying something like hundred and fifty maybe two hundred pounds. Got anything in that range?'

'We certainly do,' and her face lit up as she turned and took another tray of rings out.

Poor cow, thought Kevin, she's thinking of her commission, sack more likely. He began lifting the rings and examining their stones. Just as he was wishing his father would hurry up, the door was flung open and Archie burst into the room. The girl was shocked at his sudden appearance. Flustered she went to close the door behind him. 'We're closing sir. This gentleman is my last customer.' Archie looked contemptuously at Kevin, 'Well, while he's making up his mind, perhaps you'd be good enough to show me a couple of watches. There's one on a tray in the window I like.' He sat down on the chair beside the counter.

'Go on,' Kevin told her. 'There's still five minutes before closing time.'

She shook her head, but at the same time, picked up a key, made her way to the window. With her back turned, Kevin scooped up a handful of rings and strolled to the door. To her back he said, 'I don't think there's anything here for me. Sorry, but thanks for your time,' the bell pinged as he left.

Giving a sigh, she placed the watches in front of Archie. 'Lovely,' was all he said.

Suddenly, she gasped out loud. She whirled round shouting, 'He's stolen my rings,' and was dismayed to see Archie stuffing watches into his pockets.

Archie lifted his hand to her face, 'Shut up, or else,' he threatened.

When the two men reached home, Kevin was still shaking. He couldn't believe what they had done, and got away without trouble. Together they spread their haul onto the kitchen table. Archie picked up ring after ring holding them up to the light, delighted as the diamonds and other gems sparkled. 'You did well, there my son.'

Now more relaxed, Kevin was impressed with the amount he'd grabbed. Eight rings – all over a hundred and fifty pounds. Together with the half dozen watches, Omega and Seiko, the whole lot was worth a fortune.

He turned to Archie, 'Not bad, not bad at all. But how we going to get rid of them?' He turned quickly and faced Archie. 'I hope you're not expecting me to tote them round the pubs or something, because I ain't.'

Archie raised his eyebrows and shook his head in disbelief then grinned. 'You daft bugger. We'd be inside before you downed your first pint. No, you leave it to me. I know a bloke who...'

Much relieved, Kevin handed him the phone. 'Well,

here's the phone. Get on with it. We don't want this lot hanging about the house for too long.' Archie made the call. The next day, Kevin knew exactly what was in the packets he had to deliver.

Chapter 17

A date had been set and Becky bought two single tickets to Spain. Their plan was to have a week's holiday, find a flat to rent and search for a suitable bar to purchase. 'Somewhere on the coast,' Mike said, 'Not a tourist spot, but where holiday makers could walk away from the livelier resorts and have a quiet drink, maybe a meal. Somewhere less noisy than the popular overcrowded places,' he'd enthused.

For the last few weeks Becky had sneaked some of her clothes from home to her locker in the hospital. Fearfully, every morning she sneaked them out. Occasionally Archie would be at the door as she left, and he would cross-examine her.

She'd given in her notice, and was informed that when she returned there would be a place for her at the hospital. She told her friends that she was off to Australia to see her mother. 'I thought if anyone should start asking for me, to say Australia would put them off the scent.' She smiled at Mike, 'for good.' Still smiling she took Mike's hand. 'I can't wait, Mike, I'm really looking forward to our future.'

He kissed her as he said, 'So am I, and what's more, between us we can make it work.' He gave a chuckle, 'Of course, we won't get very rich, well not to start with, but, Becky, I'll make sure you never go without. Whatever you want, I promise.' He kissed her again as she murmured,

'I'll pull my weight I promise.'

Becky left for work a little earlier than her usual time. As she mounted her bicycle she looked back at the house and remembered the happy day she shared with Kevin when they moved in. All spoilt when, laughing and jostling together, they went to answer the door to their first visitor – their father. She sighed as she pedalled away, knowing that Archie was right to stop their relationship, but so mean in his delight at ruining things. At the hospital she abandoned the bike, collected her bulging suitcase and said her last goodbyes.

Waiting in Bristol airport, she sipped a coffee in a cardboard beaker, as a thousand thoughts chased around in her mind. Was she doing the right thing? It was still early, but she wondered if the estate agents, 'For Sale' board gone up yet? If so, was Kevin, or more likely Archie, looking for her? She glanced at her watch, six thirty-three, and was satisfied that no, they probably wouldn't even be awake yet.

Where was Mike? It was his idea to meet at the airport. 'Save money,' he'd said when she suggested meeting outside Smiths and get a taxi. Did they really have enough money? She felt in her handbag and groped for and found the bank book confirming this. Scanning the faces of people scurrying through the doors she felt a twinge of anxiety. Where was he? He promised he would be on time. The plane was leaving at eight o'clock. They had yet to hand in their luggage at the reception desk, show their passports, collect boarding cards and whatever else, she told herself. What is he thinking?

There was another musical note from the address system. They came one after another, hardly any time between announcements of departures, arrivals and lost children or luggage. After a while Becky ignored the messages, knowing that it was too early for her flight to be called. Suddenly she was alert, surely not? The message was repeated. 'Would Miss Rebecca Wilson please contact Britannia Airways', desk thirty-four.'

Becky's first thought was that the message wasn't for her. Nevertheless, a feeling of dread came over her. Surely it couldn't be Archie or Kevin? Were they at the desk waiting for her? If it so, she told herself, I'll make a scene, accuse them of kidnapping if they tried to drag me away. She was exasperated with herself at such an idea. They had come home around three in the morning so would not even be awake yet. Again the air was filled with a request for Miss Wilson, and reluctantly, dragging her suitcase, readjusting her hand luggage and placing her empty coffee carton in a waste bin, she made her way to desk thirty-four.

The smart, uniformed receptionist behind the desk smiled brightly as Becky approached. 'Are you Miss Wilson?' she asked as she reached behind her for an envelope. Becky nodded 'For you,' the woman said as she held out an envelope. 'Left here a few minutes ago.'

With trembling hands Becky took the letter, turned it over and saw it was addressed to her in Mike's handwriting. What had the woman said? 'Left a few minutes ago?' Glancing round the booking-in hall quickly, she was sure she would see him. Frantically she searched the swarm of people milling about again, but there was no sign of him. She was puzzled, surely he was here somewhere.

The receptionist leaned forward and pointed. 'He left through that door. Said he was in a hurry and that you would understand.'

Becky frowned. 'I don't understand. We are going...'

'Why don't you open the letter? Perhaps that will help,' the woman said as she turned to attend to another traveller.

Becky murmured her thanks as she walked away and found a seat. For a few minutes she sat staring at the envelope, turning it over and over again, reluctant to open it and dreading what the news might be. At last, after taking a deep breath and biting her bottom lip, she opened the envelope and began to read.

'*My dearest Becky,*' she read and was heartened briefly by the simple words, then read on. '*I am writing to tell you that despite my everlasting love, I am unable to start a new life with you in Spain. I know you will be upset and disappointed but the truth is that after five years of marriage, the last three have been hell, finally my wife is pregnant with our first child. We have had many disappointments, but now everything has changed. I realise that I also love my wife very much and cannot leave her or our child, ever. I do hope you understand and I truly wish you will find someone to make you as happy as we are.*

Goodbye, my dearest.'" He had signed it, but had added a postscript. '*Could you please forward my share of the money to the butcher's shop as my wife does not know of our affair. The money will be so useful for our child's future.*'

It couldn't be true, she thought, and read the letter again. A quiet whimper escaped her and she took rapid, short intakes of breath. The people sitting either side of her glanced at her curiously. Seeing her white face and obvious distress, one put her hand on Becky's arm and asked, 'Everything alright dear?'

Standing up Becky shook her head, gathered her belongings and walked away. For a few moments she wandered up and down the hall, trying to find somewhere, anywhere she could be alone. Glancing at a directions board, she saw the obvious place – the chapel and made her way there.

The stillness and quiet in the cool chapel did little to soothe her. At first her crying was uncontrollable, loud and raw as tears streamed down her face as she rocked herself back and forwards on the hard pew. Finally she had no more energy for this personal onslaught, and wiped her tears away. As time crept on she was unable to stop the deep sobs that welled up from inside her from time to time. Her feelings were in turmoil. Along with feeling intensely sad she felt hopeless and worthless. It was when she looked about her and saw her suitcase, her mood of self-pity changed to one of anger. Let down by someone who had professed to loving her until his dying day, someone she had made plans with for the future – Michael. Every time they were together, she tested herself for signs of love for him. Always she had to admit that her love was no more than that for a very dear friend who she trusted with her life. Convinced that some time in the future real love would happen she had, this very day, done with her past and had been looking forward to a new life. She gave a long drawn-out sound. A sound combining a groan of frustration coupled with a suppressed scream. She beat rapidly on the backrest of the pew in front of her as she drummed her feet on the floor.

Becky put her head in her hands and slumped down in the pew. All emotions spent and she was tired – too tired to think of what to do next. Leaning back she lifted her head to the ceiling and closed her eyes. It was when a hand gently squeezed her shoulder and a voice said, 'He will listen my child,' that, at last, she felt calmer.

Footsteps padded away, but she didn't open her eyes just let this new feeling envelope her. Now relaxed, she let her thoughts wander and shortly found herself smiling as an answer to her future slowly formed.

Chapter 18

Kevin stirred, reluctant to wake up, but there was a distant hammering. They'd had a good night, him and Archie. There was no doubt about it, Kevin thought, the old man is good at conning people. He felt little remorse for the victims parting with their money. Turning over in bed he smiled as recalled they had called into a crowded pub, somewhere out in the countryside, on their way home from meeting up with one of Archie's mates. It was in there that they'd overheard a man speaking to another. 'Let me down again,' he'd said, 'The job will never get done in time for me and the missus to move in.'

It was then that Archie had given Kevin a warning look and had edged his way over to the complainant. 'I know just what you mean,' he'd said. 'Builders eh? Let you down over and over again.' He'd pointed to the man's glass, 'Have another mate?'

'Thanks, yes. We're on Fosters.'

Archie nodded to Kevin to refill all four glasses. When he returned he heard Archie saying, '...left all the cupboard doors off. Couldn't get the blighters back. "On another job" they kept telling me.'

The drinks were passed round, there was a clink of glasses as the two men gave their thanks. Archie took a sip before saying, 'Best builders in the area I was told. You know the one? Beezely Builders, see them knocking about all over the place. I was calling them beastly builders in the end.' He'd given an unseen nod to himself as everyone laughed. It was then that Kevin knew the men were being reeled in, and he waited to see how Archie was going to play the game.

'So, what happened in the end? Get someone or do it yourself?'

'Exactly what you're doing now. Talking and moaning in a pub when...'

He put his arm round Kevin's shoulders. 'When this young fellow interrupted,' – and he punched Kevin on the arm. 'Very rude of you that my boy.' There were quiet chuckles from the listeners. 'When this fellow said he was a carpenter and would do the job for...well I forget. But I was that glad,' he gulped his drink, and winked at Kevin.

Where's this leading? Kevin wondered.

'All I need is a few shelves putting up. Some in the kitchen and some under the stairs for storage. Can you do that?' he asked turning to Kevin. 'Missus will kill me if they ain't up by the time she comes on Tuesday.'

'Course he can,' Archie said too promptly. 'He's a bloody carpenter. Shelves is nothing to him. Ain't that right?' and squeezed Kevin's arm in warning.

Kevin coughed, swallowed a mouthful and spluttered. 'Yes, nothing to it.'

'You got time to do this little job, lad?' Archie queried. 'Tomorrow perhaps? Help a bloke out couldn't you?'

Kevin couldn't believe that Archie had put him in this situation. I'm useless at do-it-yourself stuff, Archie knows that. What is he up too? Dropping me in it again, I reckon, but he could say nothing and nodded, as he mumbled, 'Piece of cake.'

The two men looked at each other. One raised his eyebrows then said, 'Tomorrow you say?'

'Yes,' said Archie. He stopped for a moment, 'provided you got the materials, yes?'

'No, mate. Left all that to the foreman. Useless bugger.'

'So lad,' Archie said turning to Kevin, 'Looks like you'll have to go shopping first thing in the morning. Forty pounds should cover it don't you think?'

Kevin couldn't believe it, and without batting an eyelid answered, 'More like seventy, maybe fifty, maybe fifty-five.'

'Can you cover that? I mean it's quite a lot of readies ain't it. You got that amount?' Kevin shook his head.

'Well then,' he said turning to the possible client, 'What do you say? Fifty up front and if it's more settle up tomorrow.' He smiled as he added, 'you never know, with luck there might be some change.'

The man hesitated as Archie stared at him, unblinking as if to hypnotise him. Reaching inside his jacket the man pulled out a cheque book, 'Fifty, you say?' he said as he took out his pen.

Quickly Archie said, 'Cash only mate.' The man frowned. 'Boy ain't got that sort of cash and the bank won't be open 'til ten. Blimey mate, he could be finished work at your place by then.'

Giving a sigh the man reached for his wallet. He turned to his companion and said, 'Lend me twenty can you Dave?' He handed over fifty pounds to Kevin. Wood shelving, brackets and other essential aids to the work were discussed and the address given. As they departed almost immediately, Kevin said, 'See you around eight tomorrow then.' He smiled as he drifted back into sleep.

It was gone eleven o'clock when he finally roused himself. He stretched, got out of bed and wandered over to the window. As he drew back the curtains he gave a gasp. Oh, God, he said to himself, that must have been the banging I heard earlier. He screwed up his face and rocked on his feet. Bloody, bloody hell, he thought, Archie isn't going to like this.

Two large boards, their size ensuring they could not be missed, had been planted beside the gate – notices that glared out in large, red script, 'For Sale'.

There was no mistaking Archie's rage. Kevin had showered and dressed before waking his father with a mug of tea. Sipping it gratefully, he winked at Kevin as he said, 'Why ain't you at work?' and laughed as he added, We did good last night boy. Fifty quid and the silly blighter didn't see it coming.'

Kevin sat quietly on the edge of the bed and cleared his throat. 'Dad,' he began hesitantly.

'I know what you're going to say. Going to ask for a share.' He put his mug down on the cabinet, patted Kev's arm and said, 'Course you can have some. Got a hot date?'

Kevin avoided looking at him. 'Dad,' he began again. 'There's something you should see.'

'See? Where?'

'In the front garden.'

'What? What is it? A dead creature no doubt, and you too squeamish to deal with it I bet.'

'No Dad. Nothing like that.' Kevin went across to the

window and opened the curtains. 'See for yourself. You're not going to like it.'

Archie threw the bedclothes off and stumbled across to the window rubbing the stubble of his face and muttered, 'Kids!'

At first, he said nothing just stared unbelievingly at the boards. He turned round and Kevin saw his father's white face, bulging eyes and clenched fists as he stomped across the room muttering, 'The bitch. I'll kill the bitch,' Kevin knew it would be wiser to say nothing and get out of Archie's way as quickly as possible.

It was over an hour before Archie put in an appearance. He sat down at the kitchen table and Kevin put a mug of tea in front of him. Archie took a sip and looking over the top of the mug said, 'Right. When that...' he hesitated, 'when that cheating, lying, little cow comes home tonight, you stay away. I'll sort her out, you wait and see.'

Trying to soothe the old man, Kevin said, 'Now, Dad, steady on.'

Archie reared up from his chair. 'You do as I say, or else...' he roared.

Kevin stared at him. 'You touch her Dad, and so help me...' he began.

'You're still after her aren't you? Oh, yes. I've seen the signs, sighing and waiting for her to get home. Well no more, my lad. She'll do as I bid from now on.'

Although there had not been any indication of Kevin's and Becky's feelings for each other since Archie's arrival, he knew that both of them would have to be very careful around him in future. He pulled on his tracksuit top zipping it up as he went to the door.

'And where do you think you're going, now? Off to warn

the bitch no doubt.'

Kevin shook his head, 'Mind your own bloody business.'

In an instant Archie was beside him and grabbing his arm tightly, 'That's just it. You and her are my business.'

Kevin shook him off, gave him a shove and said, 'We'll see.' There was no way he was telling Archie that he was off to the hospital to find Becky, warn her and get some answers.

The news he was given at the hospital astounded him. In his wildest dreams he could not believe that Becky had actually left him as she had always there for him. Okay, so their relationship had been destroyed, but that didn't mean he didn't care about her. True, he told himself, he had been more than rotten towards her since their father had turn up. On the other hand, he had protected her more than once from Archie's bad temper and his inclination to solve everything with threats or his fists. It was all Archie's fault. Why did he have to turn up and spoil everything? No one would ever have found out that they were half brother and sister and he had truly loved her. How was he going to tell Archie what he had just found out? The right moment will come along, he told himself, and I'll just say it as it is.

Archie began pacing just before six o'clock, the time Becky was expected home. Back and forwards between the window, whirling away from it and striding to the front door. At times he thumped his fist into the other palm muttering to himself. 'Where is she?' he demanded as he opened the door and peered up the road.

Kevin sat quietly in the kitchen, chewing on his thumb knuckle, knowing that before long he would have to tell.

Archie, his face white with mounting anger, stood in front of him. 'Afraid, that's it. She's afraid to come and face the music. And so she should be,' he growled. 'Just wait 'til she gets here.' he leaned down and prodded Kevin's shoulder, 'and you, my lad, stay out if. A couple of slaps and she'll see sense, or else...do you hear me? Leave me to deal with me own daughter.'

Kevin lifted his head and stared into Archie's eyes. 'She isn't coming.'

'What do you mean? She isn't coming. This is still her home.' As an afterthought, he added softly as the thought came to him, 'Unless she's got somewhere else to go already.' He pulled Kevin to his feet by yanking on his shirt front. 'What do you know about this? You and her planned something, didn't you? Yes, I bet you've got a hand in this somewhere.'

'Let go, now old man, or you'll be sorry.' Kevin's tone held a threat, one that Archie knew he could not ignore.

'So, you do know something.' He loosened his hold.

Kevin moved away, putting the kitchen table between them. It was alright to threaten, but he wondered if he really could take on the old man. He cleared his throat. 'She's not coming because she's gone...' he hesitated and swallowed, 'gone to Australia.'

Archie bellowed out, 'Australia?'

Kevin nodded twice.

'Australia, for God's sake. Why there? Thinks she's escaped. Well, I'm not having it.' Turning on Kevin and pointing his finger at him he said, 'You should have given her what she wanted.'

There was a shrug from Kevin as he asked, 'And what's that?'

'You in her bloody bed, you fool.'

'And if you hadn't turned up, I would be,' he shouted

back. Both were breathing heavily, Archie with clenched lips and fists, Kevin with disgust at Archie's outburst. Gradually both calmed down. Archie sat down and Kevin boiled the kettle, made fresh tea and sat opposite him. He took a sip from his mug then said, 'She's gone to Australia to see her mother.'

Immediately, Archie flared up again. 'Her mother. In Australia? What she doing there? I've been searching for the woman ever since I got here.'

'Settle down. There's nothing we can do now.' Kevin said. He pushed a tin of biscuits towards Archie before saying, 'Seems she married someone recently, and they moved out there and Becky's gone to see them.'

'How could she marry someone else? She knew I'd be around one day. We had a good thing going me and her.' He nodded his head as he added, 'Definitely had a good thing going there. Thought she'd wait.' Looking over the rim of his mug as he took a sip of tea, he asked, 'Is the girl coming back?'

'Don't know, but the ward sister said they were keeping her job open, so maybe.'

There were a few moments of quiet between them until Archie spoke. 'Tomorrow, you go to the building society. See what you can find out. A forwarding address, account number, anything. She ain't getting all the money I tell you, not if I can help it.'

The visit to the building society the next day was fruitless. 'No, sir, we cannot give out account numbers, only to the holder,' and, 'no sir, Miss Wilson said she would contact us when she is permanently settled. Even then,' the manager added, 'we would not divulge it without Miss Wilson's permission.' When asked where the money would be sent Kevin was told, 'All monies, after our legal deductions, will go directly into Miss Wilson's bank account.'

'Which is?' Kevin queried.

'I'm afraid I cannot tell you that sir. Not without...'

Kevin interrupted and mimicked, '...Miss Wilson's permission.'

As Kevin left the building he turned the silver engagement piece over in his pocket. It always surprised and pleased him to find it there. In frustration he had thrown it carelessly into a drawer some time ago, and had been startled to find it in his trouser pocket one day. There was only one person who could have put it there. Why, he often wondered? Although he denied it, there was still a place in his heart for Becky. With a resigned smile he thought, good for you, Becky. Making a stand and a new life for yourself. Touching the silver piece in his pocket again, he whispered, 'Good luck.'

Chapter 19

There was a determined look on Becky's face when she left the chapel. As she made her way to the Ladies she ignored the curious looks of passersby, but wasn't surprised when she looked in the mirror. Red eyes with swollen lids, streaked mascara down her white face, smudged lipstick and still hiccupping. After she had splashed her face with cold water she pressed a cold compress made out of toilet paper to each puffy eyelid. Carefully, she made up her face, applied lipstick, put on her sunglasses and took a deep breath – she was ready.

Sipping her coffee, she looked around the hall to locate

the different desks she was about to visit. Pulling her case along behind her, she first visited the enquiries desk of the Spanish airline she was to have flown with. Pretending to be flustered and out of breath, she gasped out to the girl behind the counter. 'I've missed my flight, haven't I?'

The assistant took her ticket, scanned it, nodded and handed it back to her.

Feigning disappointment Becky said, 'Alarm clock, traffic, all the usual excuses. I'm so sorry.'

'No problem at all,' the girl said. 'We can transfer you onto another flight.' She thumbed through a sheaf of papers. 'Ah, here we are. Another flight in an hour's time. That suit you?'

'Lord, no!' Becky answered quickly. 'I've missed everything. My contact, the interview and, I might add, a date with a dishy Spaniard,' she gave a sigh. 'Pedro Amaro,' she sighed again. 'Said he was a famous singer and he was going to introduce me to his agent.'

'Oh, that's too bad.'

Becky glanced down at the ticket and in a voice choked with emotion said, 'No, I think the best thing for me is to forget all about it.' She reached into her bag for a tissue and wiped away imaginary tears. 'My mum said it was just a foolish dream. You hear all sorts of stories about promises and that. Perhaps it was just a con. Trick after all. I don't know.' She frowned and pretended to be thinking. After a second or two she said, 'I think the best thing to do now is have the money back.'

The girl leaned forward. 'I'm afraid I can't do that. You have to go through head office,' and reached behind her searching through a pile of leaflets. 'Here,' she said, 'take this form and send it off. The address is at the top,' and smiled as she added, 'you may be lucky.' Becky took the form and gave her thanks.

'You've probably saved yourself a lot of trouble,' the girl said.

As Becky walked away she smiled to herself. Job number one completed.

The next task was to book onto another flight as soon as possible. She didn't want to hang about in the airport too long in case Archie, Kevin or even Mike thought about tracking her down. The destination she chose was Belfast. No amount of searching by the men, would find her on a flight to Australia or Spain. Just disappear out of their lives forever, she told herself.

'Yes,' the booking clerk said, 'there's a flight this afternoon, two-thirty five. Would that be suitable for you?'

'Thank you,' said Becky as she wrote out a cheque for the fare. 'That will be fine.'

After she had booked in and deposited her suitcase she saw that it was lunchtime. There was one more thing she was intent on doing. In WH Smith's she purchased a cheap packet of writing paper, envelopes and a couple of magazines. The smell of food made her feel hungry so she made her way to a food counter and ordered a sandwich. While she was eating she was mentally compiling a letter she intended to send which, she admitted, will upset the recipient, something she regretted, but it couldn't be helped. Another point that bothered her was Mike's wife. The letter Mike left her, saying his wife was pregnant had hurt as she read it. Now, she felt a smidgeon of guilt knowing that she was probably destroying their marriage, and the happy time they might have had with their child. On the other hand, Becky decided, if a husband cheats once and doesn't get found out, he will probably do so again. In the end, she convinced herself that as she would never forgive an unfaithful partner, she was doing the poor woman a favour in the long run. At first, she decided to enclose a cheque as a token of compensation. After she had written it out, it suddenly occurred to her that at a later date there was a possibility that the cheque could be traced back to her. If Mike told of her part in the affair then the police might be involved. At present no one knew where she was or where she was going and he would have a hard time trying to convince anyone that she even existed. She made a mental note to change her bank as soon as possible and tore up the letter and the cheque.

The letter she did write was short and to the point. *'Dear sir, if you check your books you may well find some discrepancies. Michael Govan will be able to give you some answers.'* She signed it *'A friend.'* In her handbag she had a book of stamps, licked one, stuck it on the envelope, and addressed it to Mr Reynolds, Private, the owner of the butcher's shop. As Mike was only the manager, he would not open it. The pillar box was almost overflowing with last minute holiday cards and Becky pushed her letter well down amongst them. There, that will sort out Mike she told herself. As for the other two, they'll be homeless before long, and she felt very satisfied with the knowledge.

Chapter 20

Becky booked herself a week's stay in a small hotel in Belfast, in order to seek a nursing post and find a flat. The idea was to purchase a modest flat where she could feel content and happy – a flat she could truly call home. She had just enough for a deposit, and knew that her bank balance would eventually be added to once the house was sold and the bank had retrieved the mortgage costs.

Going to the local library she scanned the newspapers and waited impatiently for the Nursing Times magazine that she was sure would have a suitable position for her. Within three days she found exactly what she was looking for. A small hospital some five miles from Belfast was advertising for nursing staff. All the questions asked at the friendly interview, date of birth, education, training and experience she was able to answer truthfully. Once her qualifying certificates had been inspected she was offered the position.

At first, she was offered a small bedsit in the hospital grounds which she accepted, but was determined to find somewhere of her own. Days off were spent looking at property that appealed to her from the handouts offered by the only estate agent in the town. It was five weeks later when she found exactly what she wanted – a self contained flat attached to the side of a large family home. The sitting room window overlooked a well maintained garden full of seasonal flowers. From the bedroom at the back there was a distant view of mountains and farmland. There was a long driveway from the house to the main road. Getting to work might prove a problem, but she had set her heart on living there.

After making enquiries, she learned that there was a limited bus service starting at six in the morning which would take her as far as the hospital entrance. The last bus however, left at six thirty in the evenings. Most of the hospital staff she worked with were around her age, and she had already made friends with five of them. It was Maureen who offered to pick her up and take her home if their shift pattern coincided.

'No problem at all,' she told Becky, 'Just a stone's throw out of my way. Nothing to it.'

Becky was so delighted with the offer and repeated over and over again, 'Thank you, thank you so much,' so many times that the nurses started to mimic her English accent saying 'Thank you so much,' at every opportunity.

At last, her life was getting into place. She had a home of her own, a satisfactory job and new friends. Once she had settled into the flat, the occupants of the adjoining house, a young barrister with an equally young wife, made her welcome. She saw little of them as they were both working in Belfast and at weekends preferred to take mini breaks from Friday to Sunday evenings. Yes, she told herself, at last I'm content, but she didn't admit to anyone that some nights she was so lonely that she wept.

Chapter 21

After Becky left, and they still had no news of her whereabouts, Kevin and his father stayed on in the house for another three months. The first eviction notice arrived within two months of her departure. The new owner had made it clear he wanted them out as soon as possible.

'They can't do anything,' Archie had declared.

A few weeks later the second notice was delivered threatening court action. Kevin could almost remember the exact words, very formal. *You are to vacate the premises within seven days. Failure to respond to this* notice, the owner will have no alternative but to take you to court.'

The very word court had properly put the wind up Archie, but the stubborn old fool had stayed on until, at first the gas was turned off, a week later the electricity and finally the water. It was early December – no heating or hot food and Archie got bronchitis. Kevin was worried when Archie's cough worsened. He could see Archie was struggling to breathe, and that every breath he took caused him to gasp and clutch his chest. In the end, there was no alternative and Kevin called an ambulance. At the hospital, they were told Archie had pneumonia due to lack of care and nutrition.

Kevin stayed with his father whilst tests were carried out. He wasn't sure how he felt about Archie. He certainly didn't respect him, nor he admitted, was there any special relationship between them, but Archie was, after all, his father. He bit his lip when Archie's face was covered with an oxygen mask, and he followed staff around through sessions of x-rays, blood and sputum tests. Convinced his father's life was in danger, Kevin broke down when the tubes taking various fluids into Archie were put in place. 'He's going to live, he is isn't he?' he begged everyone, over and over again.

Always, they shook their heads and replied, 'We're doing our best. Try not to worry.' Kevin sighed with relief when it was obvious Archie was getting better when he began to harangue staff about going home.

It was while he was in hospital, that bailiffs were employed to deposit their possessions into the street, and the new owner changed the locks. Kevin was devastated and, childlike in his frustration, he stamped his feet, yelling, 'I'll get you for this, Becky. Do you know what you've done?' and shaking his fist added, 'he's your dad too. He's ill.'

Sitting on the kerbside with his head in his hands, he muttered, 'God, now what?' Archie, who had taken the lead over the previous few months, was now a useless, sick old man. At first Kevin didn't know where to turn, but by the time Archie was well enough to leave the hospital, and with the help of Ryan, he had found some cheap rooms for rent in Trethorpe.

Archie had turned his nose up when he entered the shabby rooms. 'Not what you could call home, is it lad?'

'It's the best I could do, given the circumstances. I've got no cash to do better,' Kevin flashed back.

Archie flicked the faded curtains drooping over the grimy window, ran his hand along the dusty sill and fingered the threadbare blankets. 'Ain't staying here long, that's for sure.'

They were both startled when the mobile phone rang. Kevin lifted it, and handed it to Archie. 'For you. Quick off the bloody mark aren't they?'

Grabbing the phone, Archie said, 'Just got out. What do you want, mate?'

Kevin heard someone gabbling at the other end, before Archie said, 'I ain't up to it mate. Still a bit on the wobbly side if you know what I mean. Give me a week or two, then it'll be back to business.'

Kevin watched as Archie nodded, pursed his lips then shook his head as he listened to the caller.

'Well, if it's that urgent, how about I send my lad along? He's smart, keeps his mouth shut.' Archie was quiet as the other person spoke, until he indignantly blustered, 'Of course I bloody trust him.' There was more exchange between them before he said, 'Right, eleven thirty tomorrow morning, yes? I'll tell him.' He smiled across to Kevin who scowled back.

'By the way, cash in hand job? Usual rates? Pay the lad.' As an afterthought, he added, 'See that the money is put in an envelope, mate.' As he put the phone down he turned to Kevin and said, 'Put the kettle on, I'm gasping for a cuppa.'

Kevin rattled some mugs and slammed the fridge door shut. 'What was that all about?' he demanded.

'Just another little driving job for you. Nothing new except it's a collection not a delivery. I usually do the collecting bit.'

'How far?'

'How should I know? Just drive, pick up whatever, and deliver. Okay?'

'Not okay,' Kevin snapped back.

'Now don't get in a paddy, lad. We could use the money. It will start a fund to get us out of this dump.'

Standing over Archie, Kevin took his shoulders and looked him squarely in the face. 'First you tell that bloke that you trust me, then...' he gave Archie a shake, 'then you tell him to put the cash in an envelope. What was that all about? You either trust me or you don't.'

Giving a quiet chuckle, Archie wriggled out of Kev's hands. 'It's him I don't trust. If the money isn't in an envelope, loose like, then it would be easy for him to help himself to a quid or two wouldn't it?'

Kevin shook his head, not sure whether he believed Archie's excuse.

'Now where's that cuppa? I don't suppose there's any biscuits?'

The job was easy as were the others that came along.

Within a few weeks Archie was available for work, none of it legal. With their joint earnings they were soon able to move into more comfortable accommodation, not homely, but not threadbare, 'Even a few cushions,' Archie said punching one into shape.

Someone must have liked Kevin's businesslike approach to each job he undertook. It was a Saturday lunchtime when the telephone rang. Kevin left Archie to answer it. There was no mistaking the surprise in Archie's voice, as he said, 'It's for you.'

Kevin shrugged, 'Not expecting anyone to ring me,' he said as he took the phone. Archie watched as Kevin's eyes widened in surprise and saw him nod as he answered tersely, 'I'll be there.'

Archie turned away, desperate to know and trying not to show interest, but curiosity got the better of him. 'Um, some girl, I suppose. Got her into trouble? That her dad?'

Kevin sat at the table, curled his hand around his chin, nodding slowly with a sly grin. 'Something like that,' he said, 'a sort of date.' He stood up briskly, 'And that's all you're going to know,' and left the room.

Monday, one thirty at a high class restaurant, were the instructions. As he entered the near empty restaurant, he saw a man in a secluded corner put up his hand. Kevin made his way over to the man, and noticed his wealthy appearance. His suit had hand-stitched lapels, his shirt was not from a chain store and his gold cuff links, with a diamond stud, protruded from his jacket sleeves. Beckoning with his cigar to the chair opposite, he said. 'Sit down. Kevin is it?'

Kevin nodded as he answered, 'Yes, sir,' and held his hand out.

The man ignored his hand, leaned back in his chair, took a drag on his cigar and said, 'I like that. Sir. Shows respect.'

Kevin was nervous, and sat with his hands clasped between his thighs, hoping his anxiety didn't show.

Waving to a waiter, the man asked, 'Something to drink?'

Kevin shook his head, then changed his mind. 'A beer, thank you.'

'Good, keeping a clear head. Right...' The man glanced at the menu. 'What about a steak. I like a steak meself. Suit you?' Without waiting for an answer, he gave the order along with Kevin's beer and a bottle of wine for himself.

Pushing the cutlery aimlessly round and round with his forefinger, the man looked across to Kevin. 'Well,' he said, 'I expect you're wondering why you're here?'

At first Kevin felt a brief flicker of fear but quickly dismissed it. Instead, he sat up straighter, pulled his shoulders down and with a measure of defiance said, 'I've done nothing wrong. I've obeyed every instruction without question.'

The man gave a quiet chuckle. 'Relax, lad. Nothing like that.' he gave a brief smile, one that didn't reach his eyes. 'It's like this. How would...' he stopped speaking as the waiter had returned with their drinks, poured a little into a glass and handed it to the man. The man sipped it and when he nodded his approval, the waiter filled the glass. Leaning forward, Kevin watched him and was fascinated as he tipped the bottle and heard the wine gurgle into the glass. The man took another sip, licked his upper lip and sighed with satisfaction. The waiter began to re-arrange the cutlery, and the man waved him away impatiently.

Kevin noticed that the small finger on the man's left hand was missing.

The man lifted his glass, took a good mouthful and said, 'That's better. Drink up, lad.'

As Kevin raised the bottle to his mouth, the man hissed,

'For God's sake, use the glass. Where do you think you are? In a workman's café or something?'

Kevin coloured up, inwardly knowing he should have known better.

'As I was saying,' the man continued. 'The man at the top, no I don't know his name, nor the next one down nor the next, then there's me. You've noticed I've not told you my name?'

Kevin nodded twice.

'He got a report from one of his, shall we say, customers. Told him about you. How you wouldn't budge from instructions. Bloody defiant he said.' He took another sip of wine. 'Well, I can tell you the boss was impressed. So impressed...' he put his glass down. 'Yes, so impressed that he instructed that you should be hunted down.'

Kevin gasped and gave a swallow. His first thought was, is this my death sentence, but the man's voice was friendly. Bitterly, he told himself, yes I've seen it on the telly, what do they say? Softly, softly, lull them into a feeling of security.

'But, but...' he began.

'Wait. Listen to what he wants.' The waiter reappeared with plates piled high with chips, onion rings and a steak the size of which Kevin had not seen in a very long time.

'Tuck in,' the man said as he forked a large piece of steak. With his mouth full, he spluttered, 'You got a passport?'

Looking down at his plate, Kevin couldn't face the mountain of food. A feast, and he was unable to eat it. Kevin shook his head. 'Never needed one. Can't afford holidays abroad.'

'Play your cards right, son, and you'll have a villa abroad to live in before too long, never mind holidays.'

Cautiously, Kevin picked up a chip.

'Manners, boy, manners. Look around you. See anybody else using their fingers?'

Again, Kevin blushed.

'With the money you could be earning, you could live like this, like me, everyday.' He swilled his mouth with wine and, with eyes narrowed, looked keenly at Kevin. 'You interested?'

'Depends.'

'Depends! What do you mean depends?' he stared at Kevin. 'Of course it's all illegal, but you already know that. What you've been doing for the last year or so has been illegal, but that hasn't bothered you much so far has it?'

Almost ashamed of himself, Kevin answered, 'Needed the bloody money, didn't I?'

'Yes, I understand that. But now you've got a chance to get your hands on big money. Not only that, it would be pretty regular. The top man has all sorts of clients wanting different things.'

'So, what's with the passport?'

'Amsterdam? Diamonds? I'll not say more.' He tipped the remains of the wine into his glass, took a sip and looked over the rim. 'Well, you interested or not?'

Kevin grinned. As far as he could gather, he would go abroad, get well paid for the privilege and live like a lord. Cutting into his now lukewarm steak, he nodded.

'You bet.'

The man sighed with relief, the hardest part was done – recruiting a new face. 'There are a few rules you need to understand,' he cautioned.

'Okay.'

'You're definitely in? Can't tell you anything unless you're committed, understand?'

'I've been broke for so long that I'm prepared to do most things. Not murder, no, not that, nor anything to do with people smuggling, but as long as I've got some sort of security if I'm ever caught...' he grinned at the man, 'but, you can be sure I never will be...'

'Now, hang on a minute. Why do you think I never gave you my name, eh? Because, if you don't know it you can't drag me down with you can you? I'll tell you what my nickname is shall I?' He waved his left hand in front of Kevin's face. 'Pinky. Get it? Pinky, because once, just once, I made a mistake and...' he wiggled four fingers at Kevin. 'So I got a light punishment. Understand? Don't know those above me, so I wouldn't be able to tell the cops sod all.'

A shudder went through Kevin as he listened. 'You've got a point. I understand. In any case I'm no grass.'

The man looked at his watch. 'Listen up. Get yourself a passport. In a month or so someone will contact you. Tell you what to do. You won't go alone. There will be a bloke with you watching out for trouble.'

'Blimey, my own minder.'

'Don't be daft. He'll be minding the goods, not you. You're dispensable. We're talking big, big deals here.' He reached for his wallet and handed Kevin a wad of notes. 'Get yourself some decent clothes. Look like a young exec.

or something. Oh, and think about moving somewhere a bit more respectable. The boss man likes class. You're not in his class, so pull yourself up.' He glanced at his watch again, picked up his jacket and threw paper money on the table. 'That'll cover the bill. You won't see me again.' As he moved away he turned back to say, 'You'll get your own nickname soon, so watch how you go.'

Chapter 22

With a few nursing friends Becky headed to O'Shea's for a well deserved drink every Friday when they ended their shift. Becky enjoyed their company, especially when one of the nurses would relate some incident that would set them off laughing. Maureen, who was older, had been nursing the longest, had many tales to tell. Often the friends begged her to tell one particular story of her early nursing days. Maureen laughed along with them, older and wiser now.

Well, alright. Just this once mind, then I'm never going to mention it again,' but she always did when they asked.

'It was like this she began. 'In those days, we were in nursing school for six months, then six months on the ward until we qualified. It was my very first time on night duty, and I was sent to the men's ward,' she smiled. 'Sister had gone for her supper. I was on my own and it was lovely and quiet. Not like today, everything going on day and night. Anyway, someone rang a bell, and I hurried along in my new white plimsolls that squeaked on the shiny ward floor. Pity Matron's didn't, you know how they creep about. A warning like that now and again would have been useful.' She took a sip of her drink, and then went on. 'Anyway, as I was saying, I got to this gentleman's bedside, and asked him what he wanted. I had to bend over to hear and he whispered, "A bottle, miss. I'm fit to bust." So off I went to fetch the wretched thing.' All the friends began smiling and nodding to each other knowing what was coming.

Maureen took another sip of her drink, a sparkling Babycham, before continuing. 'So back I trotted with the bottle, white enamel in those days. I handed it to him, but he refused to take it. Instead, he pointed for me to put it under the blankets. Well, I was just eighteen and I was flustered, went hot and I'm sure I coloured up. I put my hand under the covers and felt around.' She demonstrated by making exploring finger movements, and everyone laughed. 'I felt around, getting more and more upset, until I found the right place so to speak, and placed the bottle in position and left him to it.'

By now, the girls were nudging each other and tears of merriment rolling down faces. Maureen grinned. 'When I got back to collect it, he was grinning and said, "Ha, that was great, really great." I can't begin to tell you how embarrassed I was, I mean, you know...'

'We know,' one girl giggled.

'God, where has all that innocence gone? Even kids out of the convent know more than that these days,' another added. All the time everyone was chuckling.

But Maureen hadn't ended her story. 'Worse still,' she continued, 'The next night all the eight bells in the ward rang together, and I raced to see what was happening. Would you believe everyone one of those blighters was asking for a bottle!' Always, at this point of the story, there was an explosion of laughter causing others in the room to turn and look over to see what was happening.

'Anyone else got a story to tell,' asked someone. Kitty, who had been nursing for six years, gave a vague wave of her glass hoping no one would actually see her.

'Look,' cried Becky, 'Kitty's hand is up.'

This caused Kitty to blush and she dropped her head. 'Oh, I'm sure you've all had the same experience,' she murmured, 'It's nothing new really.'

'Well, how do we know if you don't tell us, Kitty?' someone asked.

Another, cheered on by the others, said, 'Come on Kitty, it can't be that bad. Open up, tell us.'

Twisting the glass round and round in her hand, she looked up and smiled at them. 'I can laugh now, but at the time I was so scared.'

The girls leaned forward, their faces lit up with anticipation.

'Go on, Kit, tell us what happened.'

Kitty took a deep breath. 'Like Maureen, I was no more than eighteen and at the hand-over between shifts. I was on nights of course, and we were told the patient in bed eight had died, and was now in a side ward.'

There was a sympathetic sigh from someone.

'Anyway, during the night, around midnight, Sister left the ward. I don't know what for, but she said she wouldn't be long. So, there I was on my own when a bell rang. I glanced up to see who was ringing and...' she looked at her friends and widened her eyes.

'Oh, no. Don't tell me...?' Maureen began.

'Yes, you're right. The bell was from the room where the body was.'

One of the girls crossed herself, saying, 'Jesus, Mary, mother of God.'

'Honestly, I was that frightened, I could feel my heart thumping and I could barely breathe. It seemed, at the time, that the damn bell went on forever. I remember standing up and feeling a bit giddy, but I knew if that bell was ringing when Sister came back I'd be in trouble.'

Becky stretched out a hand towards, Kitty, 'Oh, you poor thing.'

Someone said, 'I'd have run a mile.'

Kitty laughed, 'Well, it wasn't so bad in the end.'

'What did you do? Did you answer it?'

Kitty, now the centre of attention, was enjoying their reactions and answered, 'Yes. My hands were clammy and I wiped them down my skirt, made sure my cap was on straight, God only knows why, and made my way to the side room. I opened the door, and to add to my misery, the damn thing creaked. The room was almost dark except for the candle, burning for his soul near the bed, and moonlight. I tell you I couldn't get out of that room fast enough. I turned off the bell and...' she hesitated. 'And checked, you know, to see if he was alive,' then solemnly added, 'he wasn't of course. I found out later that one of the porters had rigged up the bell and rang it from outside the window. One or two of the girls had began to have their suspicions.'

'How? I mean, well someone rang it,' asked Becky.

'Yes, they did. I found out on the next shift that one of the porters had climbed in through the window!' She raised her glass, 'and what's more I reckon that Sister was in on it. When she returned to the ward, she was definitely laughing and kept looking at me.'

'That was a rotten trick,' Becky said. 'You might have had a heart attack, fainted at least.'

'You know the rule girls – nurses aren't allowed emotions.' Swallowing the last of her shandy, she lifted her glass and asked, 'Who's ready for another? Let's toast all nursing sisters. Bless them.'

Becky was intrigued by an attractive, full of energy man, and she had seen him every Friday for the last three weeks. Perhaps he would be there again tonight. What was she thinking about? Every one of her friends knew she had little interest in the opposite sex, but she had not told them why.

Always at the bar laughing, and friendly nudging those around him, he seemed to be very popular. A tall man, taller than most men in the room, at least six feet she estimated. Although his hair was well cut, his auburn curls showed a hint of scattered silver. She noticed his long fingers holding his glass, and that he didn't swallow down his drink quickly like so many others, but took his time, seemed to be savouring it, not speaking until he had downed a mouthful. As men joined the crowd around him, he made them welcome, hailing them by name, sometimes slapping them on the back before ordering more drinks. When he moved, from leaning on his elbow on the bar, or sprawling on one of the sturdy carver chairs, or making his way across the room, he was loose-limbed yet graceful. And yes, he was here tonight and she was, she realised, secretly pleased see him.

Ann asked, 'Whose turn to go to the bar?'

'Not me!' Yvonne protested, no taller than five foot four inches, 'I'd get trampled to death under that lot.'

Molly was more forthright, 'They're on the pull. Look, look how they're eyeing every female. Asking for trouble to go amongst that lot believe me.' She gave a sniff, 'and anyway, my Brendon wouldn't like it.'

'And why isn't he here then protecting you?'

'Cos he's out on the pull himself,' Yvonne quipped.

Molly leaned over and gave her friend a friendly slap. 'He'd better not be,' she said, twirling her engagement ring round and round her finger. The three of them looked at Ann, who shrugged nervously. 'I couldn't,' she whispered, 'I don't like being pushed and shoved about, you know that.'

'I'll go,' Becky volunteered. 'I'll sort them out if they start anything. Can't be any worse than some of the men we have on the ward.' The girls nodded and muttered in agreement.

There was a large crowd around the counter just standing, glasses in hand, calling out to newcomers, chattering and laughing. Becky edged her way through, and was nearly at the bar when she was roughly jostled forward, and stumbled into the man she'd been observing.

'Wow, steady on,' he chuckled as she bumped into him, and he reached out to steady her.

She saw his friendly grin and smiled back, 'Sorry,' she said.

Looking at him she noticed he was wearing expensive, well cut jeans, a blue shirt and a fine wool, jumper in a darker blue. She realised he was staring at her, and found she couldn't look away. It was as if she were hypnotised and she knew at once he was...exciting, sensuous and dangerous.

The bartender interrupted them, 'What'll you be having Connor?' he shouted above the noisy crowd, 'usual half lager?'

Still holding her elbow, Connor turned to him and said, 'Serve this gorgeous witch first who has cast a spell over me.'

The barman laughed as he turned to Becky, saying, 'You watch out miss, he can charm the cows into milking themselves, he can. Now, what can I get you?'

The drinks she ordered were put on a tray, and while she was paying, Connor lifted it, saying at the same time, 'I'll take these across for you, and you...' he pointed at the barman, 'can line me up at least four pints for that lot over there,' and pointed to his friends.

Becky led him across the room to the girls, and she was amused to see how they were reacting as they approached. Yvonne was smoothing her hair, Kitty was brushing crisp crumbs from her top and, to Becky's mind, Molly was spellbound. Maureen gave a knowing smile. As he put the tray down on the inadequate table, he beamed at them all, and said, 'Evening ladies.'

They murmured their replies, fidgeting like schoolgirls. Becky was convinced he was very much aware of his effect on them, and secretly laughing.

He turned to her and taking her left hand in his, stroked her third finger and nodded two or three times. 'I see you're not spoken for yet,' he said softly. Becky felt herself going hot and her heartbeat became momentarily erratic, then settled. She tried to pull her hand away, but Connor hung on to it. His face was alive with mischief and grinning down on her.

She could not ignore the attraction she felt towards him.

'Well, I can alter that for you,' he said, and laughed as she finally snatched her hand back.

'You flatter yourself. As if I would look twice at the likes of you,' she countered. 'Go away with your fancy words. Go on, be gone with you.' Becky dropped heavily into her seat.

He remained grinning at her.

'Clear off,' and when he still hesitated, said loudly, 'Now.'

Openly laughing at her now, he spluttered, 'Many have looked at me more than twice, and I've looked at them and found them wanting.' He stopped laughing and leaned towards her, 'But you...'

'Had a lucky escape then didn't they?' she snapped. She stood up and placed her hands firmly on the table. 'If you don't leave now, I'm calling the manager.'

Ignoring her threat and in a more serious tone said, 'Believe me, you will not regret spending the rest of your life with me.' They looked at each other, she in anger, not knowing if he was making fun of her. She was sure she could see a flicker of laughter in his serious face.

She began to shake and taking a deep breath, 'Better still, I'll call the police. This is harassment and I want you gone.'

Yvonne quickly pulled on her sleeve, 'Sit down, Becky,' she insisted, 'You're making far too much of this. He meant nothing.'

Becky sat down heavily, muttering, 'Well I've had enough.'

Unnoticed a young man, a friend of Connor, came swiftly over to them. 'That's it Connor. You're annoying this young lady. Back off,' he said firmly, as he pulled his friend away.

'I thought you might be close by, you devil, spoil everything you do. Do you know that, Denis, you're a real spoilsport? I'd just got her going, a real firebrand that one,' and he chuckled as he shook himself free of his friend.

'You've ordered drinks and they need paying for and we're all gasping back there.'

Resignedly, Connor did as he was told, nodded to the group of girls and spoke directly to Becky, 'I'll be around. We will take this further. Now I've met you I need to know you more.'

Becky opened her mouth to make a retort, but before she could do so, Connor's arm was grabbed by his friend, and he was led away. After taking three or more paces, Denis turned his head and looked at Becky, smiled, a shy smile, and mouthed 'Sorry.'

Although he was shorter than Connor, Denis was obviously the leader at the moment. His fine hair, had a slight wave in it and was neatly parted, his back was straight and his step confident. Somehow, she didn't know why, he definitely left an impression on her as well, one that intrigued her.

As soon as the two men were out of earshot, the girls rounded on Becky.

'Do you realise you almost had a proposal there?' squealed Yvonne.

'The best looking guy around, you lucky girl,' sighed Kitty.

'And well off. He owns a farm up the gleann, smart as a new pin.'

'Gleann?' queried Becky.

'Valley to you – you English ignoramus,' answered Yvonne.

'If I wasn't engaged to Brendon, I'd make a bid myself,' said Molly.

Becky took a sip of her drink, 'Well, if you must know, he's a bit too forward for my liking.' She put her head back and added thoughtfully, 'Maybe, just maybe, I might...' She shrugged her shoulders, 'We'll see what happens, but yes,' she conceded, 'he is very, very attractive.' All of them laughed, aware that Becky was definitely interested in Connor.

It was three weeks later when Connor asked her out. 'Would you walk out with me this Sunday?' he spoke hesitantly but politely enough. Becky noticed two things simultaneously. Firstly, it was obvious Connor was nervous. He looked at his feet, glanced at her face then dropped his head again. Secondly, as usual, Denis wasn't far away.

'I'll think about it,' and pointing to Denis, she added 'Will you be taking your minder with you?'

'I thought we might take a walk around my farm. There are some lovely views and my mother will give you supper.'

'Sounds fine but...' again she looked across the room to where Denis was sitting. Although he was chatting she could see he was watching Connor, or her, all the time.

Connor followed her glance. 'Oh, if it's a chaperone you're needing, my sister will walk with us if you like.'

Becky laughed outright at the thought. 'What time were you thinking?'

'About two. Where shall I pick you up?'

She thought fast, she didn't want the other girls to know of her date – not yet. And secondly, for some reason, she didn't want him to know exactly where she was living. The pain of trusting a man was still raw.

'Outside St Joseph's.' Then as an afterthought, 'If you know where that is.'

It was his turn to laugh. 'It's where I'll be marrying you.'

'Not on your life,' she retorted.

Connor waved as he moved away. 'See you then, Sunday. Don't forget.'

On their first date, Connor took her to his farm, some ten miles from the town. There were no close-by homes, only the farmhouse. Originally a beautiful, rambling house, but now made ugly with mismatched wooden extensions erected at the sides, obviously by a do-it-yourself person. Asking Connor why they were there, his reply surprised her.

'Had to have somewhere for the hands to sleep. They take their meals with us, and mother sees to all their other needs.'

Becky raised her eyebrows, and there was a quizzical look on her face.

Connor took her hand, 'She does their washing and mending, changes their bed stuff, cleans the bathroom after them, that sort of thing. You know what men are like. Messy creatures aren't we, so we need womenfolk around us.' Becky made no comment as he took her into the house.

As they entered, she smelt a mixture of lavender polish and cakes baking, a homely smell that had been missing from her life for a good while. The furniture was heavy and solid, with grooves that could harbour years of dust she thought, but there was none to be seen. Connor took her into the large kitchen and introduced her to his mother, saying, 'This, mother,' he said pulling Becky forward, 'is Rebecca, the woman I'll be marrying soon.'

Becky laughed, 'He hopes, Mrs McDowell, he lives in hopes.' Becky liked Connor's mother at first sight, but was dismayed to see that the woman standing in front of her was tired and old looking before her time. She had a clean apron around her ample waist, her greying hair was twisted up into an untidy bun and her cheeks reddened by the heat from the range. 'You're very welcome, my dear,' and looking at her only son, added, 'and you're wise to think twice about marrying this lumpkin.'

As Mrs McDowell began setting the table, Becky offered to help. 'Let me put the cutlery out, and I can make a pot of tea. Go on, sit down for a moment. I expect you've got an evening meal to prepare later.'

Becky didn't notice the exchange of looks between mother and son – looks of approval from her and his, a look of satisfaction. As Becky was bustling about the kitchen, occasionally asking where this and that was, Mrs McDowell told her about her fourth daughter's imminent wedding. 'The last of my girls to wed,' she sighed. 'I had five girls and just the one boy, that fella over yonder,' she said pointing at a grinning Connor.

It was six months later when Connor asked, as he put his arms around her and brushed the hair away from her face, 'Rebecca, will you put me out of my misery and marry me?'

'Not again, Connor, you asked me that last week. The answer's the same.' she smiled at him as she answered, 'No, no thank you.'

Folding his arms around her and rocking her gently, he said, 'You silly woman. I really mean it. Will you marry me or not?'

Looking up into his face she could see his hope and he wasn't fooling around. 'Connor, you've never said that you love me, ever. How is a girl to know you're not teasing or leading her on?'

'Love?' he said shrugging his shoulders. 'Love grows

within a marriage. I'll love you well enough, you'll see.'

Becky was astounded by his answer. 'But...' she faltered, 'Connor, why have you never made love to me? Most couples do you know after a few weeks, sometimes after a few days, but not you. I mean, for weeks I thought, he's a laugh, good company, but I don't think he really likes me.'

'Good grief, girl. I want to make love to my chosen woman on the first night of our marriage.' He pulled her closer and murmured, 'Doesn't mean that I wasn't tempted though.'

'Yes, but...'

'No buts Becky. Oh, I know girls fancy me, and to be honest, I've taken advantage of them. I dare say you too have had your admirers, but...'

Quickly she put her finger on his lips and he grinned, 'Nevertheless, I respect you more. I wanted you for my wife from the first day I saw you.'

There was a long silence between them. Her first thoughts were, here we go again. Kevin, not entirely his fault they couldn't wed, but as soon as Archie had appeared, Kevin had abandoned her. She remembered that it took a long time before she could trust another man. It was Michael who had rekindled trust, but again she had been let down. Oh, he was genuine enough at the time, she admitted, he really had wanted to be with her, but a pregnant wife, a wife he hadn't disclosed, was his final choice. Now, Connor. Could she, dare she trust him?

'Well?' Connor's voice was tender. 'What's it to be? Shall we tell my mother you are to be my wife?'

'Connor, you're a dear man and lots of fun to be with.' She gave a small sigh, before taking his hand and saying, 'Can I have a little time to think things over. It really has been a shock. Any moment now, I expect you to say, you're only kidding.'

'That's fair enough. Do you think you could give me an answer next weekend? Then we could start making plans.'

Half laughing, she retorted, 'Honestly, Connor, you're so bloody sure of yourself aren't you?'

Chapter 23

'You girl.' The raised voice of her mother intruded upon Ethel's thoughts. Where had she got that expression from, she wondered? Girl indeed. 'Don't ignore me. I'm talking to you,' the voice continued.

Ethel turned to face her mother. 'What do you want now?' she asked putting down the knife she was cutting vegetables with.

'Don't you lip me, my girl, or you'll find yourself without a roof over your head. Do you hear me?' Victoria, now sixty-nine years old, was in a wheelchair the seat of which sagged under her weight. Ethel remembered her saying that it was easier to sit in the chair and be pushed around. Easier for whom, Ethel wondered.

'Much better than struggling with a stick with blasted painful arthritic hips,' her mother had declared.

Nevertheless, the stick was always to hand. Ethel avoided it as much as possible. A moment of forgetfulness, she couldn't remember what now, and the stick had been smacked across her back. There never was an apology and although she made a point of ignoring her mother for hours afterwards, it was with bitterness and anger that she had finally gone back to the duties of caring, dressing, feeding and toileting. Now, it was used to occasionally give an unexpected poke as she passed by.

Turning back to her present task, Ethel asked, 'What is it you want, mother? You can see I'm busy.'

'That's just it, girl.' There was an angry edge to Victoria's voice as if she were addressing a lowly servant from the distant past. 'You're so stupid. Don't you ever listen? I've told you time and time again, chop those carrots smaller and not so much onion, thank you. They upset my stomach.'

Upset her stomach, Ethel fumed silently. Always greedy and selfish, she took more and ate more that she needed, often with very unpleasant consequences that Ethel had to clean up.

'No wonder you never married. Never had the looks anyway, did you, for a fellow to look twice at you? Run a mile to get away from your sullen face. Spared someone some pretty awful cooking too I'd say, as well as your moods.'

How many times had she heard that Ethel wondered? Yes, there had been someone, they had talked of getting married, but the death of her father had made her hesitate and her chance of happiness was gone. No opportunities now of ever finding someone. She was forty-one, and burdened with caring for a very unpleasant mother, and what's more, she told herself who would want to hear, 'Do you take Ethel...' at the altar, such a hateful, old fashioned name.

It was getting dark outside and she caught a glimpse of her reflection in the window. Wispy, greying hair tied back with an elastic band with escaping strands. Long, hollow face with dark shadows around the eyes, drooping mouth – what was there to smile about, she chided herself. Like her mother's, her clothes were old, shabby and out of date.

What was really galling, beyond belief, was that the large house contained plenty of silver – candlesticks, salvers, sweet dishes all of a past age. There were also two rough sketches by Landseer. She had no idea how they came into the family, but surely they must be worth something – but her mother was adamant. 'We manage very well as we are,' was all her mother would say when the subject of selling anything was broached.

The meal Ethel had been preparing was late, and mother liked to eat her last meal of the day around six-thirty, but it was nearly half an hour later when the dish was put in front of her. The usual complaints followed.

'Too much salt,' after one mouthful. 'The meat's tough. You tell that butcher tomorrow. Get my money back.' Then, 'It's too hot to eat.' This was followed in less than a minute with, 'This is cold. Did you warm the plates like I told you?' After a few more mouthfuls it was, 'I shall be ill if you've undercooked this and you know what that means. Ruined our holiday plans with your efforts last week. Stuck here when I could be waited on hand and foot in Jersey. Call yourself a cook. Trying to finish me off aren't you? Well I'm hanging on.' Nothing the old woman was saying was true. Ethel clenched her fists, holding back what she'd like to say, but it wasn't worth further abuse.

Pushing away her half empty plate, Victoria wiped her mouth, sniffed and leaned back in her chair. Glaring at Ethel she said, 'And now I suppose, there's no afters.' She looked around the kitchen, her eyes narrowed and pointed with an arthritic finger at the sink full of dishes. 'Your next job my girl, is to tidy this place up. I'd be ashamed to bring anyone into this house. It's the same all over. What's the matter with you?' she quickly answered her own question. 'Lazy, that's what, lazy.'

Ethel bit what was left of her already chewed nails and asked herself, who would want to visit a vile old woman like her mother or me, a sorry old maid? 'There's strawberry jelly, and I thought some ice-cream?' she ventured.

'Jelly,' shrieked Victoria. 'Again?' As Ethel leaned over and placed the dessert in front of her, Victoria lifted the bowl, threw it across the room and lifted her stick.

Ethel, her heart pounding, as she lost control of her pent-up frustration, wrenched the stick mid-air from her mother. It happened so quickly, she didn't know where her energy came from. In a blinding rage, she brought the stick down hard and fast on her mother's head screaming out, 'I hate you, hate you.'

Chapter 24

Kevin was watching a formula one race when the telephone rang. Irritated at the interruption, he turned the sound down to answer it. The television was a recent purchase, one of the latest on the market and he was very pleased with it. The last deal he had negotiated had really paid off. He shouted brusquely down the mouth piece, 'Hello?' and silently cursed. 'What do you want?' he asked Archie. 'I'm in the middle of something.'

There was excitement in Archie's voice. 'Keep yer hair on and listen.'

Kevin heard Archie catch his breath. He'd been breathless and often told Kevin he didn't feel well ever since his bout of pneumonia. Kevin thought, as he had thought many times before, the old man is losing it.

Out of the corner of his eye he could see the television screen's flashing blue light. 'Get on with it. What do you want? I'm not leaving this house to run about for you again today.'

'No, nothing like that.' Archie paused before saying, 'It's like this. A job has come up. A good job. It...'

The interruption came quickly, 'Not interested. Got me own people now as you well know.'

'Just listen will you.' Kevin kept quiet. 'You there?'

Archie's dealings of late were not worth bothering with, not now he had made his own contacts, and very lucrative they were too. Got to be careful, he told himself, one mistake and...well a hiding if he was lucky, and likely a hospital job at that.

With a sigh and a hint of sarcasm, he answered, 'Yes, I'm here, waiting for this "good job" news.'

Archie gave a cough. 'Worth thousands. Honestly, thousands.'

Thousands? Kevin, now alert was definitely interested, but intended to be cautious. He had been misled by Archie more than once. 'Go on.'

'It's like this. There's a bloke set his heart on having a couple of drawings. Says they're by a famous artist. Never been seen by anyone.' Archie paused, 'You interested?'

'Depends.'

'He got in touch with a mate of mine. He can't do it, got a touch of arthritis or something so not as quick as he used to be.' Archie couldn't see Kevin shaking his head side to side, and mouthing, another old geezer like you. 'Anyway, he thought of me, told the man and the bloke got in touch.'

'Where are these drawings? Not in some bloody museum are they? Far too dodgy to break into.'

'No, that's just it. They're in a big private house and what's more, he says, the owners are on holiday for a month so the place will be deserted.'

'When? I mean, when is the job to be done?"

'Sometime this week.'

'Sounds like a piece of cake. How much exactly is he offering?'

'Not sure, at least a couple of thousand I think, but we can always up the price can't we? After all, we'll be taking the risks.'

Kevin laughed in disbelief. 'What do you mean, we? It'll be me taking the risks. I bet you'll do more than be a look-out or something easy like that. Something that won't take much effort or risks if I know you.' For a moment or two he was silent and then said, 'I'll think about it. Let you know tomorrow. Now, clear off and leave me in peace.'

Archie, his father, still a petty thief, who had recently been caught trying to rob an 'off licence', and had served a recent six month sentence for his bungling attempt. Kevin had done his best, seen to it that Archie now had a decent place to live, and provided him with a battered, cheap but serviceable car. He'd also given him a small television, 'To keep you out of trouble,' he told him. It didn't work, Archie continued with his, in Kevin's opinion, trivial thieving.

Sitting in front of the television, still showing a race with the sound off, Kevin leaned back and closed his eyes letting his thoughts wander. The old man had been getting on his nerves for quite a while now. Was it only four years ago that Archie had blundered, crashed, no bulldozed his way into his life, changing everything that might have been? How bloody green I was in those days, Kevin thought.

Instinctively, whenever he thought of Becky he felt for the silver charm, now on a silver chain under his shirt. Whenever he thought of her he felt ashamed at how much he had hurt her. Where are you now Becky, he whispered to himself.

Smiling, he thought how surprised she would be at the change in him. He wandered across to the hallway and looked at himself in a mirror and his clean shaven face looked back at him. He stood straighter in well cut jeans and a crisp blue shirt. He had put on a little weight, so that he no longer looked so youthful, and it was obvious to those he met that he was full of confidence. This is me now, he told himself. Now an owner of a four bedroom house in a lovely quiet avenue. An agency sent a cleaner and gardener once a week so the place stayed in good order, whether he was at home or not. There was a beauty of a car in the twin garage and he enjoyed holidays abroad, especially in southern France and Portugal.

There had been girls, of course, but now he had met someone, someone special. It surprised him that Sarah had shown an interest in him as she was quite his opposite. Intelligent and aware of his lack of knowledge of just about everything that she loved – art, the theatre and music, classic and modern, but she was never condescending. Patiently she explained and guided him, and to his amazement he found he enjoyed learning. They had met at 'Sarah's Ristorante', a small, busy restaurant she owned. Sundays was the only day they could be together all day, but most evenings he sat in her restaurant sipping a beer, just the one, that lasted a long time. A self-imposed restriction meant that he never, ever had too much to drink – the very nature of his activities demanded that he kept a clear head. He couldn't risk making mistakes, or the safety of his life. The time was spent watching her friendly, but respectful welcome to diners with an open smile, and coping with minor disasters in the kitchen.

Kevin was nearly always early at the restaurant and amused himself watching people coming and going. One evening, an over large, short woman entered. Kevin raised his eyebrows in astonishment at the amount of jewellery she was wearing, at least four strings of chain, in varying shades of gold as were the numerous, jangling bracelets on her wrists. On her arm was a large handbag, one of the largest he had ever seen. In a firm voice he heard her say, 'Table for four, please,' and pointing to a table in a prime position, stated, 'I'll sit over there and wait.' Kevin couldn't help watching her as she bumbled her way across the dining room, her bag swinging and just missing other diners. To finish off the little drama he was witnessing, she turned and called over her shoulder to an open-mouthed waitress, 'A glass of water if you please. No ice,' and promptly sat at the chosen table ignoring the sign that read, "Reserved".

Another time a pair of diners entered. A young, willowy girl, giggling as she and her escort, a man, Kevin thought old enough to be her father, jostled in the doorway. When they were seated, they gazed into each other's eyes, he tenderly stroking her fingers and she flicking back her hair and dropping her eyes coquettishly. Kevin found their age difference disturbing, but was glad to see that when they left and the man put his arm around her possessively, she angrily shook him off.

There was no doubt in his mind, that Sarah made him feel special, cherished even loved. At ten, sometimes eleven o'clock, he would drive her to her home, kiss her good-night and leave. No way was he going to spoil his chances of something more lasting with her. He'd wait. Getting himself a lager from the fridge, he returned to his armchair and turned off the television.

The old man, as he now referred to as Archie, had not lived up to the self-image he had boasted off, but one thing he was always firm about was, 'honour among thieves', Kevin told himself. Now he had an offer that would mean betraying honour. Archie must know that there would be some questions tomorrow, before he committed himself to taking part in a robbery.

Kevin had never forgotten Pinky. As he had predicted, Kevin now had a decent amount of money. Only because, he told himself he'd always kept strictly to instructions. Bluebell was the name of the voice that telephoned instructions. Kevin wondered how he got his nickname – was he a homo? Did he live near a bluebell wood? Did he have a pet with that name, a bird? Well it could hardly be a canary, he thought smiling at his own joke.

Kevin was surprised to learn his nickname, Kid. It began with a phone call from Bluebell. 'Is that the Kid?'

Kevin knew that it was Bluebell's voice.

'Who's asking?'

'Me, you silly bugger, Bluebell.'

'Then this might be the Kid what do you want?' After instructions, questions and answers had been exchanged, Kevin said, 'One more thing. Why did you call me Kid?'

'Because, my old son, you're the new boy on the block, and still wet behind the ears as far as real work is concerned.' Bluebell gave a chuckle, 'That will all alter, believe me. Once you get used to big money, well let's say the president likes your style, and has plans for you.'

Kevin was a little disappointed with his name, but if Bluebell was right, it could well be altered if he played their game. At the same time he was aware that he was part of a big organisation if a president was justified. Also, despite what Pinky said, members must have talked about him. This was no tin pot, chancing gang like that of his father's. As Pinky said, names are a secret.

Shaking the lager can, he tipped his head back to get the remaining dregs as he thought about his last contract. The telephone had rung early one morning last week. When he picked it up there was no mistaking Bluebell's voice. Kevin's stomach tightened partly from apprehension and partly excitement. He was to go to Amsterdam by boat. This was his second visit to Holland and was told to use passport z. He had three passports, all in different names. Two had arrived just after his meeting with Pinky last year and the third was the one he had applied for in his own name.

Passport x was used to fly to South Africa for a ten day holiday a couple of months ago. He was told that a hotel had already been booked in Cape Town. He'd been advised to enjoy himself and to make sure he did the tourist attractions. He would be contacted in due course. He'd taken the cable car ride to the top of Table Mountain and went on safari, and was spellbound watching the animals in the nature reserve. A vineyard with a wine tasting event was suggested by the management and for once, he let himself enjoy the wine offered in tiny beakers. It was a cheeky idea to visit the diamond museum, but seeing their beauty and their value, he understood how greedy women, men as well, went to extremes to own them.

It was while he was rubbing himself down on the beach after a swim, that a grinning, boy, no more than twelve years of age, approached him. A beach vendor with a heavy tray stacked with packages and a cool box, queried, 'You want ice-cream? Cold drink?'

Kevin shook his head.

The boy held out a sealed bag of boiled sweets. 'You English?'

Smiling, Kevin had said, 'I am.'

The boy had thrust the bag of sweets at Kevin. 'You take, very cheap.'

Pushing the boy's hand away and shaking his head, Kevin pulled on his shorts.

'You have bluebells in your country?'

His question surprised Kevin at first, then he realised that, without doubt, this was his contact. He was shocked that such a young boy should be part of a smuggling deal. He had expected to be approached in the hotel by someone older. 'Yes, we have bluebells,' he answered, and put out his hand for the bag of sweets.

The boy heaved a sigh of relief, handed the bag over and hastily disappeared into the crowd.

On his way to the airport for the return trip, he bought an identical bag of sweets, a toy car and a stuffed toy lion. Feeling a bit silly, he carried them with his hand luggage, explaining to the stewardess, 'For my niece and nephew.' He'd handed her the lion, 'Think she'll like it?'

'Sure to, sir. Now could you fasten your seat belt.'

There was no problem at the airport, and within days he met up with another courier who exchanged the sweet packet for a bulging envelope.

The trip to Amsterdam a few weeks later opened his

eyes to how clever the chain of exchange was. It was a three day trip from Tilbury. Free time on the first day, and return trip on the third day. 'No need to disembark at Amsterdam,' Bluebell had said. He had stayed aboard the second day, leaving his cabin briefly to have a tour of the ship and occasionally talked to and had a drink with other passengers. The day ended with dinner at the captain's table. Bluebell had told him that the cleaner of his cabin would conceal a package behind a panel over his bed. At Tilbury, another cleaner would retrieve it. 'You're the minder this time. You remain with the consignment,' he was told, 'And God help you if anything happens to that package. Understand?'

'I get the message,' he'd replied. As far as he was concerned it was great. His greatest fear was to be stopped by customs personnel. At first, just walking through the airport or seaport, filled him with dread, he sweated and kept looking round, but on this trip he had nothing to fear. He hoped he would be doing the trip again. As usual, he was paid well, this time a motorcyclist had roared up to his door and handed him the envelope.

Kevin had a dilemma of his own making. As he worked for someone unknown to him, he wondered if there were other schemes that were less dangerous to carry out, but equally as rewarding. It was now his ambition to eventually, to take over as leader or form his own team. Not in the near future, as he needed as much experience as possible and was quietly biding his time. All of these dreams were on hold as he thought about marrying and having a family, now he had found someone special. Was he prepared to give up all these ambitions and settle down? Sarah was the girl who had brought this change about.

During her working hours she wore her long blonde hair in a French pleat or pony tail, but on Sundays, let it hang down her back in waves. Not a tall person, but Kevin had noticed that she stood straight so that whatever she wore hung well on her petite frame – a picture of health and happiness.

He'd never, since meeting Pinky, questioned any of his orders nor opened any packets, he knew he was well paid for his work. He must make very sure before he made a decision about Archie's proposition. A few thousand quid would be a bonus. Perhaps, invest it in another restaurant and propose marriage to Sarah.

Relationships, especially marriage, should be based on trust, with no secrets and that was another of his problems. Should he tell Sarah of his illegal activities? In his heart he felt she would never understand or forgive him, as she was so honest and trusting. Should he make a clean break from crime or follow his plans for his own establishment? If he gave it up, how and where could he earn enough to give Sarah the lifestyle he wanted for her. He had no qualifications, and no useful contacts outside of the criminal fraternity. Archie too, could do with the extra cash he told himself. After an hour or so of these deliberations, he decided to go ahead, but the stakes were high. Sarah and Bluebell were never to find out, so he must be very careful.

Kevin could hear the excitement in Archie's voice when he telephoned him the next morning to say he would do it. 'Just this once. Understand?'

'Thank gord for that,' he said, and Kevin heard his sigh of relief. 'I won't let you down son, but it means a lot to me.' He gave a little chuckle. 'You and me,' he said, 'a team again.'

'Forget it, Dad. It won't happen. I mean it. This is a one off. Don't ask again, alright?'

'Alright, alright. Keep your 'air on. I'll get back to you when I hear what's what. Ok?'

'Don't take too long about it. I could be off again very soon. Never know when a job comes up, so buck up.'

Archie gave a sniff. 'What sort of job?'

'Mind your own business,' Kevin snapped back and heard Archie give a little grunt.

Archie phoned the same evening. 'We're on,' he whispered.

'What on earth are you whispering for?'

'Am I? Sorry about that. Anyway, the guv says tomorrow would be the best time. It's nearly a week since the two women left the place, and they're not due back until the end of the month. That means they won't find out for another two weeks at least.' He paused. 'With luck, they'll not find out for a good while, by which time we'll be in the clear.'

'Tomorrow, then?'

'Yep. Oh, and by the way, he says, the guv, he says to wear marigold gloves and plimsolls so you can burn them afterwards.'

Kevin exploded. 'Does he think I'm a bloody amateur?' he snorted. 'Marigold gloves. Tell him I'm not washing up and if he turns nasty tell him to stick his job.'

'Now, now, lad,' said Archie softly trying to soothe Kevin. 'He don't mean anything by it. He's never had dealings with the likes of us before and he's a bit nervous. If we get caught...'

Kevin shouted, 'If we get caught, I'm done for and I

don't mean prison, more like a concrete overcoat or worse.'

'Don't be daft. What can go wrong? Pick me up at, let's say around nine tomorrow night. Don't fret, it'll be a doddle. Empty house, in its own grounds way out in the country, couldn't be easier. Bye.'

Chapter 25

There was a three diamond engagement ring on Becky's finger, after two months agonising of over her decision. Carefully, during quiet moments on night duty she weighed up everything she could think of, making a list of Connor's good and bad points before she'd consented to his proposal. Each time she added something to the 'bad' list she determined on a good one. The good list showed, she thought, that he had a sense of humour, there was never a time when she was in his company that he hadn't made her laugh. There was certainly a promise of financial security, as she was very aware of how hard he worked on the farm. This probably accounted for his good health and, she had to admit with a little thrill, his honed body. There was also the respect he'd shown her over the sex, and although a little disappointed, she couldn't help wondering what it would be like, but he still insisted that the first night of their marriage would be special. She'd smiled a little as she wrote that down on her list. Added to the list was his good temper, not like Archie who, as soon as he had raised his voice, had put her on her guard. Nor was he weak, always the leader, unlike Kevin. Mentally she told herself to stop making comparisons, see Connor as himself. He was so certain of her reply. Perhaps she ought to put arrogance on the 'bad list' which as she looked at it, gave her some misgivings. Was he trustworthy she wondered as she thought of Michael? She was still not always sure of his sincerity, feeling that he was hiding a joke at her expense, but she was unable to exactly define what.

It bothered her that he seemed happier with his Friday night drinking friends, mob she called them, not putting her first or spending time with her. This thought made her wonder how serious was his commitment. This fault, his love of drink bothered her most, one that surely could be controlled later when they were wed, not yet a serious habit, she admitted, like Archie's and the awful consequences of heavy drinking. Memories surfaced – her mother's fear and beatings – and her stomach churned every time Connor came close to being drunk. Thankfully Denis was always at hand to save Connor from injuring or making a fool of himself. Always, when she mentioned it he excused it as, 'Just being with the lads,' then with his usual charming smile added, 'but when we're married it'll just be the two of us.' Silently, she hoped that didn't mean she would be taking over Denis's role of minder. She shook herself mentally, you're going too far she told herself, don't be so ridiculous.

On the other hand, it was obvious he respected and cared deeply for his mother, and Becky longed and hoped for the same devotion. He certainly showed affection towards Becky, but still no mention of love.

It was suggested that they would live at the farm, and she agreed after extracting a promise from him that he would repair and paint the lovely house back to its former glory. Connor had hinted that she should give up nursing, but she hadn't entirely promised to do so, telling him she would think about it. After all, she reasoned to herself, I'd be bored stiff on the farm all day. The wedding date was set for October. Connor had insisted on the date as it would be after the harvest was in, and the ground ploughed ready for the following year. It was still another four months away. They had grown closer, and Becky was happy.

They had arranged to meet on Friday evening in O'Shea's, Connor's favourite bar. Due to an emergency and lack of staff, Becky had stayed on late at the hospital, and was over an hour late. As she entered the bar, she could see across the room Connor surrounded by his good humoured friends, and she smiled as watched him laughing along with them. She bought herself a drink, took a sip then quietly approached the crowd around Connor, and sat down. The group at first hid her from him, but she didn't mind, he was obviously enjoying himself, and she daydreamed about her wedding day as she twisted her ring round and round. Connor had plenty of female relatives to choose from for bridesmaids, and she knew she would have to be careful when choosing, so as not to offend other relatives. Another problem that seemed to have no solution, was who should give her away? Connor had decided to pay for the reception, wedding dress, flowers and honeymoon. He hadn't told her where they were going, always laughing when she asked and saying, 'Wait and see, nosey,' before kissing her on the tip of her nose.

It was when she heard someone say, 'So, Connor, you're getting wed?'

The remark jolted Becky, but she smiled when she heard Connor confirm that was so.

'For the love God, man whatever for? Surely the girl was more than willing like all the others. No need to shackle yourself, like that.'

There was loud laughter from all around, 'Come on Connor. You're the last person to be thinking of wedded bliss,' another said slapping him on the back.

'Which, believe me, it isn't,' another voice chipped in.

'Been making promises to the girl?'

Connor shrugged his shoulders, 'one or two,' he answered.

There were a number of opinions voiced as to what the promises might be.

'Like, giving up drinking with the lads? That's always the first to go.'

'Not Connor. He'll be here you wait and see, every Friday as usual.'

'Yes, give it week or two, that's when the nagging starts.'

'Bet you didn't promise to give up the girls, though eh, Connor?'

Connor was laughing along with them all.

'He bloody hasn't,' someone said, causing more laughter.

Becky stood up on tiptoes as she was too short to see over the heads of the men, but between their bodies she could see Connor who was still not aware of her presence. She saw him take the last swallow of the drink in his glass, and wave across to the barman for a refill.

Grinning at his friends, he swiftly looked about the room, but still didn't see her, and indicated that they should come closer. He didn't bother to lower his voice when he said, 'It's like this lads. Got a mighty big area to farm, you know that.' Becky saw him give a slow wink. 'A farm that'll need sons one day, and that girl has the makings of dropping quite a number in the next few years, I shouldn't wonder.' There was a roar of laughter.

Becky gave a gasp, began to shake, and fearing she might faint held on tightly to the back of a chair. It took a moment to pull herself together – then anger welled up inside her. Not only was she angry with him, but mostly with herself. Again, she thought, another man betraying me. First Kevin, not entirely his fault, but he could have supported me more against Archie, but she reminded herself that he was always weak, backing out of even minor confrontations. Then there was Archie, her father, who had made it clear that he wanted nothing to do with her. All those schemes she and Michael had planned. His declaration of loving and taking care of her, all gone with a brief note – he'd chosen his, unknown to her, pregnant wife. After two years, she'd allowed herself to trust Connor, and again she was betrayed. She hated them, all of them. A sob choked her as she heard Connor add, 'And something else, my mother's getting too old to wait on the farm help hand and foot, from morning to night. She's finding the dairy work too much these days, and my sister's away to wed.' He paused, took a swallow of his drink before adding, 'Anyway Becky's already taken to the chickens. Time my mother retired, been doing it since she wed some forty-five years ago. Remember, Becky's a nurse, used to long hours on her feet and used to hard work. She'll do fine.'

Becky had heard enough, and with tears running down her face, began to tug at her ring, intent on throwing it back in Connor's face with a few choice words. The ring wouldn't budge but she flew towards him, her fists ready to punch him over and over again. Pushing the first person blocking her way, and using her elbow and through pressed lips, ordered, 'Move.' There was no mistaking her tone. All the men, some who were shocked and others amused, heard and took a step back to let her through.

A low voice, barely audible, said, 'I'm out of here.'

Someone moved away and another joined him, saying, 'I'm with you, Liam.'

Becky had taken no more than four strides, and suddenly stopped in her tracks. In amazement she heard Denis's angry voice. 'You're a bastard, Connor.' He had grabbed Connor's lapels and pushing his face close up said, 'How could you speak like that about a wonderful girl? You've absolutely no respect at all for anyone. She's not one of your "here today gone tomorrow" type. I've seen how you've treated her, laughing at her expectations.' He let go of Connor, and added, 'She deserves better.'

Connor shrugged himself back into his shirt. 'Jesus, you know I didn't...'

'Intend marrying her?' And with that, Becky watched with her mouth open in awe as Denis, his eyes blazing with anger, lifted his right fist and punched Connor in the face. 'That's for Becky,' and followed this with another punch from his left hand. The hand found Connor's nose who staggered and fell backwards onto the floor. Looking down on him his voice filled with contempt Denis said, 'And that's to end our friendship. You've used me enough.' As he strode away he added, 'You disgust me.' He grabbed Becky's hand and dragged her after him. Looking back just once, Becky saw the group around Connor quietly disperse, one or two shaking their heads, others muttering to each other. One pulled Connor to his feet, then left to join the others.

She glanced back again. There was a look of bewilderment on Connor's face as his fingers explored the damage to his nose, and he shook his head at the same time. As he lifted his head he saw her and held out his arms, palms uppermost, as if pleading. Denis had already pulled her through the door and they were outside in the cool evening air.

When they reached his motorcycle parked outside, Denis turned to her. 'You all right?'

Nodding she said, 'You hit him!'

'I did, didn't I?' And with a wry grin began rubbing his knuckles, 'And it bloody well hurt.' They looked at each other and began to laugh. It was when Becky's laughter turned into tears that Denis put his arms around her.

'It's alright,' he whispered. 'It's alright.' he wiped away her tears with the palm of his hand. 'Honestly, Becky, he's not worth it. You truly deserve some one better. Trust me, he would have made your life a misery.'

'I know,' she answered, 'but I just thought he might... you know...be more loving and caring once we were wed.'

'He can be very charming, promise you anything, he's the same with everyone. Then they find out how shallow he is, and believe me, they soon depart.'

'But there's always a crowd round him, he loves it.'

'Becky, he has generous pockets. How many of those blokes did you see buy a drink. That's mostly what they hang about for – whatever they can get from him.' He paused, 'Of course, some of them just love the situations he gets himself into, situations that I rescue him from time and time again. They don't get involved, but...like tonight, notice anyone going to help him?'

Becky's sobs had lessened. 'But you've stayed with him, since school, he told me.'

'Did he tell you why?'

She shook her head.

Denis gave a deep sigh. 'It was his mother. We were only wee lads at the time, around nine I think. Anyway, he fell in the river. It'd been raining hard, and the water was fast...' He paused, let go of her and sat down on his motorcycle, pulling her down beside him onto the passenger seat. 'As I was saying, 'he fell in, the river and like an idiot, I jumped in after him.' He clasped his hands, turned and looked at her. 'By heavens, that water was cold. It was just luck that I grabbed him and well...'

'But he owes you! You don't owe him anything.'

For a moment, Denis gazed down the narrow street then turned back to her before saying, 'It was his mother, you understand. She was hysterical when she found out, him being the only boy.'

Becky was indignant as she asked, 'She didn't blame you did she? I mean has he always been so, so...casual about his actions and real danger? Did he never think of the consequences?'

'As I said at the time we were only little boys, but yes, that's Connor's way, always has been and no doubt he will continue the same.'

'So, what's this all about his mother?'

'She made me promise that I'd always keep an eye out for him and never let him get into danger,' again he sighed. 'And an almighty burden that's turned out to be.' He stood up, pulled her to his feet and straddled his motorcycle, 'Come on, let me take you home. Climb up behind me.'

When she had settled, he said casually, 'Now, put your arms around my waist and hang on tight.' As soon as she was seated, he kicked the starter, the bike roared into life and they set off. Becky was exhilarated as Denis manoeuvred the bike at speed, causing her to lean into corners in tune with his body. The draught cooled her cheeks and she laid her head on Denis's back, feeling somehow relieved at the turn of events. As soon as she dismounted outside her door he said, 'Goodnight,' and left her. For the few moments it took, she watched the red tail light until it vanished.

After making herself a coffee she began tidying up the kitchen and was surprised to find herself humming – I should be unhappy, weeping and wailing, she thought, but somehow I feel as if I've escaped a prison sentence. Giving a wry smile she told herself she probably had. What surprised her more was how she felt when Denis put his arms around her. It was a long time before she had truly felt safe, comforted or cared for. Always with the others there had been a nagging doubt, but with Denis it was somehow different.

Chapter 26

As the house was empty, it was agreed that around nine would be the best time to carry out the robbery. This suited Kevin as he had promised to pick Sarah up after her shift around ten thirty. He decided it would be wiser to take Archie's car. Should, just by chance, anyone see something suspicious and note a car, the robbery would not be traced back to him. His own BMW was after all said and done, far too good for the job.

There was an eerie silence about the grounds once the noise of the car engine had died away. The unlit house looked gloomy and uninviting. 'Come on, let's get this over with,' said Kevin as he bent over to tie the lace on his leather shoe. He patted his pockets, located his leather gloves and slid his hands inside them, smoothing each finger for a comfortable fit.

With barely a sound Archie prised open the unresisting door with a crowbar, splintering the wood so that it gleamed white in the moonlight. To Kevin, the noise was like a pistol shot and for a moment unnerved him. In an angry whisper he turned on Archie, 'Are you daft or something? Do you want to get us caught, you old fool.'

Archie flashed his new false teeth, 'Nobody about, I told you, got the place to ourselves. Take as long as we like.' He stood back and pushing Kevin ahead added, 'after you, me lord.'

Kevin stumbled into the hall, Archie followed him and shut the door. They were in a hall lit only by the moon's ghostly, meagre glow filtering through two small windows in the door. Kevin hesitated, trying to allay his unease. There was something not right, the atmosphere held secrets, and he had a feeling of danger that had nothing to do with his associates or Pinky's missing finger.

Turning back to Archie, he whispered, 'Did you bring a torch? We're not going to risk putting the lights on. They could be seen for miles.'

'Yes,' Archie replied, and promptly turned it on flashing it around the hall they were standing in.

'Keep it low,' Kevin hissed, and keep your voice down.' He glanced nervously along the passageway. Every door each side of the passage, painted in mediocre brown, looked forbidding.

'And who's to hear?' retorted Archie. 'I keep telling you

we have the place to ourselves.'

Carefully, quietly and methodically they searched each room without success. Each room needed attention as nearly everything was covered in a fine film of dust. Loathe to touch anything, but knowing he had to, Kevin kept brushing his hands down his trousers. Archie, wearing cotton gloves, was tempted to help himself to some of the silver objects lying carelessly around the room. Archie had an itch over his eyebrow, and removed his glove to scratch when he saw a pair of candlesticks. With awe he picked them up. 'Look at this. George the Third I reckon, they were into silver in a big way in them days.' He caressed a salver, put it down, then lifted an intricately woven open-work cake basket. He gave a low whistle, 'The silver in here is worth a fortune,' he said.

In exasperation, Kevin strode across to him and roughly shook his arm. 'Put it down. Forget it. Now.' He heard Archie mumble something under his breath, and taking no notice said, 'I'm going into the next room and if the draw-ing isn't there, I'm off.' As he left the room Archie spotted a set of spoons and stopped, tempted to take them, but decided against it. Kevin would not be happy, probably cause a scene, might even make him take them back.

Utterly exhausted Ethel had fallen asleep and woke to find herself still sitting in the dark and began once again to weep tears of regret. She repeated over and over again that she was sorry as she reached for the dead woman's hand. Suddenly she straightened her back. Had she heard a noise the hallway? She held her breath for a few seconds and then picked up the walking stick when the soft sound of movement, a shuffle, was repeated. There definitely was someone or something in the hall. Without turning on the lights she crept to the kitchen door, listened and cautiously made her way to the hallway.

Kevin made his way along the passage to the furthest door, tripping slightly over the curled edge of a runner and swore. He smiled grimly to himself, just as well there isn't anybody at home, he thought as he regained his balance. Archie flashed his torch once more around the room and clicked it off. No more than a few seconds behind Kevin, he stepped quietly into the ill lit passageway. Unable to believe his eyes, he was just in time to see someone creep up behind Kevin, and lift a walking stick to strike him. He never knew where the speed came from but in a few quick-steps, all in silence, he grabbed the weapon from Ethel's grasp and without a second thought, brought it crashing down on her head. The blow caught her unaware and Archie watched as, with a surprised grunt, her knees buckled and she pitched forward. With her hands outstretched she fell onto Kevin, scrabbling at the nape of his neck, as she folded unconscious at Archie's feet.

Feeling the sudden weight of her on his back Kevin yelled out, 'What the hell...?' She dragged on the fine chain around his throat snapping it as she fell. The silver charm slid off and, along with the chain, disappeared into the darkness, but Kevin didn't feel it leave.

Archie moved towards the end of the passageway and turned on the lights. Kevin began to protest, but Archie, facing him, said calmly, 'It's alright boy, you can be sure there is no one here now. That racket would have brought any other living soul that's around running to see what the noise's about.'

'What's going on?' demanded Kevin, as he rubbed the soreness the chain had caused as it rasped along his skin.

Then he saw the body of a woman at his feet. A sudden feeling of dread came over him, he felt the bile rise in his throat as he looked at Archie, still clutching the bloodied walking stick. Seeing his stricken face, Archie quickly dropped the weapon, the crack noise it made as it hit the floor shattered the quietness about them.

'What have you done, you stupid, bloody fool?' Kevin bellowed as he bent over Ethel. 'Christ, if you've killed her, I'm done for proper. How could you be so, so...?'

'It was her or you – she was about to give you a head-ache with that stick. Thank your lucky stars I saw her in time.'

Dreading having to feel for a pulse, Kevin hardly able to hold his temper, knelt down beside her and gingerly put his face down to hers. 'She's so still, I reckon you've bloody killed her.' For a few moments he stayed then began to panic. 'She's not breathing.' Archie hurried to his side as he stood up and looked down at Ethel's body. Kevin, tense with fear, felt the hot, itchy sweat in his armpits. With shaking hands he grabbed Archie and pulled him up close. Through clenched teeth, he said, 'You're in this alone. I was never here, you understand. You say one word about tonight and I'll kill you myself.'

Archie, with a little chuckle pushed him away. 'Calm yerself,' he said as he pointed to Ethel, 'She's breathing alright. Look, see, her chest is still going up and down, just as normal. No, she's out for the cold, but you're right, we'd better scarper before she comes round.'

In the car going home, Archie grumbled, 'Well, that was a waste of time. Three hours if you ask me, what with travelling to get there. I've a good mind to charge for our time. Bloke's got plenty of money. I reckon he owes us.'

'Shut up! Shut up,'

'What you so bloody het up about? We got away didn't we?' A few moments later he added, 'What was that stupid cow doing there, anyway? I had it in good faith that she'd be away.'

'I don't care,' flared Kevin. 'I knew there'd be trouble. I knew it. I sensed it as soon as I saw the house. Cold, dark something not right there I tell you.'

When Archie dropped him outside his door, Kevin turned and pointed at him. 'Don't you ever, ever ask me to help out again. Understand?' He slammed the car door. 'And another thing, if you get caught, I mean it. I'll deny you're my father and I wasn't there. Got it?'

Archie didn't answer, but put his foot down on the accelerator and speed away. Good, thought Kevin, at that speed this time of night you're sure to get picked up.

Chapter 27

When Ethel roused in the darkness, she wasn't sure what had happened. Carefully she pushed herself up into a sitting position and felt the back of her head. Feeling the stickiness on her hand coupled with throbbing pain she realised that she had a wound of some sort. Rolling over onto her thighs, then her knees she placed her hands on the floor to lever herself up. Once she was on her feet she experienced a wave of nausea and giddiness and clung to the wall for support. With one hand clasping the back of her head and the other feeling her way along the passage wall she made her way to the kitchen. She turned on the light, gasped and immediately retched. Horrified she took in the scene – her mother slumped in the wheelchair with congealed blood down her neck from the injuries, not one, but many, about her head. Ethel retched again and again and raced for the sink as she moaned, 'Oh God. Oh God, what have I done?'

After swilling out her mouth she sat down abruptly in front of her mother, alternatively staring at the body, hoping for a sign of life, and dropping her head into her hands, knowing that there was none. Desperately, she wondered, how can I explain this to anyone? It was half an hour later when she made up her mind what had to be done.

It was obvious that the events of the evening would have to be reported. A little blood was still oozing from her wound and what had run down her neck was sticky. Timing was important, so she plugged in the hairdryer, and trained it onto the blood until it looked as dry as her mother's. She looked around the kitchen and satisfied, dialled nine, nine, nine.

'I've been attacked, me and my mother. I think she is unconscious,' she screamed down the phone.

The voice at the other end of the line told her to 'Calm down,' and asked for details of names and address, and details of the attack ending with, 'Do you have a dog?'

Ethel almost laughed thinking to herself, if I had a dog it would have alerted and protected me, but only whispered, 'No,' to the operator.

'An ambulance and the police will be with you directly. Could you please turn on the lights and open the door for them.'

Making sure there was a measure of hysteria in her voice, Ethel replied, 'No, no, I can't do that, they might still be around.'

'I understand, but they will identify themselves when they arrive, so please be ready to let them in. In the meantime, please do not touch or remove anything from the scene. The ambulance has been dispatched, and will be with you shortly. Please stay on the line until they arrive.'

Three police officers arrived first. As they entered the house, Ethel watched them, their eyes taking in every detail, as they walked along the passageway. One asked if she was alright. Another other asked, 'This your blood?' as he pointed to the stains on the wall.

'Yes,' she faltered. 'Yes, when I came round, I had to get to my mother as soon as I could but, but...' and she began to weep.

Once they had reached the kitchen the officer insisted she sat down.

One of the officers gave a cough and pointed to the walking stick. 'Is that what you were hit with?' he asked.

'It could be, couldn't it?' she answered. 'It's got blood on it so I suppose...' and she trailed off.

When the three men entered the kitchen they wandered around the room, and one pointed to the smashed dish on the floor in a puddle of melted jelly and ice-cream. One of the officers went across to her mother, and, as Ethel watched, he bent over her then glanced at his fellow officers and shook his head. 'I'm afraid she's...' was all he said and Ethel felt faint under his gaze. A thousand thoughts crowded her mind, the foremost being, did he suspect her, before she passed out?

When she came round she found herself being wheeled out to a waiting ambulance, and heard the attendant arguing with a policeman that, 'No way, she's not fit to be questioned. Needs attention to that head wound. Could be brain damaged for all we know. The quicker she gets help the better.'

'Go with her,' one of the police officers ordered a young constable. 'She just might say something that would be useful. Then get back here as soon as she's admitted.' Ethel closed her eyes thankful for the respite and determined to say nothing. The constable accompanied her, and stayed with her until she was safely in a hospital bed.

Early the next day, having had the wound stitched and a drug induced sleep, she was told that there was a policeman who wished to interview her and she began to tremble.

'There, there my dear. Don't upset yourself,' the nurse said, as she helped Ethel into a sitting position. A man in a neat suit and tie entered the room, and was immediately cautioned by the nurse.

'Only a few minutes, sir. Miss Carter is still in a state of shock.'

In a gentle tone the man at her bedside introduced himself as police detective Richards. He cleared his throat before saying, 'Miss Carter, I'm sorry for your loss.'

Tears filled her eyes and she turned her head away from him.

He gave her a moment to recover then said, 'We believe your mother, she was your mother?' Ethel nodded and he went on, 'We suspect that she was murdered by a person or persons unknown.' Ethel inwardly cringed, person, she thought. Does he mean me? 'Now, I need your help. May I ask you a few questions about yesterday evening?'

Wiping her eyes she lifted her head and looked into his serious face. 'Of course,' she answered.

Taking a notebook and a pen from his inner pocket, he

began with a few routine questions. 'Do you have a husband, boyfriend?'

'At my age?' she countered.

Richards smiled, 'Just routine, just routine. Well, let's just say is there anyone who might wish to harm you?'

Ethel shook her head.

'How about your mother? Has she any friends? Do you know of anyone who might, erm...wish her ill?'

Ethel was thoughtful for a moment before answering. 'There was a time when mother had a number of friends. They used to come round for a game of bridge.'

'Used to?'

'Oh yes, that is until, I don't really know what was said, but there was a tremendous quarrel and after that...well, visitors were few.'

'Would any of them wish her harm?'

Ethel was beginning to relax. He was searching for someone and it didn't seem to be her. 'Good heavens no! All genteel ladies and all of a good age. I daresay one or more of them must have died by now.'

'I believe you told one of my officers that you heard a noise in the passageway and went to investigate. Right? What sort of noise? Footsteps? Voices?'

She shook her head. 'No, it was like a tiny bump sound almost as if someone had tripped.'

'And so you thought you'd see what it might be?'

She gave a nod.

'Did you arm yourself?' he smiled as he added, 'Hopefully not with a kitchen knife.'

Again she shook her head. 'No, though I did pick up mother's...' she swallowed back her tears, 'mother's walking stick.'

'Yes, we found the stick which means, at some time, we shall have to take your finger prints to eliminate you from our enquiries.'

Inwardly she sighed with relief. So no one thinks I might have killed mother. 'Well, it is my home, so my prints are bound to be all over the place.'

'Quite so. Did you think there was more than one person in the passageway?'

'I didn't see anyone of course, someone behind me obviously, but there might have been someone in front. Sorry, I just can't remember at all,' she lied.

'Do you have anything at all of value about the house? Jewellery, money perhaps?'

'No, except there are a couple of Landseer's, the Victorian painter,' she added as she saw a questioning look on the officer's face. 'Some sketches somewhere in the house, just scraps of paper really. Been in the family for some time. I can't think of anyone who might know of it. There was only my mother and myself. I do have a distant cousin in Australia, but I'm sure he doesn't know about them. I certainly don't think they can be worth very much.'

'Oh, you'd be surprised. Some people just like owning something, nothing to do with its value.'

Ethel lay back into her pillows, it was funny how tired she felt suddenly and closed her eyes.

'I'm sorry,' said Richards, sympathetically, 'I've tired you. Just one more question for the time being.' He pulled out a plastic bag from his jacket pocket. 'Does this belong to you?'

Opening her eyes she looked at the silver charm he was holding out to her and shook her head.

'I thought not. The initials are R and K cleverly intertwined. Yours are E and C so...' He trailed off as he returned the piece of evidence to the bag. He stood up. 'Just one more thing, can we take away for the time being some of the silver items? We think we might get some fingerprints off them. Someone will give you a receipt and they will be returned as soon as possible.'

He looked down on her, handed over his card. 'I will let you know of our progress, and when we apprehend your attacker. But, in the meantime, should you remember anything that you think might be of help, please get in touch.'

It was as he left that she did remember something. 'Mr Richards,' she called out as he was halfway down the ward. 'Mr Richards.'

He turned and saw her beckoning and returned to the bedside. 'Yes, Miss Carter? You've remembered something?'

Pulling herself up onto the pillows, she said, 'Not exactly. Not about last night. You see, the house should have been empty and I hadn't turned the lights on, so...'

The inspector turned his head to one side and there was a curious note in his voice. 'Oh,' he said, 'and what happened?'

'Yes, we were to go on holiday, mother and I, but she became ill at the last moment, and we had to cancel. So you see, I thought that maybe somebody knew and hadn't expected us to be there.'

Inspector Richards took out his notebook. 'Perhaps you can tell me who you booked with,' and he wrote down the name of the travel agent company she gave. 'Did anyone else know you were to be away? Newspaper delivery? Postman? Milk? Any other regular delivery services?'

Ethel gave him the names of all she could think of who might have been told of their holiday dates.

'Thank you Miss Carter, this information could be helpful. At least it will help to eliminate people from our enquiries once we have interviewed them.' He stood up and offered her his hand which she shook and he left.

As Ethel lay in her bed she had mixed feelings. Of course she was sad at losing her mother. When she was a child Victoria had been someone she had loved without question, and her mother was full of love for her, always there, advising and supporting her. The latter years had been difficult for both of them. Victoria constantly in pain and deprived of her independence and Ethel committed to unending hours, of caring mostly without thanks, with much criticism. Guilt was another feeling and now she was experiencing remorse. Murder! She had committed murder. It was on the spur of the moment, she hadn't intended a fatal blow, just...Ethel didn't know what – a taste of her own medicine perhaps. Killing her own mother would not gain her any public support if she was found out.

Now her thoughts switched to whoever had entered her home and injured her. Grievous bodily harm, and they might so easily have killed her. That would probably be the charge, so why shouldn't she let the police think they had also killed her mother? She knew there were at least two people involved. It was a bit of luck that the walking stick was the weapon for both crimes. The death sentence had been abolished, they wouldn't hang. That thought gave her a measure of relief, and they would most likely only serve half of any sentence handed down to them, anyway. What's more she thought, this probably wouldn't be the first of their criminal activities. They deserved to be charged. Determined to toughen up and not to weaken her resolve to put the blame elsewhere, she cautioned herself to be extremely careful when answering any more questions from the police.

It was two weeks later and Ethel had decided on a holiday. It had been really great to go out and buy some new, cheerful clothes, clothes she knew her mother would never have approved off. As she was holding up a green flowing dress against herself and looking in the mirror and deciding whether to take it, thinking that maybe there might be some dancing and maybe – the doorbell rang. It was difficult to hide her surprise when she saw inspector Richards whose smile was friendly when she opened the door. Her stomach churned as she convinced herself that some new evidence had surfaced and pointed the enquiries in her direction.

'May I come in? I shan't take up much of your time.'

'Of course.' She stood back to let him enter. There was a tremor in her voice and her hands were shaking as she asked, 'Have you come with some news?'

'No, not yet I'm afraid.' He looked at her and noticed she was trembling. 'You're not over the shock yet are you. I'm so sorry to disturb you. I just want to clear up a point then I'll be on my way.'

'Can I get you a cup of tea or something? Coffee?'

Richards shook his head. 'No, no thank you. I'll be brief. You..., please sit down Miss Carter.' Ethel felt behind her and found the back of a chair and sat. 'Good.' He cleared his throat and said, 'You mentioned earlier that the house was in darkness, that you hadn't turned on the lights. Why was that? What I mean to say is that you and your mother were having supper. That's right isn't it?'

Ethel nodded.

'Well, do you always eat in the dark?' He gave a quiet laugh as he continued, 'I know the idea is quite ridiculous, but you must admit it was a strange remark you made at the time.'

A sigh escaped from Ethel, she pulled at her skirt, and then smiled up at the inspector.

'I can see your point,' and taking a deep breath said, 'We usually eat late, around seven or so and mother had eaten quite a large meal. It wasn't unusual for her to take a nap, often quite a deep sleep before she wanted her dessert. And that is what she did that night. Fell asleep, so rather than disturb her, she's, she was quite frail you know, I...'

Richards gave a slow nod and said, 'Go on.'

'Well, I didn't turn on the light, just fumbled my way around the kitchen, clearing up a bit, even dropped her ice-cream.' She hesitated. 'Then I decided to sit down and wait for her to wake up.' Pausing again she took another deep breath, and with a catch in her voice said, 'and that is when I heard...'

'Ah,' he exclaimed. 'Now I understand. Yes, I can see it now. House could easily have looked empty from outside. Thank you, Miss Carter. I'll be on my way.' She half rose from the chair. 'No, no. I'll see myself out.'

Well, most of that was true, Ethel told herself when he had gone, and she returned to her packing.

Chapter 28

Kevin hated himself. For two days after the fiasco and he anxiously prowled around his home, biting his nails and when he remembered the prostrate body of the woman on the floor, with a bleeding gash on the back of her head, he shook. What was troubling him the most was the loss of his pendant. He remembered the searing pain on the back of his neck when the woman fell against him, but he hadn't realised the chain had snapped and the pendant was missing. He had searched the clothes he had worn that night, but could not find it and was now convinced it must be at the scene. Newspapers were delivered and, at first, there was only a brief report stating that a woman was in hospital recovering from a brutal attack in her home. It was obvious from the photograph in the paper that it was the place of their miserable burglary attempt. This was followed the next day with glaring headlines: 'Elderly woman bludgeoned to death', followed by an account of how she was found sitting in her wheelchair dead, by her daughter who had survived the attack. It was believed that a burglary had been interrupted. Nothing had been taken, so the motive was not clear. The police suspect there were two persons involved and were seeking witnesses.

There was never any violence or threats in the criminal activities Kevin was involved in. He'd made up his mind when he was first approached that there was no way he would ever become like Archie. He recalled how uncaring Archie had been when he struck the woman. There was no mention of any clues, so, he thought he must have lost the silver token somewhere else.

Throwing the newspaper across the room, the pages separated and drifted to the floor. Angrily he kicked at them. Murder! Kevin shuddered. He dared not get in touch with his father, wanting desperately, to tell him to keep his mouth shut. What if he bragged in his local, what if he inadvertently said, 'Me and Kevin...?' Archie never kept his mouth shut when he had a grievance, and when Kevin had left that night, he was still harping on about not being paid. That would be his starting point Kevin told himself, and then it would lead to what and why? He was angry, frustrated and fearful and regretted bitterly that he had been tempted to make some easy money.

The phone rang for the umpteenth time. It was sure to be Archie, and Kevin ignored it. It was after the fifth time, in immediate succession, that Kevin angrily snatched up the phone and, convinced it was Archie, snapped, 'What? I don't want anything to do with you.'

'Shame about that,' answered Bluebell.

Sighing with relief, Kevin muttered, 'Sorry.'

'Who the hell has upset your cosy little life?' Bluebell quickly added, 'Don't answer that. You nearly lost out on a nice little earner,' he sniffed. 'Well, in any case, there ain't anyone else the boss would trust with this one. Plenty of cash, after my usual ten percent.'

Kevin sat down. 'So? Tell me about it. Usual conditions – no violence or slave trading – you know what I mean?'

'Nothing like that. Tickets are at the travel agents. Take your passport, the French one. Little place in France, you'll like it. A delivery job. Nothing dangerous, as long as you ask no questions. Just routine, alright?'

Alright! Alright! Too bloody true it's alright, a jubilant Kevin thought, but his voice belied his joy, and indifferently he answered, 'Alright, yeh.'

Bluebell went on. 'Fly out in the afternoon, day after tomorrow. Letter with the details will be with you in an hour or so, by hand. Remember, no questions.'

The phone went dead when Kevin replied, 'Bye, mate

and thanks.'

Two things came to mind on hearing of this new job. Firstly, it would get him out of the country. If the police came he was certain he wouldn't be able to deal with the situation. He was sure he would go to pieces. Even though neither his father nor himself were guilty of murder, they were at the house on the fateful night. He was convinced the evidence stacked up against them. Mentally he cursed Archie again. Secondly, he was determined this would be the last time he would carry out somebody else's dirty work. Having made the decision, he realised he would be free to lead his life as he wanted. With lifted spirits his thoughts tumbled as he began making plans, but first he had to see Sarah.

Chapter 29

At first Becky was angry with Connor for his lies and deceit, and angry with herself. What was wrong with her? Taken in by his charm and promises? She reminded herself she had been cautious, not too sure of his love yet willing eventually to trust him. How could she have been so gullible again? I'm a fool, she thought, never again.

As the week wore on, Becky realised that despite the Connors of the world, she did in fact enjoy the company of men and was determined in the future that there would be nothing more than a drink, a chat and sometimes a meal or outing if she was ever asked. Never would she make any lasting promises of commitment, never.

The following Friday, her nursing friends, Kitty and Molly asked her to join them for their usual night out.

She'd bought a new outfit and had carefully made up her face. When they met up Kitty said, 'Becky, we thought we'd go to Flynn's for a change. You know...,' she looked at Becky who was smiling at her. 'Well, you know, we thought, that...'

Molly interrupted, 'So you don't have to see Connor. That's what she's trying to say. We don't mind really. Flynn's will make a change.'

Exasperated, Becky said, 'For heaven's sake, O'Shea's fine.'

'There's a live band at Flynn's. We thought that might cheer you up.'

'What makes you think I'm unhappy, Molly? I'm fine, honestly.'

'I'm thinking Connor might be there and...'

'So what? He's no power to upset me, none at all and I prefer O'Shea's.' Satisfied the girls made plans to meet up at eight o'clock.

'I'll let Maureen know. She has a sore throat at the moment, but sure to be fit to meet up.'

Connor was there when they arrived – a subdued Connor with no more than three of his former mates. Rather sheepishly, they half raised their hands on seeing her, and Becky watched as they nudged Connor letting him know of her presence. He looked across to her, lifted his hand and began to walk towards her.

'You going to be alright?' questioned Kitty 'I'll see him off if you like.'

Becky shook her head. 'No, it's fine. He owes me an apology, and he knows it.'

'Hello, Becky,' he said standing at the side of her chair.

'Connor,' she murmured back without looking at him.

'Good to see you. I was hoping you'd be here tonight. Can I get you a drink?' He turned to group of girls. 'Ladies?'

'No thanks,' said Kitty and the other three shook their heads.

Connor cleared his throat. 'Er…Becky…' he looked around the crowded room. 'We need to go somewhere quiet to talk. Outside I think would be better.'

There was a hint of a chuckle in her throat when Becky answered, 'No need Connor. There really isn't anything to say is there?' She paused, 'Except of course, your apology.'

'Of course I apologise,' he exploded. 'With all my heart.' All of the women were looking at him expecting more. 'Becky, please, can I speak to you in private?'

'No Connor, we're finished. Closed chapter in both our lives. Now, please go away and leave us in peace.'

He began to walk away, but turned back. Gently he cupped her cheek in his hand. 'Despite everything you heard and, I might add, when I was the worst for drink at the time, despite all our ups and downs Becky, I truly love you.'

In a regretful and gentle tone she answered. 'It's done, spoiled. Go away Connor.' As he left she gave a sigh, stood up and turned to her friends. 'White wine all round, girls? Let's party.' On her way to the bar she looked around expecting to see Denis, but he was nowhere to be seen. He had kept his word and had abandoned Connor too.

Shift patterns at the hospital meant that the friends couldn't meet every Friday. There was also a re-allocation of wards for the nurses, and Becky found herself on the children's ward. The nursing was different, and often difficult for Becky not to get emotional as babies and youngsters suffered. Their parents, desperate with anxiety,

203

begged for help and asked endless questions, fearful of the answers. Becky often felt it was easier to nurse the new born or very young. Although they were equally as distressed as the older children, with their heart-rending cries for, 'mammy', the babies voiced their distress with pitiful crying and whimpers. Becky often found herself guessing at their need for comfort and nursed, cuddled and sang softly to them, which she thought helped. Ruefully, she admitted that it certainly helped her. She also appreciated the team she worked with always supporting each other through the good and bad times. The good times was seeing the improvement being made in a child, and clapping them out of the ward on discharge. The bad times occurred when a gravely ill child did not respond to treatment and had a long journey to recovery.

The visiting rules stated that only two persons were allowed at the bedside of the patient. One evening there were three around a little girl, Laura, recovering from an operation. Becky went over to the visitors to remind them. 'Only two at a time, I'm sorry,' she said.

The extra visitor was a male and as he stood up and bowed to her, he grinned. 'I shall obey your command,' he said. 'Perhaps you will take my hand and guide me to the waiting room.'

'Liam,' remonstrated the patient's mother. 'That's enough.' She turned to Becky. 'Ignore him dear, he's just a smart arse.'

As Becky and Liam left the ward, he lifted his eyebrows, and looked at her intently, starting with her eyes, down over her face, then returning to gaze into her eyes. Becky stiffened, acutely aware of his scrutiny. 'This way,' she said curtly.

He stepped in front of her and stopped her. 'So, Sister, what's your name?'

Dodging round him she retorted 'Staff Nurse Wilson to you.'

'Oh, a little madam,' he murmured as she left him at the door of the waiting room.

Liam turned up every evening to visit his niece and, it seemed to Becky, he always managed to find her and say no more than, 'Good evening staff Nurse Wilson.'

To which she always coolly replied, 'Good evening.'

On the day of the Laura's discharge, Becky had all the necessary papers and medication ready for the parents. Liam had accompanied them. The moment came for good-byes, and Becky had a farewell hug from Laura. The little girl ran to Liam, cuddling him about the legs until he picked her up.

Later the same day, Becky was beckoned to the telephone. 'It's for you. A man's voice,' her colleague said with a grin.

Becky sighed. Connor had phoned a few times and each time she had made it clear that there could be nothing further between them. Picking up the phone and suspecting it was Connor again, she snapped, 'No, I will not marry you. Please stop pestering me.'

She had a shock when an unfamiliar male voice answered, 'I haven't asked you yet.'

'Oh, oh,' she stammered. 'I'm so sorry. I thought it was...'

There was a chuckle at the other end of the line. 'It's alright. He's a fool, whoever he is to let you go.' There was a pause before he said, 'It's Liam.'

'I thought it might be. What can I do for you? Is Laura alright? You can bring her back in straight away if there's a problem.'

Again there was laughter as Liam said, 'Laura's fine, but I have a problem. Would you care to hear it?'

'Not really, but I can't stop you I suppose.'

'My problem is this, and it is enormous. How do I ask a pretty nurse out for dinner tonight without my head being bitten off?'

It was Becky's turn to laugh. 'Well, you could suggest a respectable Italian restaurant that serves cold white wine. Perhaps somewhere quiet out of town.' She heard him sigh with relief.

'I know the very place. Now how do I know when she is free?'

'If I'm right about the person you have in mind, I'd say around eight o'clock on Friday.'

'Shall I pick her up in my, my...' he searched for the right words, 'in my modest little car?' Oh, and where?'

'Outside the hospital. It will save me, her, going home to change.'

'Friday it is then,' he said. 'And thank you staff nurse.'

As Becky walked towards him on Friday evening she saw his face light up and a spontaneous smile that caused tiny wrinkles around his eyes. He's really quite friendly and pleased to see me, she thought. This was confirmed when he said, 'I wasn't sure if you'd come. I, er, well I can be a bit pushy sometimes,' then added hastily, 'but I so wanted to know you better.' He ran his hand over his auburn hair, tugged at his tie, then offered her his arm, and linked hers confidently and firmly. Still smiling he ventured, 'May I say how lovely you look this evening?'

The colour rushed to her face and she was glad she had made an effort with her dress and make-up, but said no more than, 'Thank you.'

'My car's over there,' he said pointing to a dark green two-seater sports car. 'I thought we'd try bistro Carlos, a family run restaurant. The food's freshly cooked by Mama and tastes wonderful.'

Sitting at the table enjoying the food that lived up to his prediction of being wonderful, Becky admitted to herself that he was extremely attractive. Lively, dark brown eyes and, as he looked into hers, she sensed his sincerity. Clean shaven with a hint of expensive aftershave, and even white teeth except a front one was a little crooked. She smiled to herself thinking – not quite perfect. The conversation flowed as they discussed books and films and he told her of his family. He leaned back in his chair, picked up his glass and looking across to her asked, 'And you, Rebecca? You've not told me anything about your family.'

Although she smiled at him, she hoped he didn't notice the confusion and embarrassment his question had caused her. Carefully, she put her fork across her plate. 'My mother is in Australia and...that's it,' she finished lamely. 'Just my mother, who has remarried and writes to tell me frequently how happy she is, and keeps asking me to join her.' A lump had come up in her throat. At that moment she dearly would have liked be with her mother. She hadn't realised how much she was missing her.

Liam stretched his hand across to her and briefly gave a light touch on her arm as he saw the faraway look on her face. 'You miss her, don't you?'

There was a nod from Becky and she picked up her fork in order to finish her meal. For a few moments neither spoke but then Liam, brightly and cheerfully told her how he'd misheard directions and found himself at the edge of a lonely lake somewhere in the country. Not knowing where he was he slept in the car and was woken early by a curious cow whose head was poking through the window – mooing. 'Honestly, I'm sure she was telling me I was trespassing,' he chuckled.

Becky laughed. 'I can just picture that.'

'I tell you what. Her breath was very, very bad,' and they laughed together.

Becky liked him. He made her laugh. A man with a sense of humour who could take a joke about himself, could never be dull she thought. Although they dated frequently, they were no more than good friends and the arrangement suited Becky. Liam had explained earlier on during a meal at their favourite restaurant that his career often meant he had to go abroad for weeks. 'Can't be helped,' he'd said smiling at her, 'but it does make things awkward for erm...well, for lasting relationships.'

Becky sighed with relief. 'Liam, I ask no more of you than an occasional meet-up. Suits me fine. My last relationship, as you call it, ended in disaster.'

'Hah, you mean that chap who kept asking you to marry him?'

Giving a sigh, she said, 'I don't want an intense involvement for a long time, if ever.' She linked her arm through his as she added, 'so, you're off the hook.'

There was a mocking serious look on his face as he looked into her eyes, 'Pity,' he said, 'I was hoping...'

'Shut up.'

As predicted, their on and off relationship fizzled out, although she saw him occasionally when he was back in Ireland, but as he went away more and more, Becky saw less of him and felt free to date others.

Chapter 30

It was a Friday evening and with a mug of tea in her hand, curled up in her favourite armchair, Becky smiled to herself, glad for once to be able to relax and looked forward to the weekend. She was not on duty until Monday morning and there were no outings planned. Tomorrow, she thought, she might go shopping followed by a film.

It was six months since she and Connor had separated, and it was over three weeks since Becky's last date – a date that she would rather not ever repeat. It was with Dr Donald Moran, and she smiled knowing many nurses harboured romantic thoughts about him. There was no doubt that he was attractive, with an almost oval shaped face with a well defined jaw line, a smooth chin and keen, blue eyes that when he looked at you, 'Made you buckle at the knees,' one nurse was overhead to say. All these attributes made him appear incredibly handsome and undoubtedly, sexy.

Leaning over a patient one day, she was surprised when Donald, Dr Moran placed his hand low down on her back and, without moving his hand, asked, 'Is there a problem, nurse?'

She sensed he was staring at her raised bottom, and stood up abruptly as she shrugged his hand away. 'No. No problem.'

Donald had given a little cough. 'Er, I thought you looked en...' He raised his shoulders, and smiled. '...a little uncomfortable.'

'Entertaining, I think you were about to say,' she

snapped back as she marched away.

Donald followed her down the ward and into the office. 'Have I offended you Nurse...?' he asked raising his eyebrows.

Knowing she could be severely reprimanded if she said what was in her mind, she answered briefly, 'Nurse Wilson.'

'Let me buy you coffee in your break.'

'Don't bother.'

But he did bother. He found her in the cafeteria and sat down opposite her. 'Look here,' he said. 'It was really very silly of me to, well, I suppose make a move on you. I would be glad if you will accept my sincere apologies.'

Sitting quietly for a few moments, she sipped her coffee without looking at him. Knowing that he could make her life a misery on the wards if she refused, she gave a small nod.

He put his head to one side and with a disarming smile asked, 'Dinner?'

The restaurant Donald took her to was the best the town had to offer, with an extensive menu. I wonder if he treats all his dates like this or is he out to impress me and is genuinely interested in me, she thought. By the end of the evening she was convinced that it was only Donald Moran he was truly interested in. Throughout the meal she was entertained, bored really, by his telling of the more gory operations he had performed, how many lives he had saved, how the top management had congratulated him, and his ambitions to become the most respected surgeon in Ireland. 'Yes, a couple more years I reckon,' he said, leaning back in his chair and lighting a cigar.

Becky had raised her eyebrows when he lit up as she was

still eating, and was irritated that he had not asked if he might smoke. Seeing her look he hastily said, 'Sorry, sorry. Would you care for a cigarette?' while she was still finishing her dessert.

'No, no thank you.'

'I can see you disapprove, but a man like myself is entitled to indulge in some pleasantries, don't you think?' He leaned forward, and she was grateful that he turned his head away as he blew smoke into the air. 'I also treat myself to the opera, always the best seats. If I'm out for the evening, I might as well spoil myself don't you agree?'

Becky remained silent as she thought how pompous he was.

'So, now...What do I call you? Nurse Wilson is more than formal on a date, don't you think?'

'Becky,' she snapped.

'Well, I suppose Becky is better than nurse. So many of you, I'm spoilt for choice.' He chortled at his own little joke. 'But,' he had raised his eyebrows and turned his head a little to one side, 'I trust your real name is Rebecca?'

Inwardly fuming she replied, 'Rebecca Ann.'

As his hand stretched out across the table towards her own, she snatched hers away. 'I thought an evening at the opera would suit us fine. I've booked seats to see, *L'elisir d'amore* written by GaeTano Donizetti. Do you know it?'

It was a lie, but she couldn't help it as there had never been an occasion or time for opera in her life. She gave a little hmm before saying, 'Of course.' Was that a flicker of irritation or disappointment on his face she had wondered?

Having paid the bill, Donald helped her on with her coat, whispering in her ear as he did so, 'It's a love story sung in Italian. Who knows by the end of the evening I might serenade you and there might be more if you're a good girl and...'

'Shall we go,' Becky interrupted.

During the early stages of the performance, Donald translated for her, until he was reprimanded by more than one member of the audience. Becky sighed with relief and began to enjoy the colour, music and interpretation of the opera.

When they reached her door at the end of the evening he'd said, 'Well, Rebecca my dear, are you going to ask me in for coffee?'

She shook her head saying at the same time, 'No, I don't think so, do you?'

Noting the tone in her voice he stammered, 'I thought, I thought you liked me,'

'Dr Moran, I don't believe we have anything in common, and I see no point in meeting up again.'

'I don't understand.'

Becky could see the bewilderment on his face and asked, 'What do you know about me? Not once did you ask anything about me. I know your past and your ambitions. Most of the evening was about you.'

'But,' he began running his hand through his hair, '...but I thought...'

Briskly, Becky turned the key in her lock, opened the door and said, 'Goodnight.' She watched him walk down the path. At first his shoulders sagged, then she saw him straighten up as if, he's thinking, there's always a more willing nurse. 'By the way, she called after him, 'You forgot to add Prime Minister to your list.' One thing was for sure, she was going to let the others who longed to date him, know exactly what to expect.

There had been others before Donald. Becky sighed as she recalled Eamonn. It was a chance meeting in the hospital. Eamonn worked in the Admissions Office, and Becky immediately liked his quiet apology when he had bumped into her. He was flustered thinking he had injured her, and repeated again that he was sorry. Once convinced that she was not hurt in any way, she had seen him take a deep breath before saying, 'Please let me make it up to you. A coffee perhaps?' He hesitated, 'or a drink after work?' There was almost a hint of pleading in his request, and rubbing her shin she agreed to meet him later.

Their first date lasted no longer than forty-five minutes in the nearby pub. It was obvious to Becky that Eamonn was nervous. Little was said between them and when he did speak he seemed unable to look directly into her eyes. Instead he looked ahead over her shoulder or at his glass which he twisted round and round in his hand. When she asked him a question, his replies were simple – a yes, or no and occasionally a shrug. From the few fuller answers he gave, she learned he was fond of animals and law abiding, and she had decided that he was a very decent person.

The date was going nowhere, so Becky finished her drink and stood up to leave, 'I've got to go now,' she'd said.

Eamonn immediately stood, put out his hand to shake hers, then coloured up as he stammered, 'Perhaps we could meet up again? Saturday? Go to the park perhaps?'

To this day she had no idea what possessed her to say, 'That would be lovely,' and was rewarded to see a smile spread on his face, as they confirmed the time and place.

The outing was not at all what Becky was expecting. Instead of a brisk walk which might have given Eamonn an opportunity to open up to her, he had explained rather hesitantly, 'I hope you don't mind but every weekend I enjoy my hobby of kite flying,' and promptly unpacked a colourful Chinese dragon kite with a long tail to assemble. Once he had done so he turned to her and with awe said, 'Isn't it beautiful?' She had nodded, and before she could say a word the kite was airborne.

At first she was fascinated by the twirling gyrations of it, but after ten minutes of being ignored she had tugged at Eamonn's arm. 'Eamonn,' she began, 'It's cold standing around, can we go for a cup of tea now?'

He had angrily shaken her hand off his arm. 'In a few minutes. I...' and he had run a few steps ahead of her as the wind had billowed and the kite had sped it upwards. Out of breath he'd turned to her saying that he usually spent an hour or more every Saturday flying his kite.

'Right,' she'd said, and prepared to wait a little longer. The kite floated down to the ground and Eamonn ran over to it, adjusted the tail, and searched for a current of air to lift it skywards.

Becky caught up with him. 'There's a party tonight, Eamonn, I would love you to come along with me.'

'No.' was his immediate answer. Then, 'No thank you. I'm not a party person. No one talks to me and, if they do they're not interested in me.' He'd sat down on the grass and feeling awkward standing over him, Becky sat down beside him. He'd begun reeling in the cord, his head bent away from her. 'Do you know,' he mumbled, 'no one showed the slightest bit of interest in kites at the last party I went to, nor the one before that. No one and...' He stood up to release the kite again. 'And what's more I'm sure everyone was laughing at me.'

Busy as he was with his kite, Becky could see he was

upset. 'You can't be sure of that,' she said. 'They could have been talking about anything, not you at all.'

When he turned to her she had seen the misery on his face. 'Look at me,' he'd invited. 'What do you see?'

'I...' she began.

'A clerk, and not a very good one at that. The easiest job going for the likes of me.' He shrugged as he added, 'No looks, no dress sense. Jeans and cardigans suit me fine, not suited, like all those doctors about the place.' He'd smiled at her. 'No, Becky, a social life is not for me.' He frowned before going on. 'I was hoping that was how you might be. You know, a quiet home-loving person, someone I could perhaps call "my girl".'

Becky took his free hand. 'You know Eamonn, it doesn't have to be like that. If you...'

'No Becky.' He withdrew his hand and said, quietly. 'Let's call it a day.'

'But...'

'We're not suited Becky, not at all.' And that was the end of their dating.

However, when she compared him to Patrick, Eamonn was seen in a much more favourable light. Patrick was a police officer and she admitted to herself, charming. He'd been driving past her early one morning as she walked towards the hospital some three quarters of a mile away. 'Hey, nurse,' he'd called out from the driving seat of the patrol car, 'Care for a lift?'

Gratefully, she had got into the car, but was horrified when, without warning, he accelerated. When they arrived at the hospital in less than two minutes, she was shaking.

There was a smirk on his partner's face. 'Got another one, Paddy, well done.'

Becky was furious. Firstly she berated Patrick for driving 'like a psycho,' then she turned her attention to the other policeman. 'And you,' she said pointing her finger at him, 'should stop him. It would serve you right if you both end up smashed in this car one day.' She paused for breath. 'And what's more if you end up in my ward, I'll see to it that you really, I mean really, suffer. Both of you should have more sense.' Having said her piece she turned and stalked away.

She was surprised when Patrick caught up with her. 'Hold on a minute missy,' he said severely, 'a word if you please.'

Fearing she had overstepped the mark she stood still, but defiantly asked, 'What now?' and noticed his broad shoulders and even white teeth when he grinned down on her.

'Allow me to apologise,' he began and when she shook her head and tried to move away from him, he put up his hand as if halting traffic. 'I'm so sorry I scared you.'

'You certainly did,' she snapped.

'Don't be mad. It was only a bit of fun.'

'Fun!' she stormed. 'You almost killed me.'

'Steady on. I'm fully trained you know. Chasing villains all day we are.' He lowered his hand. 'Now, Miss...?' Becky didn't volunteer her name. "I will take you bowling on Saturday night to make amends. Meet some of the fellows?' Seeing the look on her face, he added, 'There'll have their girls or wives with them.' She didn't answer, but she was still thinking how attractive he was. The silence grew between them until he said, 'Be there. Mill Town Road.'

'I'll think about it. Now I must go or I'll be late,' she said and almost ran to the hospital entrance.

'Outside the bowling alley at eight on Saturday,' he called after her.

As far as Becky was concerned, the Saturday date was a disaster. They entered the venue together, but it wasn't long before Patrick abandoned her to be with his friends. All of the men were drinking and their banter grew louder and louder.

'You with Paddy?' one of the girls, sitting in the booth at one end of the bowling alley, asked.

'Paddy? Oh you mean Patrick.' Becky smiled, 'Well, sort of. He invited me, but...' and shrugged.

Another girl leaned towards her, 'He's a loose cannon, that one. Watch out, take him as he is or you'll probably get hurt.'

'Utterly selfish, the pig,' another added and some of the girls nodded their heads in agreement.

Inwardly, Becky could see their point, but preferred to make up her own mind about him. It was when Patrick lost his temper, stepping up to someone with fists at the ready and swearing filth at the offender, that she saw how dangerous he could be. Thinking about it, she realised that he had bullied her into this date. Becky made up her mind, indicated to the others that she was going to the Ladies when Patrick's taunting voice called after her, 'We all know where you're going.'

Without a backward glance, she made her way to the exit and called a taxi. She hadn't seen him since, nor did she want to.

Becky stretched, stood up and began walking to the kitchen to rinse her mug when the phone rang. Picking up the phone she said cautiously, 'Hello?' On hearing the voice that replied, she felt such a wave of happiness engulf her. It was as if she had been in limbo for the last six months just waiting to hear from Denis.

Chapter 31

There was no escaping the fact that what had started as a cold was now more serious. There was an ache in Archie's ribs when he coughed; he was hot, then cold. The wheezing and bubbling hadn't cleared up despite the antibiotics the doctor had prescribed. He definitely wasn't getting any better. That boy would sort me out he told himself, but knew this was unlikely to happen as Kevin wanted nothing more to do with him. He'd made that very clear after the burglary that went wrong. Archie was still annoyed that they had come away empty handed. I could've picked up some tasty bits there he told himself.

His chest was heaving as he tried to breathe and still muttering he asked himself, how many times have I phoned this last week? The boy was a bit soft. He'd come if he knew I was ill. He's probably on one of his jaunts. Kevin's work often took him away he knew that, but he didn't know where. If he asked he always got the same answer, 'Mind your own business,' or something similar from the secret little bastard. Crikey, he thought, I'm going mad as well, talking out loud to myself.

Supporting himself against the wall, he made his way to the kitchen and searched his cupboard for something to eat. There was nothing. No back-up tins that Kevin always made sure were available, no eggs, not even a slice of bread. Archie sniffed, not hungry anyway, he said to himself, as he crept back into bed, and pulled the covers over himself. Sleep eluded him at first. As soon as he lay down he began coughing, then gasping for breath until finally, exhausted he fell asleep.

A continuous knocking on his door finally wakened him.

It's me boy, he happily convinced himself. I knew he'd come round in time. 'I'm on me way,' he croaked, as he fought to locate the sleeves of an inadequate dressing gown. Funny how just hearing the knock he felt a tad better. The knocking began again. 'I'm coming lad, hang on a mo,' he whispered as he struggled to the door.

There were two men, who produced cards and identified themselves as police detectives – Jenkins and Wells. Archie reeled and lent against the door jamb. Fearing the worst he asked, 'Something happened to my lad, officers?'

They looked at each other before Jenkins said, 'Are you Archibald Johnson?'

'You know damn well I am.'

'Mr Johnson,' Wells said, 'we'd like you to come with us to the station. Help us with some enquiries.'

'Like what? I ain't done anything.' The effort of talking brought on the pain in his ribs. 'Well, not today. Can't you see I'm ill?' he whined.

Brutally, Jenkins said, 'Get some clothes on, Archie. We're taking you in for suspected murder.'

Archie's face drained of colour. He began coughing. 'Murder!' he finally gasped out. 'What you talking about? I ain't murdered anyone.'

'We'll discuss it at the station. We know you were there, your fingerprints were found on a pair of silver candlesticks. Remember?' Then he intoned the familiar caution, 'Anything you say...'

Archie staggered back to his bedroom muttering all the

time, 'It's not me, not me.'

The two men followed him. 'Get your coat,' one said.

Detective Wells grinned. 'Looked at your records old man. Stretch to Newcastle and back.' He gave a little snort, 'Innocent, my foot. Grievous bodily harm, more than once recorded.' He took Archie's arm and led him out to a waiting car, and as he pushed him into the back, 'Well, all we need now is your confession, then I can go home to my wife.'

'If he co-operates.' the other detective added, as he slammed the car door.

'Cup of tea might help,' Archie said as he slumped back in the seat, 'and a bacon sandwich.' The two men laughed, confident that they had got their man.

At the police station Archie was logged, and after a disappointing interview for the two officers, he was allocated a cell by the custody sergeant, a well built man, nearing retirement. Taking down a bunch of keys from behind his desk, he led the way.

'Right, in you go, sir,' the sergeant said giving Archie a gentle push into the cell. The two detectives slouched along behind them one smoking the other with his hands in his pockets.

Archie heard one say, 'Got the bastard. He'll not see the outside world again in this lifetime.' Leaning forward he sneered, 'See you in the morning Mr Johnson. I'll be interested to hear what you have to say.'

The other chortled. 'Not that it really matters. We've got you and you're going down for murder.'

Horrified, Archie protested, 'Didn't do it. Not me.'

'Why are you trembling then?'

The sergeant smiled briefly and shook his head. 'That's

what they all say, but...'

Archie glanced behind him, watching the two jubilant detectives walk away talking about their evening plans. Detective Jenkins gave a little skip and said he was on a promise. 'Lovely little lass I met a week ago. Should come up with the goods tonight I reckon.'

Wells said he was going out with his wife, to meet their daughter's new boyfriend. 'Give him the once over. Not having her mix with some of the thugs we get in here.'

The door was slammed closed behind Archie's shaking body. Wearily he lay down on the narrow ledge attached to the wall. The thin mattress covering it wasn't comfortable but it didn't matter, he felt so ill, and was past caring, all he wanted to do was sleep.

The mug of tea on the breakfast tray was hot, strong and sweet and Archie was surprised to feel a little better after drinking it. The porridge wasn't to his liking but it was easy to swallow. Within the hour he was feeling ill again. It was after nine o'clock before anyone came.

The duty sergeant, Clarke, shook him. 'Up with you, Johnson. Wells and his sidekick are waiting for you.'

Archie groaned.

'Come on now. It won't take long. Own up to the charge then we can settle you in a proper prison. You know, meet some of your mates no doubt.'

Archie struggled to sit up and placed his feet on the floor. The officer took his arm and pulled him up. 'You're a bit hot. Feeling a bit under the weather?' Still holding on to Archie's elbow, he drew himself away as far as possible and turned his head away. 'Lot of people have got flu. Hope you're not one of them,' he said as he led Archie to the interview room.

'Morning Mr Johnson,' Jenkins smirked. 'Let's get this over with.'

Archie mumbled, 'Didn't murder anyone. You got the wrong bloke.'

Detective Wells sighed. 'Let's not have any rigmarole. He pushed a small silver tablet attached to a chain with a broken clasp towards Archie. 'Seen this before?'

Archie's eyes widened and he stopped himself gasping out loud, hoping they hadn't seen his immediate reaction. Silly little sod, he thought, told him to get rid of that bloody thing years ago. Wearily, he shook his head. He was determined to keep Kevin out of this. The two detectives were relentless in their questioning, and he either refused to answer or shook his head. Twenty minutes later Archie's head began to spin, their voices seemed distant to him. More than once he was shouted at, and gazed blankly back, shaking his head trying to clear it and concentrate. Their voices droned on and on. Both of the men were surprised when Archie finally keeled over fighting for breath.

Jenkins fetched Sergeant Clarke and said, 'Get him back to the cell, give him a coffee and we'll continue in half an hour.'

'Not with this one, you won't,' Clarke answered.

'Half an hour. He's trying it on. Well it won't work.' Jenkins lit a cigarette. 'Hear that Johnson? Half an hour, then see if we don't get a confession out of you,' and stalked off angrily.

Detective Wells shrugged his shoulders. 'Seems he didn't get much luck last night I reckon,' and grinned.

'This man is ill and I'm calling for an ambulance,' Clarke said.

'Don't be daft, man. He'll do anything to avoid a charge.

Get him fit, go on. Thirty minutes and I want him back here. Right?'

Clarke glared at detective Wells, and said nothing. Too near retirement to take notice of the likes of DI Wells and Jenkins, he would do it his way, by the book. Those two idiots pressing for a conviction from a sick man, was asking for trouble. A good lawyer would take them apart in court. They would be in bigger trouble if no one helped Johnson and the man died on the station premises. He helped Archie to his feet and escorted him back to the cell. 'Wait there, Mr Johnson,' he said softly. 'Soon have you feeling better.'

Archie didn't get better. He knew nothing about being taken to hospital, or the various tests and attention he received. Once all hope was gone, he died a lonely, pathetic old man.

Chapter 32

'I'm going away for a few days, Sarah,' Kevin began when he met her that evening. 'Well, maybe more like a week, I can't be certain.'

Sarah smiled, 'One of these days, you'll tell me what these mysterious trips are about.' She looked up at the ceiling, and put her finger under her chin. 'I think,' she said slowly then lowering her head and looking at him, 'I think you're a spy.' Giving herself a little shake and delighted at the thought, she said, 'On her majesty's secret service. That's it.'

Anything but, Kevin groaned to himself. How could he ever tell her the truth? How could she not suspect something unusual about his disappearances, sometimes lengthy when after each absence he came back loaded with gifts for her? But she hadn't had she, he reminded himself. She thought he was a spy? Well he wasn't going to lie to her. 'No, Sarah, love, I'm not a spy, just boring business, more like a courier I would say.'

Thoughtfully, she countered, 'But surely, delivering and collecting shouldn't take a week? I mean are the people you work for...' she paused, 'sloppy?'

Kevin was beginning to feel uncomfortable about the direction this conversation was going. 'No, no, just a matter of supply and demand. Someone somewhere wants something usually in a hurry. I deliver and sometimes wait for a return packet. No point coming back empty handed.' That will do for now he thought.

The restaurant was almost empty and Sarah left him for a few moments, when she saw a raised hand from one of the remaining clients for the bill. When she returned, she said, 'See, on the ball. I had the bill ready and everything went smoothly and quickly. I'd soon be bankrupt if I was careless just for one moment.' She moved away from him and began collecting dishes.

As he walked over to her, he made up his mind. When he reached her he bent down and kissed the back of her neck. 'Don't worry,' he whispered. 'I'm going to give it all up. Find myself a different job.' She gave a sigh, turned and put her arms around him. 'When I get back I'll tell you all then.'

Instructions had arrived by hand just before he left to go to Sarah's. Kevin had been curious about the courier and although he had watched carefully for someone coming to his door, he missed the chance to see who it was. He had shrugged his shoulders, careful as usual he thought. It no longer mattered who, or what or where or when, he'd made up his mind to make a permanent break. As he had told Sarah, the note said the job would take at least a week. To begin with he was to go to Paris, to a small hotel and wait for a contact. The hotel booked for him was in the suburbs of Paris, and the friendly hosts made him feel welcome. He felt uncomfortable knowing that they were being used. Fortunately, their English was good and on the second day, Kevin decided to see a bit of Paris and asked their advice.

'Take any bus from the corner,' the proprietor said, 'It will take you all the way to the centre of the city.'

His wife had stood beside him, smiling and nodding. 'Yes,' she interrupted, 'ask any French person and they will direct you to...' she was thoughtful for a moment. 'The Eiffel Tower, yes? You want to see?' Kevin had nodded. 'You go now. Ask for directions for whatever you decide on. That's the best way.'

Feeling there might be a problem with the language, it proved to be far easier than he anticipated. With the aid of a map and his index finger pointing to where he wanted to be, he visited most of the tourist attractions. It seemed to him that whenever he spoke to someone, they were more than willing to practice their English.

It was late afternoon and he decided to walk alongside the river Seine. As he wandered he came across a small church in a park with neat laid out gardens and a fountain. Quite near the church was an ancient tree propped up with concrete pillars and he stopped to admire it. On the plaque at its roots he read that it was thought to be the oldest tree, a locust, in Paris. Reading on he learned that it is believed by some to be the "Lucky tree of Paris" which will bring good luck to those who gently touch the tree's bark. Knowing that once he returned to the UK he intended to make a clean break with the past, he surreptitiously leaned forward and lightly touched the trunk. As he continued his walk he experienced a feeling of...he knew not what, homesickness perhaps, regrets about his past? It was so true, he said to himself, this is one of the most romantic cities in the world. There were couples, arms entwined or holding hands, caressing each other and stealing soft kisses. Perhaps it was loneliness and he made up his mind that this is the city, the country he would bring Sarah to if she was willing.

When he returned to the hotel, tired and ready for a bath and meal, he was met by the proprietor who bustled up to him and ushered him into a small lounge. 'A visitor for you monsieur,' he intoned.

The visitor, a small man with mean looking eyes, waved his cigarette at the owner. 'Go,' he ordered. 'We have business.'

'But, some cognac...?'

The man stubbed out the cigarette as he answered sharply. 'No.' he turned to Kevin. 'Sit down. This won't take long.' He pulled out an envelope from his inner pocket. 'This is a note to identify you to the person you are to meet. Also instructions.'

Kevin stretched out his hand for the document.

The man held onto it for a moment and said, 'You know that this contract must be done in the utmost secrecy. You speak to no one.'

Kevin nodded. 'Go on. I understand.'

'Good. Read carefully. I go now and I will not see you

again.'

Kevin wasn't sorry to see him leave. There was something unpleasant about the man that disturbed him. Once he was in his room, he read the note. He was to make his way to a village north of Paris, and take a late evening meal in the Templerie Bistro. Someone would approach him, hand him a package and take him to a small field, where an aeroplane would be waiting to fly him back to England. Kevin slumped back in his chair, relieved that the task was not too arduous and, providing everything went to plan, he would be home within a day or two.

It was nearly eleven o'clock and Kevin wondered what was meant by a late evening meal? Around nine he'd placed his order and had finished eating by ten-fifteen and no one had made contact. It didn't happen very often, but at the moment he wished he had a cigarette – anything to fill in the time. He flipped through the limp morning paper, then thrust it aside unable to read a word, even the cartoon defeated him.

Just as he decided to use the toilet, a man about forty years of age entered the restaurant carrying a large hold-all. Kevin knew straight away that this was the person he was waiting for. It amused him to see the man in the traditional French costume – black beret, a spotted kerchief around his neck and a black cheroot in his mouth. The man was exuberant, shouting greetings to the few remaining diners, thumping the patron on the back, ordering cognac, which he quickly swallowed, all the while looking around the room. Kevin raised his hand the man hastened over.

'You the English bloke?' he said, as he extended a tobacco stained hand.

Kevin nodded.

'Paul. You ready to go? Paid?'

Again Kevin nodded.

'Follow me, my friend,' and calling out 'adieu' to every-one, led Kevin out into the dark street, where he had left his car with the engine running.

The journey took less than fifteen minutes, and Kevin knew, to his cost, what travel sickness felt like. Paul drove fast along an unlit roads and Kevin's late supper protested as he braked and swerved round corners, allowing the car to bounce over unseen rocks or dip into potholes. Kevin, legs feeling like rubber, clung to the side of the car for a few moments when they finally arrived at the airfield. Across the far side of the field which was partly obscured by the fine rain, he saw an aeroplane – a very small aeroplane and he felt a small tremor of fear as he thought of flying over the channel in such a flimsy looking craft, instead of the usual sturdy planes he was more used to.

Together, Paul and Kevin walked across the field, Paul still firmly holding the hold-all. The rain changed from a mist to a sudden squally shower and Kevin was dismayed to see the plane being easily buffeted by the strong wind. He turned his collar up and trudged alongside Paul. When they arrived at the plane, Paul said, 'You've no idea have you where you are? Just as well, I say.'

'I learned a long time ago not to ask questions. I get on with the job, get paid and am satisfied,' he replied.

Paul changed the bag into his other hand and stretched his free hand towards Kevin. 'All the best my friend'

As they shook hands, Paul thrust the hold-all at Kevin. 'All in there as ordered,' he said.

Kevin gave his thanks, but as he turned to climb into the

aeroplane Paul added, 'I've put some ammo in as well. Tell the chief. Might come in useful.'

Ammo? Ammunition? Kevin was horrified. So that's what this is all about, he thought, gun smuggling and by the weight of the bag more than one. For a moment he was so shocked that he stood still on the short flight of steps, his head pounding and his heart thumping. He heard the engine roar into life and the pilot yell out, 'Come on if you're coming. We got to get out of here.'

The journey home was as awful as he had anticipated, a total nightmare. The wind and rain had increased and as the plane lifted, the turbulence made Kevin feel as if they were about to fall from the sky. Grimly he clung to his arm rests, his knuckles showing white. His stomach seemed to sink and his ears popped when the plane experienced a sharp drop or jolting. The pilot looked back at him and grinned. 'Great isn't it? This is what I call flying,' he shouted above the engine noise.

Kevin swore under his breath. Not only was the flight causing him misery, he was greatly distressed by the revelation of the bag's contents. Always he had tried to avoid violence. The very idea of taking someone's life was repugnant to him. In his mind he could still see the lifeless body of the woman Archie had clobbered. There had been accounts of the murder on the television, and in the newspaper. He lived in dread that their presence at the fateful house would be discovered.

Chapter 33

The next morning looking in the mirror, Kevin was satisfied with his appearance. At first, he teamed his shirt with a tie, then abandoned it preferring an open neck. Jeans of course, a good quality pair and the new shoes he'd treated himself to in Paris. He'd got himself ready far too early before he was to meet Sarah. He paced nervously about the room, looked longingly at the decanter of whisky and decided against it. He wanted a clear head and to be honest. Trying to calm himself, he sat down and picked up the newspaper and attempted to finish the crossword, but his concentration was ambushed by the negative thoughts hammering in his head. Flowers, he thought might be a good idea, or a bottle of wine, then decided against it, thinking she might think such gifts were a bribe. I'll buy her anything she wants afterwards, he told himself, if she, if she...What if she found his past unforgiveable?

Although it was still too early to meet Sarah, he decided to go and wait at the restaurant. As he waited his apprehension grew. Out of habit he watched the clientele. I know just how he feels, he thought as he spotted a man behind a couple, waiting for a table. A young man, tall, too thin, slightly balding, wearing thick glasses that he constantly pushed back into place and shrinking further into his shabby jacket as a noisy crowd jostled behind him. Surreptitiously, he studied each face. Satisfied that he hadn't recognised anyone, he relaxed, but was alarmed every time the door pinged when opened. Swiftly he turned towards it, his body stiffened and there was naked fear in his blinking eyes. He turned away, then slowly half-turned back to inspect the newcomer. Suddenly there was a loud bang and clatter. Simultaneously, he saw Sarah rush towards the kitchen and the man jump, bewildered, looking frantically around. I must have been like that when I began being dishonest, no wonder Archie thought me a wimp, Kevin wondered why the man was so nervous. Was he being chased, had he been mugged or maybe committed some crime and was now afraid of the consequences?

Sarah came out of the kitchen laughing. 'Only a shelf fallen down, the one holding some of the smaller pans. Nothing broken,' she explained to Kevin. When Kevin looked again the man had gone and he would never know what had caused such anxiety, but he knew what was causing his own.

When they finally arrived at Sarah's flat, there was soon a delicious smell of cooking in the air that he identified as her favourite herb, oregano, and he smiled to himself.

'So, what's for supper? Smells like something Italian.'

Smiling she turned to greet him and put up her face for a kiss. Kevin kissed her briefly before she turned back to the stove. He watched her lifting pan lids, give each pan a stir then lift the spoon to taste the contents. 'Hmm, not bad,' she said, 'just left-overs from the restaurant, but I'm adding this and that, a sort of experiment.'

Kevin took a deep breath, lifted his shoulders, then quietly asked, 'Will it spoil if we leave it for a bit?'

'Course not, I'll turn the heat right down. Go and open a bottle of wine, I'll just wash my hands and I'll be with you.' she looked at him keenly. 'You had a bad day?'

'It might be,' he muttered.

'Ciao,' she said lifting her glass as she settled beside him on the sofa.

Giving her a little poke in the ribs and a small lopsided smile, he answered, 'Cheers and, my girl, you're no more Italian then I am.'

Laughing outright, Sarah said, 'But the customers like a little bit of authenticity.'

Taking her glass out of her hand, he put it beside his own on the low table in front of them, and turned to her.

'I meant what I said earlier, Sarah. I love you.' He was pleased when she moved closer to him, and put her head on his shoulder and whispered her love for him. Holding her close he said, 'Before we go any further Sarah, I have got to tell you of my past.'

'No, you haven't. There's no need, I love you Kevin, that's all we need.'

'Sarah, you need to know the truth about me, so that you know what, I mean, who you are chancing your life with.'

She sat up quickly. 'Have you killed anyone?' she asked. She said it as a joke but at the same time, he sensed there was a hint of anxiety in her question.

For a moment there was a silence before he quietly said, 'No, nothing quite as awful as that.'

'Well, then there's nothing to worry about,' she said falling back against him.

Kevin gave a little cough and Sarah looked up into his face. 'You're nervous, aren't you?' Still gazing at him she took his hand. 'It's alright, you know. You haven't got to say anything but if it makes you feel better, I'll shut up and listen.'

Kevin kissed her lightly on the forehead before taking a deep breath and saying, 'Sarah, I want very much to marry you and...' he paused, 'and when I do ask you officially, I desperately want you to say "yes".'

Sarah gave a quiet chuckle. 'Of course I'll...'

Quickly Kevin put his finger over her lips. 'Wait,' he implored. 'Wait, until you hear what I have to say before deciding anything.'

'I love you Kevin Johnson, and anything you say or have done will not make me change my mind.'

Jumping up suddenly, Kevin raised his voice, 'Just bloody listen will you?'

Surprised at this outburst, Sarah nodded.

Kevin sat down beside her and clasped his hands between his knees. Hoping that he didn't sound full of self-pity or attempting to justify the reasons why, he began to tell her almost everything. He told her how Archie had led and encouraged him, firstly in petty thievery graduating to serious burglary. 'I was young, Sarah, and I have to admit, easily led, lazy too.' He lifted his head and compressed his lips before saying, 'Archie died last week, I found out today. The police called round to tell me.' Sarah sighed and stroked his arm for a moment. 'Truly, Sarah, he was...' he thought for a moment for the right words, 'I do believe, truly evil.' he finished up. He went on to tell her how latterly, he had been part of an organised smuggling group and now, finally, he had broken all contact with his associates. He told her how badly Becky, his sister, had been treated by Archie, and how he had done nothing to defend her, how broken she was and that she had disappeared and he had no idea where she was. He didn't feel able to tell of the true relationship between Becky and himself. 'Now you know most of my history,' he finished. 'I'm sick to my stomach at what I have done in the past, but now...' Kevin glanced at his watch and was surprised. Had he really compressed his life story into only eight maybe ten minutes?

He turned to look at Sarah and she briefly looked back into his face before turning away. The silence grew between them and unable to bear it any longer, Kevin whispered, 'Sarah?' There were tears on her cheeks when she turned back to him and he wiped them away gently with his thumb. 'Sarah, please, say something.'

Choking back a sob, she said, 'Please tell me, I mean I want to know if, well if you smuggled people into the country?' She was glad to see a horrified look on his face.

'No, no. Nothing like that, ever, I swear.'

'Drugs?'

Kevin shook his head. 'I think it was mostly jewellery, works of art maybe. The packages were always well wrapped, sometimes large and bulky but mostly small.'

'You swear you've told me about all of your, your...' she was at a loss to find the right word, then said, 'bad ways?'

Still not sure whether to mention his love affair with Becky, he hesitated.

'Well?'

'There is just one more, perhaps...' he began.

'Oh, Kevin!' she burst out. 'I don't want to hear anymore. Let's put it behind us. Never mention any of this again shall we? Whatever it is, it doesn't matter.'

Thankfully, he took her into his arms, kissed her tenderly before asking, 'Sarah, will you marry me now you've heard about my past. With you, my future can only be wonderful.'

'Of course I'm going to marry you. There was never any doubt in my mind.'

Chapter 34

Becky gave a contented sigh, stretched and leaned back in the car seat. Denis was driving and turned his head towards her briefly and smiled. Life was good, she told herself. Whoever would have thought a few years back that she and Denis would be the parents of two lovely boys and be holidaying in France? She turned round to check the children in the back. They smiled at her, one looking so much like Denis and the other, she couldn't help thinking, not unlike her mother. Of course, he would never agree, always insisting that they both took after his side of the family.

Denis looked at the range of dials on the dashboard. 'We'd better stop at the next garage for some petrol,' he said, 'just in case we get caught out in the wilds.'

They pulled into the forecourt of the next garage, and when Denis went to pay, an old woman, in a clean but shabby dress covered by a spotless apron, came to the car window with a tray holding small bunches of lavender tied together with a thread of blue cotton.

At first she spoke rapidly in French, and David, the elder of their two sons, carefully tried out his school French. 'Bonjour, madame.' He pointed to his mother and added, 'mama,' then pointing to William said, 'mon frère.'

The woman sighed before asking in English, 'You Angleterre?'

'Oui, madame.'

There was a moment's silence, and Becky could see the

woman searching for the words to speak to them in English. Tapping her own hand she pointed to Becky, then reached through the open window and tried to pull Becky's hand into hers. 'I tell mama God's will,' she said with a smile.

Becky hastily withdrew her hand close and shook her head, but the woman insisted, and both David and William began begging their mother to have her fortune told. Reluctantly, she finally gave in and let the old woman trace the lines of her hand. The woman lifted her head and smiled. Madame,' she said. 'There is joy for you soon. Something lost is found.'

'Great,' laughed Becky as she fished in her handbag for some coins, 'I hope it's a fortune.'

As the old lady shuffled away, she called back, 'No, I think something better.'

The journey seemed endless. 'I'm hungry.' It was nine-year old David.

Denis laughed. 'Tell me when you're not.'

'It's ages since I had anything to eat,' David grumbled.

Becky wriggled in her seat. 'I'm getting a round bottom. You said it wasn't far,'

'Well, it didn't look too far on the map.' Denis changed gear, the hill was steeper than he'd anticipated. 'There,' he said jubilantly. They had reached the top of the hill and below them was a small town. 'Told you we were nearly there. We'll find somewhere for the night, and tomorrow boys, we'll be at the seaside.'

When they, Denis and Becky, decided to have a holiday abroad, they poured over maps and brochures and decided to motor to Beaulieu-Sur-Mer, a seaside village on the French Riviera between Nice and Monaco. They had been excited as they planned the trip during the long cold spring. Becky thought it was very brave of Denis to drive so far. Denis could tell that she was nervous, but keen to travel somewhere new, where hopefully she could bask in the sun. They had told the boys that the beach was sandy and the water warm and shallow, that there was a floating deck and, as they were all good swimmers, they would be able to reach it and dive to their hearts content. There was also a beach club for the children and plenty of restaurants and pavement cafes.

David had teased William his seven-year old brother, who was passionate about sausages and chips that his French dinners would mainly be frogs' legs and snails.

The car was brought to a halt outside Bienvenue Bistro just outside the town. 'That means welcome bistro,' David told them, proudly showing off his limited French again.

They all got out of the car, stretched and looked around them. 'Welcome,' a pleasant woman's voice in clear English said. 'Have you come far?'

David, always ready to speak without thinking whispered loudly, 'Mum, she speaks English.'

The woman laughed, 'And you, no doubt, are from Ireland. I can tell by how you speak.'

David nodded before saying, 'I'm starving.'

Becky gave him a little shake. 'David,' she remonstrated, 'where are your manners?'

'It's alright. Come along in. We have a good choice on the menu, something to suit everyone I think,' and leading the way, the family trooped in behind her. They were quickly served by a young man with coffee for the adults, and fruit juice for the boys as they relaxed and waited for their meal. It was obvious that the bistro was very popular which was not surprising as the meals were reasonably priced and the atmosphere was lively and cheerful.

'Where are you staying?' asked the woman when she returned from the kitchen.

'We're hoping to find something like a bed and breakfast, and travel on first thing tomorrow,' answered Becky.

'Well we don't do B&B. My husband and I decided to settle in France, oh, must be seven or eight years ago, and as I worked in catering in London we thought our own bistro in France would be lovely. As it happens everything has turned out very well for us, but it's just food though. Sorry.'

'Pity,' said Denis. 'It's quite homely here.'

'Thank you. Thank you so much for saying that. It makes everything worthwhile. We have worked so hard.'

'Perhaps you know of somewhere local? Just for the night,' queried Becky.

'There's a lovely small villa just a mile or so away. I'll get my husband to make some enquires if you like. See if they've got any vacancies.'

Becky and Denis both nodded and Denis, sighing with relief said, 'Thank you. We'd appreciate that.'

Some French tourists entered and immediately, speaking in French, the woman welcomed them, pointed to an empty table and hurried away to fetch them wine. As she passed by, Denis and Becky, now enjoying a glass of wine, David tugged at the woman's sleeve. 'You speak in English to us and French to others.'

'That's because I am English, but now I have lived here for some time, I can speak French as well, so it is easy for me to talk to everyone.' She smiled down at David. 'Shall I bring you some chips?' and wasn't surprised when both boys nodded with enthusiasm. 'With an egg? Or two?'

'Two eggs!' William turned to Becky. 'Can I Mum, can I have two eggs?'

Becky laughing said, 'Yes, but you've got to eat them, not leave them on your plate.'

The meal was perfect, Denis sighed with satisfaction. It had been a long day and, looking at the boys who were nearly asleep, declared he was ready for bed. They heard a male voice call out, 'Johnnie,' and saw the woman hurry to the back of the bistro. After a few moments she came across to their table and smiling said, 'My husband telephone Monsieur Arnolde and he has a couple of rooms available, if you don't mind the boys sharing a bed.'

Laughing, Becky said, 'Look at them, just about to fall asleep. They won't be bothered where they lay their heads down. Sounds perfect to me.'

Leading them to the door she pointed to the left. 'Straight up the hill for about a mile, then take the left – it's only a track really – and you will see the villa just ahead.' As they thanked her she said, 'Please call by in the morning, we are not so busy then. Have a coffee with me and my husband. We love to see people from the UK and he would enjoy a chat with you, I know.'

Although it was only a mile, they travelled between lavender fields on one side of the road and rows and rows of vines on the other. When they reached the top of the hill, they were spellbound by the view across the valley. The old villa they were to spend the night in was a delightful two storey stone building, with traditional green shutters framing the windows. Inside were thick stone walls, tiled floors and exposed wooden beams.

The proprietor had made them welcome and his wife

made a great fuss over the children, and noting how tired they were, led them to their room. 'In here,' she told them as she opened the bedroom door, 'It is believed that once a queen slept in this room.' She turned to Becky who had followed her up the stairs, 'Of course,' she smiled, 'we cannot be sure, but it is a lovely thought, and many of my guests have tried to find out more,' and sighing she said, 'Well, maybe one day we might find out if it is true.'

The next morning after breakfast and many goodbyes, Becky reminded Denis of the invitation to revisit Bienvenue Bistro and seeing his reluctance added, 'Come on. We can stay for an hour, we've plenty of time.'

When the car pulled into the courtyard that doubled up as a car park, a ginger cat was sunning himself and a number of chickens were scratching the ground, and a barking, friendly dog rushed out to greet them. They heard Johnnie's voice call out, 'Now, what's your problem, Laddie, barking like that. No need, be quiet.'

As soon as everyone was out of the car the boys began making friends with the courtyard occupants. Johnnie came out of the front entrance, wiping her hands on her apron along with her own two boys younger than David and called out. 'Come in. Come in. I was hoping you would call back.' She led Becky and Denis to a small table overlooking the yard, and all three watched as the children began to get to know each other. 'I'll just get us all a cup of coffee, tea if you prefer?'

'Coffee's fine, thank you,' Becky answered for both of them.

'Call me Johnnie, everyone else does.'

'I was wondering about that. Why Johnnie? I mean, well that's usually a boy's name.'

Johnnie laughed, 'Not my real name. The locals call me Johnnie as it is part of my surname. So Johnnie stuck. Shan't be long, I'll get Paul to join us, he's mending the back fence. Something he promised to do ages ago.' It wasn't long before she bustled back with a tray holding four mugs of coffee and a plate of croissants. She was followed by a tall, tanned man brushing his hands down his jeans ready to shake the hands of his wife's guests.

Denis and Johnnie heard Becky gasp. As she stood up they could see tears in her eyes and although she had begun to shake, her face beamed with joy as she stared at the man coming towards them.

He had stopped, and everyone saw his mouth drop in surprise, then smile broadly. 'Becky,' he breathed in disbelief. 'Becky is it...is it you? Really you?'

She whispered, 'Yes.'

He hesitated, then lifted his arms and both Denis and Johnnie watched, astonished, as without a moment's hesitation, Becky rushed across the room to be folded in Paul's embrace.

It seemed to Denis, bewildered by his wife's behaviour, that they clung together for a very long time. He turned to Johnnie who had raised her eyebrows and shrugged, letting him know that she, too, didn't know what was going on. It was when he saw Paul bend his head into the top of his wife's head and drop a kiss that he stepped forward. Paul lifted his head and saw Denis approaching.

'Sorry, sorry,' he stammered.

Becky turned and laughing, pulling Paul after her said, 'Darling, this is my brother, Kevin, Kevin Paul Johnson.'

And Kevin, drawing Sarah close added, 'And this is my long lost sister, Rebecca Ann.'

Acknowledgements

Anne and John Samson at TSL Publications have, again, given me their unstinting patience and encouragement.

Also, many thanks to Kay Seeley for her sensible advice.

Thanks also to Jenny Hunt, and as ever, my long-suffering family.